Daniele Varè w_____
of an Italian nationalist exiled with
Mazzini by the Austrian regime.
Although he was brought up in
Scotland where his parents met,
Daniele Varè returned to Italy when he
was still young and entered that
country's diplomatic service. He
served in Vienna, Geneva, Copenhagen
and Luxembourg. However, his chief
posting was in Peking where he
arrived in 1908 and where he served
for twelve years. During his time there
he saw the overthrow of the Manchu
dynasty, the country swept by civil
war and the effects of the Russian
Revolution and the First World War as
exiles fled into China from abroad.
Many of these experiences became the
subject matter of his novels and tales.

Daniele Varè left the diplomatic
service in 1932 in order to devote
himself to writing. Many of his books
were published in both Italian and
English.

The Maker of Heavenly Trousers was
first published in 1935 and was
reprinted several times: it was
followed soon after by its two sequels
The Gate of Happy Sparrows and *The
Temple of Costly Experience*, and by
the author's autobiography, *The
Laughing Diplomat*, in 1938. Daniele
Varè died in 1956.

Also by Daniele Varè

THE GATE OF HAPPY SPARROWS

and published by Black Swan

The Maker of Heavenly Trousers

Daniele Varè

BLACK SWAN

THE MAKER OF HEAVENLY TROUSERS
A BLACK SWAN BOOK 0 552 99240 2

Originally published in Great Britain
by Methuen & Co. Ltd.

PRINTING HISTORY
Methuen edition published 1935
Second edition published 1935
Black Swan edition published 1986
Black Swan edition reprinted 1987

This book is set in 11/12 pt Mallard
by Colset Private Limited, Singapore.

Black Swan Books are published by
Transworld Publishers Ltd., 61 - 63
Uxbridge Road, Ealing, London W5 5SA, in
Australia by Transworld Publishers
(Australia) Pty. Ltd., 15-23 Helles Avenue,
Moorebank, NSW 2170, and in New
Zealand by Transworld Publishers (N.Z.)
Ltd., Cnr. Moselle and Waipareira
Avenues, Henderson, Auckland.

Made and printed in Great Britain by
The Guernsey Press Co. Ltd., Guernsey,
Channel Islands.

Contents

		Page
	PROLOGUE	ix
I.	THE HOME OF THE FIVE VIRTUES	13
II.	KUNIANG	23
III.	THE AWAKENING OF SPRING	36
IV.	DOMESTIC TROUBLES	55
V.	DONALD AND THE SILKS	61
VI.	ELISALEX	69
VII.	'LOVE-LOVE PIDGIN'	78
VIII.	THE MANDARIN COAT	91
IX.	THE SATYR AND THE NYMPH	99
X.	THE FAMILY MAGICIAN	108
XI.	THE CROWN OF MONTEZUMA	115
XII.	THE METTRAY SUCCESSION	119
XIII.	BUDDHA'S HANDS	127
XIV.	'LOVE PIDGIN'	139
XV.	INTERLUDE	147
XVI.	KINGDOM COME	154
XVII.	THE IVORY CAGE	162
XVIII.	HOME-COMING	171
XIX.	IN DUKE LAN'S PALACE	174
XX.	THE SHADOW OF A DREAM	188
XXI.	THE UNTOLD STORY	197
XXII.	GOLDEN SLIPPERS	214

Prologue

It was Kuniang's idea that I should write this book. Kuniang is full of ideas, and they generally entail some added activity on my part. I cannot say that she complained, but she implied that my books and magazine articles on Chinese history and folk-lore were long and rather dull. Kuniang had every right to say so, poor girl, as she used to copy them out for me. In doing so she discovered, as others have discovered before her, that history in China repeats itself even more often than elsewhere.

What she actually said was: 'Why don't you write something about live people, instead of all this about emperors and sages of the Sung dynasty?'

'They were live enough in their day.'

'But they've been dead for such a long time!'

'Would you prefer me to write a novel?'

'It might be more amusing. What *is* a novel exactly?'

I took out the *Oxford Dictionary*, Volume VI, from its shelf near the window, and read out:

> A novel is a fictitious prose narrative or tale of considerable length, in which characters and actions representative of real life of past or present times are portrayed in a plot of more or less complexity.

Kuniang looked doubtful. Evidently the definition seemed to her too arid.

'That sounds almost as bad as the other stuff,' she said. 'Why don't you just write about people like yourself and me and Little Lu?'

So that is what I have done in the following pages. I

began to write when nothing much had happened to us all, and the reader may find that the first part of this book is lacking in incident. But we made up for that as we went on.

Perhaps it is because I have lived so long in China, but I am fond of tranquillity. I like to linger over my actions and my thoughts, as on a quiet evening one lingers after dinner over the nuts and wine. But those hectic days are pleasant enough, I admit, to look back upon. And no doubt but the story makes better reading – or perhaps I should say that it suits the taste of the present generation better – than the annals of long-dead emperors and sages such as I used to transcribe for the edification of a few sinologues like myself.

If this were a Chinese play, and I an actor in the leading role, I would come forward to the footlights (waving a horsehair fly-whisk to chase away the evil spirits) and respectfully introduce myself to the audience, mentioning all my titles and qualities:

'I am your humble servant . . .'

But though I am willing to write, as Kuniang suggested, about myself and her and Little Lu, there is one thing that I would prefer to leave undefined, and that is my own identity. In the following pages the reader, if he has patience, will discover many intimate details of my life. But he will find no mention of my name.

The Maker of
Heavenly Trousers

1   The Home of the Five Virtues

Social position is a delicate structure, which sometimes rests on strange foundations. My own social position, such as it is, has been much enhanced by the fact that in front of the house in Peking, in which I now live, are two marble lions. Such lions are only to be found at the gates of the imperial palace, before the principal temples, or in foreign Legation compounds.

Needless to say, the lions were not placed there in honour of myself. They date from far-off days, when my residence was a temple, dedicated to two Tartar generals 'faithful and brave'.

The lions are seated, each on his own pedestal. Their mouths are open and their expression is meant to be very fierce, yet has something jovial about it, like the snarling of dogs at play. They have marble collars, adorned with tassels and bells, and under the left paw is an ornamental ball, also of marble. If they were females, they would each have a young cub, lying under the parent's paw, in place of the ball.

I have often noticed that the two lions at the entrance to my house are both males, whereas the couples in front of other old temples and palaces consist always of a male and a female. It was my Chinese teacher, Mr. Tang, who gave me the explanation of what might seem a flagrant violation of the Rites.

During the reign of the Emperor Yung Chen, a certain sculptor was given a commission to make two pairs of marble lions for the imperial household. In executing this commission, the sculptor and his assistants worked simultaneously at both couples of lions, so that they were all finished at the same time. The sculptor then went to the Forbidden City to inquire where the two pairs of lions should be placed. But the Emperor had forgotten the matter, and the answer to the sculptor's query was long delayed. At last there came a message from the Chief Eunuch, to say that one couple of lions should be placed at the entrance of the Shuang Liè Ssè (this was the name that my house bore in former days). The other couple was to be set up in the courtyard of a Manchu palace in the Western City.

The removal was duly effected. But the four lions, who had been brought up together, were much distressed at the separation. Like the toys in *Puppenfée* (who at midnight come to life and dance), they began to pay secret calls on one another, choosing the dark and stormy nights. At that time the streets of Peking were not lighted: each wayfarer carried his own lantern. During several months the lions were able to leave their pedestals and to hold their nightly meetings unobserved; but as time passed and nobody interfered, they became careless, and made so much noise that they disturbed the neighbours. One night, the pair of lions who lived in the Western City were paying a visit to their friends in the Shuang Liè Ssè, when the guardian of the temple door, awakened by the noise, jumped out of bed and ran out, armed with a heavy stick. He saw some dark shapes, which he took to be oxen, and struck at them with all his strength. The two lionesses managed to get away. But the lions sprang, each on to a pedestal, and assumed once more the attitude that the sculptor had given them. From that night onwards there were no more friendly calls. The two male lions remained at the Shuang Liè Ssè, and the two lionesses never left their palace in the Western City.

II

One of the troubles of having a house in Peking, outside the Diplomatic Quarter, is that one is afflicted with a Chinese landlord. As a matter of fact, my landlord, Mr.

Yu, is a Manchu, but it comes to the same thing. He is an estimable person, but a bore. It is his custom to pay me a formal call once a year, and then to drop in informally every day for a month, until I lose patience and point out to him, as delicately as possible, that the two hundred silver dollars, which I pay him monthly (it used to be sixty, when I first came to China), are for the rent of his house only, without the benefit of his company. After this, during the remaining eleven months of the year, I do not see him again.

Mr. Yu drives about in a brougham, with sides made almost entirely of glass, so that it looks like an aquarium on wheels. Behind the coupé is an iron step, on which stands a *ma-fu*, or groom, who jumps down to precede the horse round every corner, running in front, like the figures of the hours in Guido Reni's *Aurora*. When Mr. Yu enters the house to pay a call, the horse is taken out of the shafts and led away. According to Chinese ideas, a visit should be very long.

On various occasions, during his calls on me, Mr. Yu has sampled most of the refreshing beverages that are consumed in the West. But red wine is too sour for his taste, and champagne too effervescent. He approves of my cigars, and the last time he came he imbibed large quantities of raspberry syrup, which he took undiluted in a tumbler.

Our conversation consists of platitudes of an almost tragic banality. But after having taken leave of me (the rule is that I should escort him, not to the entrance, but as far as the second of the courtyards), he always finds some excuse to stop and talk with the servants. From them he inquires into the minutest details of my daily existence: how I earn my income; what I pay for this, that, and the other; what I eat; and so forth. I believe that, to keep up the prestige of the household, the servants describe me as a millionaire of gargantuan habits: a deep drinker and a reckless spender.

The house that I have rented from Mr. Yu is in the south-western corner of the Tartar City. It stands within the angle of the outer wall, strengthened at this point by a tower, with embrasured windows which look out over the plain towards the Western Hills. Even where no corner tower is superimposed upon its massive structure, the Tartar Wall rises high above the neighbouring houses. It shelters me from the south and west winds, which is no great advantage, as the dominant and most obnoxious wind blows from the north. Perhaps for this reason, the north is considered inauspicious in Peking. Palaces, temples, and houses all face south.

It is very quiet where I live, far from the centre of the town and from the various attractions that draw sightseers from abroad. The few friends who come to see me complain of the distance, and ask why I did not choose a more civilized quarter, by which they mean the part of Peking that boasts of foreign-style houses, cinemas, and chemists' shops.

Nearly all the houses in this neighbourhood are of the old Chinese type, and except that panes of glass have replaced the rice paper in some windows, everything is much as it was after the fall of the Ming dynasty. Young China, with its Mauser pistols and inferiority complexes, has hardly penetrated into this forgotten corner of the old imperial city.

The various buildings that make up my residence cover a large area, but there are not very many rooms. The house consists of one-storied pavilions, united by corridors, which are open on either side, like pergolas. These corridors are little more than stone-flagged paths, raised some three feet from the ground and protected by sloping roofs which rest on red lacquered columns.

The courtyards are four in number, and they are paved with stone. It is the custom, in summer, to roof them over with matting, spread over a scaffolding of wooden poles. This temporary roof helps to keep the courtyards cool.

Behind the last of the pavilions, which I use as a study, there is a garden, with an artificial hillock, surmounted by a little kiosk. There is also a lake with a small marble bridge, arched like a camel's hump, all in miniature, like a picture on a Chinese fan.

In each courtyard are four pines, planted formally in the corners. At the end of June the gardener places pots of lotus at the doors of the pavilions, and the lake is also covered with velvety leaves and pink lotus flowers. Sometimes I amuse myself by putting a few spoonfuls of tea into the lotus flowers, just before they close at evening. And I carefully pick the tea out again next morning all scented with the perfume of the lotus.

A stag and a heron, life-sized in bronze, keep silent company on a terrace in front of the first pavilion. And a bronze incense-burner, on a marble base, serves as a reminder of the days when this house was still a temple, and once a year a fair was held in and around it, in honour of the two Tartar generals who figured as tutelary gods of the Shuang Liè Ssè and of the neighbourhood. On summer evenings, when the air is still, I sometimes light one or two of those little bundles of incense sticks which they sell at the gates of the temples. And I drop them into the burner. The white, scented clouds float at a man's height from the ground, and the surrounding pavilions and lacquered colonnades seem to rest on the incense smoke, as if conjured up by jinns in *The Arabian Nights*. I like to think that the two old warriors appreciate my tribute, and that they come back, in the spirit, to visit their old sanctuary.

There are two marble stelae dedicated to them, and which stand in a little pavilion of their own, in the second courtyard. The stelae rest on the backs of tortoises with leonine heads.

One of the two generals was called Mei-ti, and he had a son, a beautiful youth, whom the Emperor loved, as Hadrian loved Antinous. But, by reason of his orgies, the Emperor neglected the affairs of state, and lost prestige. Mei-ti protested, but his protests were of no avail. So after shedding tears and making lamentations (in strict conformity with the Rites) Mei-ti killed his own son.

Thus the plaything was destroyed with which the Emperor had wasted too much time.

The porter's lodge, consisting of two small rooms near the entrance, is occupied by the *k'ai-men-ti* and the *tingchai*.

The *k'ai-men-ti's* title might be translated 'Warden of the Doors'. He is of very little use to me, but his place in the household is important, for he levies a tax on all goods that are brought into the house, and the proceeds are divided among the various servants. It is probable that he also takes toll of the Chinese who come to call on me. I do not benefit by these exactions and would prefer to dispense with the *k'ai-men-ti's* services. But this would be against all precedent.

The *tingchai* is the letter-carrier, and goes round to execute small commissions in town. Formerly I had an excellent *tingchai*, but he was too clever for such menial work, and left my service to become a writer of anonymous letters.

It is a mystery to me why he could not write letters, anonymous or otherwise, while in my service. He had plenty of leisure. Nor do I understand how it is that, the letters being anonymous, he can derive a satisfactory income from them. I suppose that he really has become a specialist in blackmail, and in this capacity has found employment with some criminal association or political club.

The *tingchai* now in my service is a boy of about seventeen years, somewhat wanting in intelligence and afflicted with so painful a stammer that it is almost impossible to make out anything he says. I was induced to take him into my service after repeated appeals from his grandfather, who in former days was a Manchu Bannerman, and is now reduced to the position of caretaker to some minor pavilion in the Summer Palace, with a stipend of three dollars a month. On this sum (if one can believe what he says) he has to keep a family which includes two wives, two mothers-in-law, and two sons with families of their own! My present *tingchai* is the only grandson over twelve years old.

At the back of the pavilions that enclose the first court-yard are the servants' quarters. The servants, or 'Boys', are all related to one another and their family name is *Tò*, which means Virtue. The number one Boy is called *Tò-tai*, or Exalted Virtue. Number two is *Tò-yuè*, Virtuous Moon. The gardener is *Tò-shan*, Mountain of Virtue; the cook is *Tò-hai*, Ocean of Virtue, and the *ma-fu*, or stableman (who lives out) is *Tò-ching*, or Pure Virtue.

My authority over these worthies should be absolute. But, as in most autocracies, the master's will prevails only within certain limits, and the Boys run this house less for my convenience than for their own advantage. The only foreigner in a community of Orientals, I feel less at home than they do, so much so that, in the neighbourhood, my house is known as the Home of the Five Virtues.

Exalted Virtue, in his capacity of number one Boy, enjoys the privilege of keeping his own family in my house. The other Boys have to keep their wives and children elsewhere. The family of Exalted Virtue consists of a mother, a wife, and a number of small children, of whom, on an average, one is born and one dies every year.

It would be contrary to all sense of decorum to mention Exalted Virtue's wife by name. When he wants her, he calls out: 'Mother of Little Lu' (Little Lu being the eldest child). And it is thus that I also address her with requests for the sewing on of buttons or the mending of socks.

The Mother of Little Lu reminds me of the inscription on an old seventeenth-century print, which hangs on the wall in my study, representing a very imposing matron taking the air on the seashore at *Neapolis in Italia*. Across the sky is a scroll, on which is written: *Ornamenta mulieris: silentium, modestia et domi manere*. The same might be said of this Chinese housewife, who is so modest, poor woman, that she does not even possess a name.

*   *   *

The mother of the Five Virtues is the one person, of all those who live in my house, whom I most cordially dislike. They call her *Lao Tai-tai*, which means the Old Lady. Of course, I might say that I do not want her in the house. But then her progeny would have to show their filial piety by going and living with her elsewhere, which would be inconvenient.

Whereas the Mother of Little Lu stays at home and never spends a *tungdze* except on the most indispensable of household necessities, her mother-in-law is always gadding about, spending money (her son's money), and she is the cause of more than half the troubles that come upon the family of the Five Virtues. Her sons can thank their stars if, when she comes back after her daily peregrinations, she brings back only some small toy for Little Lu, or some candied fruit for herself. On one occasion, after being out all day, she reappeared escorting an enormous camphor-wood box, transported by two men in a cart drawn by a half-starved mule.

'What can she want with a box of that size?' I asked.

Exalted Virtue replied gravely that it was to keep her clothes in.

'But she doesn't possess enough clothes to fill a handbag!' I objected (This, by the way, is not strictly true. The Old Lady has quite an extensive wardrobe, whereas the Mother of Little Lu has only just enough to keep out the cold in winter.)

'It is not for the clothes that she wears now,' answered her son, 'but for those which she will wear when she is dead.'

I might have guessed it! It is true that she is always buying the most expensive raiment: dresses of silk, embroidered coats and shoes, to be put on her dead body on the day when she will be placed in the enormous coffin which, many years ago, cost her family the equivalent of two months' wages. The coffin, all lacquered in red and gold, is now stored away in a temple in the Chinese City. I once asked Exalted Virtue how much he paid for the storage of his mother's coffin. He answered that payment was made in kind: so much

20

sugar and tea and flour was paid yearly to the priests of the temple. Doubtless it was my larder that provided the required tribute.

The dead, in China, are more important than the living. But the Old Lady is not dead yet, and all my knowledge of local beliefs and customs cannot persuade me that she is justified in buying the most expensive ornaments, such as jade bracelets, earrings and pendants, in order to impress the spirits in the world to come.

Although all mortals are more or less self-centred, I am sure that no one is more convinced than Little Lu that the universe rotates round his own person. When this story begins Little Lu was six years old. In the small cosmos that is contained within these walls, he has always reigned supreme. As to the world outside, he considered it much as the Emperor of China viewed the lands of the Outer Barbarians, north of the Great Wall and beyond the 'four seas'. During the winter months he wore several coats, one on top of the other, and shed them gradually, as the days got warmer. Thus it happened that, from November to February, his small body, wrapped in successive layers of quilted garments, became almost round, and his figure resembled a sphere, surmounted by a button, which was his head. In July and August he went about with nothing on but a pair of trousers of a peculiar cut. They were suspended from his shoulders and covered his chest, but left his back bare, almost down to the knees.

Winter or summer he wore no hat, save as an ornament on great occasions, and it was a mystery to me how he never got sunstroke. His head was shaved, except for a circle of hair round the crown, with four cardinal points from which started little braids of hair, tied with various-coloured ribbons. Only when he was four years old did he begin to grow a real pigtail.

For everyday wear, Little Lu and his smaller brothers and sisters had clothes made of blue cotton. But every now and then they would appear in rich robes of silk and brocade; then Solomon in all his glory was not arrayed like one of these. The occasions for so much splendour were furnished by the birthdays of his

21

grandmothers, of which Little Lu had three: paternal grandmother, maternal grandmother, and number two wife of his paternal grandfather. Sometimes the children's dresses were designed to represent a tiger, with black and yellow stripes encircling their small bodies. Their round faces looked up from under the masks of savage beasts, with pointed ears and long white fangs. Their shoes, embroidered even on the soles, represented white rabbits or black pigs, with little tails at the heels, like spurs.

2 Kuniang

I

This neighbourhood has changed but little since I first
came to live in the Shuang Liè Ssè. But on the road that
runs along the inner side of the Tartar Wall, about two
hundred yards from my door, there used to be a house
that, fortunately, has been pulled down. For it was an
eyesore to the whole neighbourhood. The building itself
was small and unpretentious, but it was surmounted by
a tower, entirely disproportioned to its size, with castel-
lated top and a white enamelled clock half-way up. During many years the hands of that clock pointed always to
twenty minutes past three, as if to show that, in its
immediate surroundings, time stood still.

The outer walls were painted pink, and though the
houses round and the wall opposite all looked old and
faded, those pink walls never lost their youthful and
vivid complexion.

The house had been built – so I was told – by the Chinese agent of a German firm, who wished to own a residence in 'European style'. But he did not live in it
himself. On the ground floor was a tailor, by name
Ah-ting-fu, who had set up a sign in English, although
written on a tablet such as are usually inscribed with
Chinese characters. Like the ideograms on an Oriental
signboard, the lettering of the English inscription was
done in relief and lacquered black, on a background of
old gold. There was no name on the tailor's sign, but
merely the announcement that he was a

In a small apartment on the upper floor lived an Italian family: father, mother, and little girl. The father was an employee of the Kin Han, that is to say, of the railway that unites Peking to Hankow. He was a good-looking man, with a jovial face and an optimistic outlook in life, which nothing in his circumstances seemed to justify. His name was Cante de' Tolomei.

To-la-yè, as the Chinese called him, or Signor Cante, as he was known to other foreigners, was not the only employee of the Kin Han who lived in my neighbourhood. There was another, a Russian, who occupied a large Chinese house, with a garden, a little farther down the road. I knew the Russian family by sight (most foreigners in Peking know each other by sight), and I used to bow to the mother when we met. She was a great big woman, like a cart-horse, with enormous hands and feet. I had once lunched with her – that is to say, at the same table with her – in the restaurant-car of the Peking-Mukden express. I still have a vivid recollection of that meal, for I had asked the lady to pass me the butter, which she very kindly did, giving me one or two pats in her fingers. Not wishing to appear rude, I felt obliged to eat the butter that had been so literally 'handed' to me.

The father of the Russian family had a job in the railway's offices in Peking, but Signor Cante was almost always away, down the line. His headquarters were close to the bridge over the Yellow River, just north of Kai-feng Fu. Owing to the disturbed conditions in the Central Provinces he kept his wife and daughter in Peking. I may have seen the wife, once or twice, but I hardly remember her. She died of typhoid in the summer of 1908. The little girl was then seven years old, having been born in January 1901. She went to a day-school, kept by some French and Italian nuns and situated to the north of the Diplomatic Quarter. On Sundays and other holidays she had to play in my garden.

She came to the house for the first time – so I seem to remember – in search of a kitten that had wandered from home. Having made friends with the 'Warden of the Doors' and other servants, she formed a habit of strolling in at odd moments, and playing about in the courtyards and in the garden, without any one troubling about her. I asked Exalted Virtue who she was, and he answered simply 'Kuniang', which means girl, so that I was not much wiser. When he explained that she was Signor Cante's child, I told the Boys to be kind to her: a needless precaution, for the Chinese are naturally fond of children, and Kuniang soon had all my servants at her beck and call. One Sunday morning, running down a garden path, she fell and grazed her knee. I took her to my room and bathed her wound and gave her a piece of chocolate; after which, she grazed her knees so often that I wondered if she did not do it on purpose, to have the chocolate. Nobody ever called her anything but Kuniang, though her Christian name was Renata.

At first she played about by herself, or with the *k'ai-men-ti's* dogs. But when Little Lu grew to an age when he could follow her about, he constituted himself her *cavalier servente*, and never left her side. Little Lu was only five years old when Kuniang was twelve, but this discrepancy of age did not form an obstacle to their reciprocal affection and esteem. They chattered together for hours in a mixture of Chinese and pidgin-English, and apparently had a great deal to say to one another. I do not know what they talked about, for a shyness descended upon them when I drew near. At times they quarrelled, and to judge by the yells that echoed through the courtyards Little Lu would come in for some hard smacks.

Kuniang taught Little Lu to play the old Italian game of *morra*, which, strangely enough, is well known also in China. The two players 'throw' a number, by putting out so many fingers of one hand, while each shouts, as loud as he can, the number which he guesses will be formed by the sum of his own fingers and those of his opponent.

Little Lu never won, but he never tired of playing. Times out of number I have stopped, as I passed by, to watch that strange couple on the steps that led up to one or other of the pavilions: Little Lu with chubby fingers sticking out of his long sleeve, and Kuniang with a blue cotton pinafore and her hair in braids. A seraphic smile would break out over Little Lu's face whenever he scored a point, but more often he would get a scolding. They spoke in English, but called out the numbers in Chinese, and one would hear something like the following dialogue:

'*Wu to.*'

'*Pa pao.*'

'Silly little fool! What is the good of calling "eight" when you only throw one? I have not more than five fingers in one hand.'

Sometimes Kuniang would bring the children of the Russian family with her into my compound: a boy, named Fédor, who was a year older than herself, and a girl, Natasha, who was a month or two younger. At first they were timid and kept very quiet. But as they became more familiar with the surroundings they grew bolder. The two tortoises that supported the memorial tablets to the Tartar generals were brought to life as hobby-horses in an imaginary merry-go-round, or as chargers in serious warfare. The lake in my garden, usually so tranquil, became busy with ocean traffic. Big liners and Chinese junks accomplished wonderful voyages into the realm of make-believe, and suffered shipwreck on the rocks and shoals of uncharted seas. A long cane of bamboo was used to bring help to vessels in distress. The children would take off their shoes and stockings and wade in among the frightened gold-fish.

More than once a sudden scream and a splash informed me, as I sat at work in my study, that some one had slipped and fallen. After which wet garments would be spread out in the sun to dry, while the owners continued to play, in a costume that rendered caution unnecessary.

Though I liked the sight of little boys and girls in my courtyards and garden, after a bit they ceased to come, all except Kuniang. This was after Fédor had had the effrontery to pull Little Lu's pigtail, which by then had reached the length of seven inches. Little Lu was touchy about his pigtail, and there were protests and recriminations, in which the Old Lady, for some reason, had her say. Possibly the Russian children, who were little savages, were rude to the Old Lady. I do not know all the facts of the case, but ever after there was a silent feud between the Five Virtues and the Russian family.

II

As a child, a motherless child, Kuniang was so thin and gawky and dishevelled that such incipient charms as she possessed were hardly discernible. But in time the nuns of her convent school managed to instil in her some sense of tidiness and of decorum. The first impulses of the eternal feminine did the rest.

Kuniang's mother had been a Scandinavian, and this may account for the beauty of her hair, which kept its curl even during the dry Peking winters. It had golden lights in it, such as one reads of in fairy-tales. Her eyes were darker than is usual in people with fair hair. They were Italian eyes: grey and quiet and gentle.

On her forehead, just above the left eyebrow, was a birth-mark, dark red and shaped like a crescent moon. When one knew Kuniang well one got used to this blemish, which was in no way disfiguring. The Chinese are always ready to give nicknames, alluding to physical characteristics, and they naturally hit upon such a name for Kuniang, calling her Fan-go Kuniang – Fairy of the Moon.

During one of those torrential downpours which occur almost daily in the 'rainy season', Kuniang and Little Lu ran for shelter into what was then a lumber-room in the second courtyard, opposite the pavilion, which I keep as a guest-room. Among the empty boxes and trunks and household goods the two children found an old typewriter which I had not used for many years. Kuniang was at once inspired by a burning desire to write with it, and later on in the day she screwed up her courage to ask me if she might do so. Apparently the typewriter was still in good order, so I gave the required permission, and told Exalted Virtue to have it cleaned and oiled and placed on a suitable table, with some paper to write on.

27

Kuniang must have spoken to her father about it, for the next time he was in Peking he came to see me, to make his excuses. He seemed afraid that Kuniang might be giving too much trouble. I assured him that it was all right, and I confirmed the permission to use the type-writer.

From that day onward Kuniang's games of *morra* with Little Lu alternated with experiments in typewriting, and I used to hear the hesitating tap-tap of the keys as she practised her new accomplishment. One afternoon, meeting her at the door of the lumber-room, where the typewriter was now installed for daily use, I asked Kuniang if she wished to become a stenographer. This is a profession which, in China, is well paid and often leads to the altar.

Kuniang answered in the negative, adding, for my information, that she intended to become a *Yao Ch'er*.

I thought I must have misunderstood her. *Yao Ch'er* is an expression which indicates, in the Chinese language, an ancient and dishonourable profession, the oldest, in fact, that is open to women.

'You intend to become *what*?' I exclaimed in horror.

'A *Yao Ch'er*,' said Kuniang confidently. 'How do you say it in English?'

'Never mind that! And who put such an idea into your head?'

'Little Lu.'

'Little Lu? And what does *he* know about it?'

I did my best to speak naturally, so that Kuniang should feel at her ease. To have shown myself shocked would have had the effect of drying up the poor child's confidences. It is too much to hope that even a little girl should be unacquainted with things when living among an Eastern people. As Anatole France says: *L'innocence n'est past une vertu. C'est un bonheur.*

Kuniang explained:

'Little Lu has been with his parents, to see the houses outside the Chi'ien Mên, where they keep girls. I do not know what they are called.'

'Neither do I in Chinese. But why should Little Lu have been there?'

'The Chinese go there, and drink tea, during the festivities for the New Year, after they have been to the temples and have paid their debts.'

'And they take the children?'

'Yes. It is great fun. I wish they had taken me.'

Kuniang's information was correct. Later on I asked Exalted Virtue about it. He had been on an expedition to the house mentioned, and his brothers, his wife, and the children had accompanied him. Little Lu had much enjoyed the excursion and had spoken of it afterwards to Kuniang, inspiring in her the desire to become as one of the ladies he had described.

'But it cannot be an easy profession,' said Kuniang to me, and she sighed.

III

I don't often go to sleep in the daytime, except in the height of summer, but I had been for a long ride, to the Temple of the Blue Tiles, south of the Chinese City. And I had lunched and well. About three o'clock I lay down on the sofa in my study to read the *Peking Gazette*. The news of the day (March 13th 1913) was the decision of the newly fledged Chinese Republican Government to organize a military expedition into Mongolia, with the avowed object of opposing Russian influence in that region. The preparations included the setting up, at Kalgan, of great hangars for aeroplanes, and the immediate departure of two hundred specially built motor-cars, which were to carry twenty-four men each across the desert. I knew enough about China to realize that this was all 'look see', and that there never would be an expedition into Mongolia. But somebody would get a nice, fat 'squeeze' out of the preparations, even if they never went further than the publishing of a few decrees. The matter was therefore of scant interest, except to the authorities concerned. So, after a few minutes' reading, I fell asleep.

It must have been little more than half an hour later that I began to wake up, but even before I was fully awakened I was aware of a figure sitting close to me, cross-legged, like the Buddha, on the floor. I stared sleepily for some time without realizing that it was Kuniang. She had come in while I slept and was evidently waiting to say something to me. I sat up, rubbed my eyes, and stared at her. To my astonishment I saw that her cheeks were wet with tears.

'Anything wrong, Kuniang?' I asked kindly.

She did not answer, but held out her hand, offering me something that glittered. It was a piece of crystal – indeed, two pieces, for it had been broken in two. I recognized a little crystal seal that used to lie among the pens and stationery on my desk.

'Why, this is my seal,' I said. 'What has happened? Did you break it?'

Kuniang nodded dolefully.

'But what were you doing with it?' I asked.

'We took it, Little Lu and I, to put a seal on a letter, which I had written with the typewriter. I know that we ought not to have touched anything of yours. But we had no seal, and this one is the double *Fu*, for happiness.'

Kuniang was right. It was not my own seal, but one I had bought at the fair, which is held after the Chinese New Year, at the Liu-li-chang. It had probably been engraved on the occasion of a wedding, for it had the character for happiness twice over, meaning a double happiness, or conjugal felicity.

The seal was of rock crystal, the base plain, with a roughly chiselled figure of a pekingese dog on the top. A little cord of plaited brown silk was threaded between the dog's back and his tail, which was arched over him. It was not in any way a valuable 'curio', but it was pretty. I was sorry that Kuniang had broken it.

I guessed that she must have dropped it on the marble flags of the courtyards, while running excitedly from my study to her typewriter, or vice versa. The crystal block was split vertically into two pieces, so that the double *Fu* was cut in two by an irregular fracture. But, when held together in the hand, the two pieces joined perfectly, re-forming the complete seal.

Kuniang sat gazing at me dolefully.

'Shall I get a hair brush?' she said.

I thought I must be looking untidy, after my snooze.

'No, thank you,' I said. 'I am going to my bedroom in a minute. I can brush my hair there.'

'I meant for me. To spank me with.'

'What made you think I would spank you?'

'Natasha always gets spanked when she breaks anything.'

'I suppose her parents do that. But you don't really belong to me.'

'I know. I don't seem to belong to anybody.'

She said it so sadly that I felt quite sorry for her. It might have been kinder on my part to have administered the spanking that her intimacy with Natasha had led her to expect.

The two pieces of crystal still lay in my hand. It would have been possible to stick them together again. But Kuniang's last words, '*I don't seem to belong to anybody*', had put an idea into my head.

'Kuniang,' I said, 'do you know what a token is?'

'It sounds like the silken cord that the old Empress used to send to people, to show that they must hang themselves.'

'You are still thinking of punishments. I meant the kind of token that people in olden times used to send to one another, as a sign that they were in trouble. Suppose that we consider this broken seal as a token, and you and I each keep half of it. Whichever of us two wants help should send his half to the other who will be obliged to come to the rescue. Do you see the idea?'

'It sounds like a kind of game,' said Kuniang.

'Call it a game, if you like. But it would imply an obligation for both of us. Whenever you are in trouble, you must bring me your half of the seal. If I need help I will send you mine.'

'You could never need *my* help!'

'How do you know? There is a fable about a mouse helping a lion, and you will be a big girl some day. As long as I keep my half of the seal, I will have the right to claim your assistance. You may find it very awkward when the time comes. Do you agree?'

'Yes. I agree,' said Kuniang. She was all smiles again.

31

'By the way,' I said. 'Wasn't Little Lu mixed up in this business? He does not seem to share your desire to expiate his sin.'

'No. He had quite a different idea. He wanted to arrange that you should find a window open, as if by a gust of wind, and some papers and your broken seal on the floor. Then you would have thought it was an accident.'

'And you would not connive at his deceit?'

'No. It did not seem fair to cheat you. I would much rather have been spanked.'

'Well. You can run away now. And don't forget your promise to help me if I send you the broken seal.'

She took her half of the crystal and departed. As the door closed on her, I wondered how many children would have refused Little Lu's suggestion, to make it all appear as an accident. Little Lu would certainly come to a bad end. Possibly in the Government.

IV

One evening, as I was coming home from a ride in the country, I noticed workmen putting up scaffolding round the house where Kuniang's father had his dwelling and Ah-ting-fu his shop. I did not stop to inquire why they were doing so. The matter did not interest me. But, when I got back to my study, Exalted Virtue came in and announced what evidently seemed to him an important piece of news, namely that the pink house with the tower was going to be pulled down.

'Thank goodness!' I exclaimed. 'But why? It was only built a few years ago and looks solid enough.'

Exalted Virtue knew all about it.

'Chinese mandalin, next door, he buy. He catch plenty dollar. He no likey that house. He say *feng shui* velly bad. Bling ill luck.'

I might have guessed it. The stringent rules of Chinese geomancy had been violated in some way by the foreign-style building, or more likely by the tower that over-looked the houses on either side. The spirits of wind and water had been offended and had brought misfortune on the neighbourhood. Now the house had been bought up and was to be demolished. I felt rather pleased about it, and said so.

'But Missy Kuniang, she must go 'way,' said Exalted Virtue.

'Her father can easily find another house. There are plenty to let.'

'Yes, Master. But Missy Kuniang fata no in Pei-ching. He go Kai-feng Fu in fire-carriage.'

So that was the trouble! Signor Cante was away, at his work on the line, and they were pulling down the house about poor Kuniang's ears. I inquired whether she could not stay at the convent school, near the Diplomatic Quarter, but apparently there had been a case of smallpox in the school, and the nuns would not take in boarders.

The result was what might have been expected, for it was quite evident that the Five Virtues considered it my bounden duty to offer hospitality to Signor Cante's daughter, at least until her father came back to Peking. I might have offered her the 'guest-room', but I preferred to have the pavilion cleared out, which had been used as a lumber-room (it was there that the typewriter had been found). Some of Signor Cante's own furniture was put in, from the house that was being dismantled. Kuniang was installed there until further notice.

After which, for some time, I saw less of her than before. I suppose she kept out of my way, fearing to make her presence felt. My cook provided her meals, and I told Exalted Virtue to let me know if she wanted anything. I received a grateful letter from Signor Cante, who said that he could not return to Peking for the time being. As soon as possible he would arrange for Kuniang to go back to her relations in Italy. He evidently had no intention of taking another apartment in Peking. His work kept him away most of the time, and after his wife's death there was no one to help him look after Kuniang.

The pink house took longer to demolish than I had expected, possibly because the work of demolition was impeded by heavy rains. One day, as I was riding past, I stopped to speak to Ah-ting-fu, who was carting away the

33

few remaining fixtures of his old shop. I asked him where he was going to set up a new establishment. He answered that he meant to join forces with his brother, who had a shop in the Hata Mên. At that moment the sign near the door caught my eye, with its quaint inscription in English. I asked Ah-ting-fu what he was going to do with it. He said he did not know, adding: 'Heavenly trousers, in Hata Mên, no can do.'

I felt sorry for the poor old sign. It had made me smile so often, when passing before the pink house.

'I will give you a dollar for it, if you like,' I said.

Ah-ting-fu looked surprised and answered courteously that if Master wished to have his sign, he hoped that Master would honour him by taking it as a gift. I realized that to accept this offer would certainly cost me more in the end. By all the rules of Chinese etiquette, if I did so, I must place an order for clothes at Ah-ting-fu's new firm. But I accepted, none the less. The sign was taken down and placed in a rickshaw, which then followed me home.

When I reached the entrance of my house, the *ting-chai* was standing in the doorway. I made a sign to him to take the wooden tablet out of the rickshaw. He did so, and walked behind me, carrying it under one arm, as I went in search of Kuniang.

We found her eating a bowl of rice and chopped pork outside the kitchen door. She was squatting down, like a Chinese, and using chopsticks, which she manipulated with great dexterity. Little Lu was beside her, similarly employed. A tiny bowl of soyabean sauce, placed on the step beneath the kitchen door, served as condiment. Kuniang and Little Lu dipped their chopsticks into it, before putting the morsel of rice and pork into their mouths.

'Won't that spoil your lunch?' I asked, as I drew near.

'This *is* my lunch,' said Kuniang. 'When I have finished this bowl, I am going to have some *tang-bulers*, and then I'm going out to see Papà. He has just arrived in Peking. He is staying with the Russian family.'

I was rather taken aback by this revelation of how Kuniang took her meals. She had never done so with me, partly because my own meals were not served at regular hours, but whenever I happened to want them (such are the habits of a bachelor in China). This irregularity was not possible for a girl, who had to attend classes and to go to bed at a reasonable hour.

Meanwhile, Kuniang had noticed what the *tingchai* was carrying.

'Why,' she exclaimed, 'You have got Ah-ting-fu's sign.'

'Yes. He has no more use for it, now that he is part-owner in an important shop in the Hata Mên. So he has given it to us. I thought you might like to put it up somewhere. It might make you feel more at home, to see it hanging outside the house you live in, as it used to do.'

Kuniang seemed pleased with the idea, so I told the *tingchai* to give her the sign. Then I left them and went off to have a bath and change my clothes.

An hour later I was surprised to find Kuniang and Little Lu and the *tingchai*, all standing in front of my study door, staring with interest at something that hung just outside. It was Ah-ting-fu's sign.

'But why on earth,' I asked, 'have you put it up there?'

Kuniang answered: 'I thought it would bring you good luck, as it did to Ah-ting-fu. It is a great advance, to have a shop in the Hata Mên.'

'You ought to have put it over the door of your own pavilion. That is what I meant you to do.'

'But I want you to have the good luck.'

'That is very kind of you, Kuniang. But don't you think it rather unsuitable. I don't make trousers, not even heavenly ones.'

'What does that matter, if the sign brings you good fortune?'

This argument was unanswerable. But I still feebly remonstrated.

'If you leave that sign before my door,' I said, 'in less than a week the story will be all over Peking, and I shall be known ever after as the "Maker of Heavenly Trousers".'

And that is exactly what has happened.

3   The Awakening of Spring

I

The verb 'to darn' is explained in my pocket dictionary as follows: 'To mend by imitating the texture of the stuff, with thread and needle.' But this definition does not correspond to the work accomplished by good Chinese housewives. When they mend a sock, or put a patch into an article of clothing, they do not try 'to imitate the texture of the stuff'. Their art makes no attempt at concealment: it even takes a certain pride in revealing itself.

On the worn heel of a woollen sock of mine the Mother of Little Lu once embroidered two scarlet bats. On the seat of an old pair of silk pyjamas she put a patch which was a life-study of no small artistic merit. On the right was a monkey, cut out of a piece of yellow silk, with a long, long arm that stretched across to reach an apple on the other side.

Although she is most willing to do her best, I cannot always count on the services of this gifted needle-woman. One day (it was towards the end of February) I called Exalted Virtue and asked him if the Mother of Little Lu would be so kind as to mend a glove of mine, which had come unsewn along the seam of the middle finger. Exalted Virtue told me that it would not be possible on that particular day.

I asked: 'Why not?'

'Because to-day is the second day of the Second Moon. The Dragon lifts his head. If one moved the needles, one might prick his eyes.'

It was a certain warm feeling in the air that gave me

the explanation of this cryptic sentence. In my court-yards the marble flags glowed in the sunlight, and the lilac bushes had swollen buds. In the sheltered corners of my garden the wild prunus was flowering; soon the cherry, the pear, and the almond trees would follow suit. The woodpecker had arrived from the south. I could hear the drumming of his beak on the trees. His green plumage heralded the green that would come later – much later – on the branches and on the lawns.

The Dragon lifting his head is a first sign of spring: what the Germans call *Frühlingserwachung*. There is a play of that name, by Wedekind. 'The Awakening of Spring' is the story of a very young girl who comes to grief because she does not know enough about life. This could not have happened if she had been brought up in China. In the East, when the Dragon opens his eyes, it is in a world that knows all there is to know about him, and a bit more.

And good housewives are careful.

II

When the Five Virtues decided for me that Kuniang should come and live in my house, she was not yet four-teen. She went to school in the morning and returned in the evening, so that I saw very little of her. Sometimes she caught a chill, and Signor Cante's doctor (a naval doctor from the Italian Legation Guard) was called in to prescribe. If she had to stay in bed, or indoors, I would go and sit with her, and take her books and illustrated papers. I never failed to be astonished at her capacity for reading in three languages, even though I knew that, like myself, she was born of parents of different nation-alities. She preferred English and American books to all others, and was so pleased when I gave her *Tom Sawyer* that I followed it up with *Huckleberry Finn*.

Kuniang was sixteen when she left the nun's school, and after that her education continued in a very haphaz-ard way. Signor Cante could not possibly take her with him along the railway line, where various generals and marshals, who had turned civil war into a profession, were continually doing battle. If he had confided her entirely to my care, leaving me to provide for her as I thought best, there might have been more continuity in Kuniang's upbringing. But this, in Signor Cante's estimation, would have been asking too much of my kindness. So he was always entrusting his daughter to somebody new, and the most she learnt from successive teachers was to adapt herself to their different mentalities. I think that the Chinese environment also taught her to make the best of things in an unsatisfactory world, so that, while still in her teens, Kuniang appeared to have attained a patient philosophy of her own, considering the vagaries of others with a certain aloofness, even when they touched her personally.

One day she came in to see me, after my own lunch, at the hour when the curio-dealers and vendors of silks and velvets waited on me to offer their wares. There are certain silk merchants in Peking who consider me their special prey. Ever since I took up my abode in the Home of the Five Virtues, they appear daily, or almost daily, and invade my premises, in the hopes of inducing me to make some purchase. They spread their wares on the floor of my study, or on the veranda outside, and then we haggle for an hour over the price of a cut velvet or a piece of old damask.

'How is it that I see so little of you now?' I asked Kuniang, when the silk merchants had departed. 'You used to come in to see me quite often when you were small.'

'It was generally because I had fallen down and hurt myself,' said Kuniang. 'But I very rarely graze my knees now.'

She was sitting opposite me in an arm-chair, with her legs hanging over the arm of it. Her knees, although unhurt, were very much en évidence, and there was a distinct lack of continuity between the edge of her frock and the rolled tops of her stockings. The fashion of very short skirts, which was just coming in, found in Kuniang an enthusiastic supporter, or else she was growing out of her clothes.

'Have you no other troubles,' I asked, 'that might

justify an appeal for help? Remember that you have the half of my crystal seal.'

'I have nothing to complain of. Papà has just stopped my going to the history classes at the American Mission School. I am glad of that.'

'Didn't you like the missionaries?'

'They were quite nice and friendly. But too much joss-pidgin. I suppose that is what they are for; but though I expect it from a priest or a nun, I don't from the father of a family. The teachers were always offering to lead me to Christ, and then going off to Pei-ta-ho for the sea-bathing, while I remained here in the heat. If anything went wrong, they told me to trust in the Lord. But they did not seem to trust him much themselves. They never had more than three children.'

'What had that got to do with it?'

'Somebody told me that the Mission gives them an allowance for every child up till three. I don't mean the child's age. I mean they may have three children at the Mission's expense. After that it is up to them.'

I pondered over this explanation for a few minutes and then asked:

'This cannot be the reason why your father has stopped you going to the history classes?'

'Oh, no. It was because I was not learning enough, which is probably my fault. I think Papà wants to consult you about my education. He asked if he might call on you before he leaves for Kai-feng Fu.'

'Of course he can. I have been expecting him since you told me he was in Peking. I wish I could see him more often. Somebody told me that he had distinguished himself, during the recent troubles in Honan, and that the railway bridge over the Yellow River would have been destroyed if it had not been for him.'

'Yes. General Feng's soldiers wanted to blow up the bridge, after they had got across, so that they should not be pursued. But Papà was standing on it and refused to move, though they threatened to explode the dynamite. He told them that, if they blew him to pieces, all those pieces would haunt them for the rest of their lives. I don't know if they believed him, or thought it was a good

39

joke. But in the end they exploded some dynamite to the side of the bridge, where it did nobody any harm. In this way the General's orders were obeyed, and the bridge was none the worse.'

'And your father is now known as the Chinese Horatius. I hope you will bring him in with you, to-morrow or next day.'

'He would not want me to be there,' said Kuniang, 'if it is about me that he wants to talk.'

'Have you been doing something you shouldn't?'

'If I had he would never tell you. He would not want you to be bothered. He is always reminding me that I must give you no trouble. And if there were anything wrong with me, he would not be likely to know about it. I do my best not to bother him. He has so many anxieties when he is away down the line.'

'That seems rather hard on you. I am not to be bothered, and your father is not to be bothered. You are too young to fend for yourself.'

'Oh, I can manage,' said Kuniang comfortably.

III

Cante de' Tolomei. To me that name was a joy for ever, even when engraved on a pasteboard visiting-card, such as was handed to me next day by Exalted Virtue, on a polished brass tray. It recalled the fifth canto of the *Purgatorio* and the so gentle figure of Pia de' Tolomei (*'Ricordati di me che son la Pia'*).

In the days when Kuniang and her parents still lived together in the pink house with the clock tower I used sometimes to stop and stare at their brass plate on the door. The Dantesque name was then combined with Ahting-fu's heavenly trousers. They rose together out of the grey dust of a Peking street, and the incongruous elements seemed to form a puzzle or a rebus, of which some day I might find the solution. I felt somehow as if there must be a reason why a name recalling the glories of Siena in the fifteenth century, and coupled in Italian history with the names of the Medicis and the Farneses, should have reappeared in a street under the battle-

40

ments of the Tartar Wall, even though the bearer was only a modest employee of a Chinese railway. Visions of hill towns, of cypresses and olives, of towers and cupolas, of open squares and arches curving over narrow streets, all came back to me, recalled by the magic of a name. And I saw again the pure renaissance lines of the Tolomei Palace in Siena, and the great iron rings on either side of the door, where people used to tether their horses.

I wondered what the Sienese would have said if some day Signor Cante had arrived up at his ancestral mansion (as he did at the Home of the Five Virtues), not on a fiery steed or in a motor-car, but in a rickshaw?

When he was shown into my study he appeared rather less jovial than usual. But he cheered up when I congratulated him on his exploit of the bridge.

'That is really why I have come to you,' he said.

I looked at him in surprise, not understanding what I could do about warring armies on the Yellow River. But he explained:

'Life is getting more difficult every day in the Central Provinces. I am well used to Chinese revolutions. I seem to have had one every spring since I came to China. I have had trouble with the White Wolf and the Red Spears and the Christian General, not to mention the Harmonious Fists in 1900.'

'Do you mean the Boxers?'

'Yes.'

'You seemed to have survived them all.'

'I have up till now. But I am beginning to feel that my day is over. It is odd. I should know more of them now than I did ten years ago, but I am no longer so sure of myself. I don't feel so utterly superior to the Chinese as I did when I knew them less. And when one begins to have doubts it is time to go home. Only I can't go home. So one of these days there will be a bundle of clothes lying among the loess on the hill-side, or circling round in a backwater on the river, and that bundle of clothes will be Cante de' Tolomei, with a bayonet thrust through his middle.'

'But, my dear Signor Cante, why not get transferred to

41

Pao-ting-fu, or to Hankow, or to Peking itself? You have served the Kin Han faithfully for many years. They will take you away from where you are now, if you feel that you are no longer up to such dangerous work. I know some of the directors myself. Shall I mention it to them?'

'Thank you for the offer. But the truth is that I don't *want* to come away.'

'Why not? Is life so pleasant on the Yellow River?'

'It is not. But it is *my* life. It has got into my blood. I cannot give it up. You know what it is to get China, or some part of China, into one's blood. It is a vice, like taking opium. We know that it is bad for us, but life would not be worth living without it. I come from the loveliest country in the world, and when I think of the wine, both red and white, that we drink where I was born, and the horrible stuff I have to drink here, I wonder what possessed me ever to leave home. It is years since I have been to Italy. Not since Renata was born. And she, poor girl, has never seen her own country. I would like to see it all again, and to take her. But to stay there, no! When I think how small it all is, I cannot imagine how anybody manages to live there at all. Dante wrote about his exile. Exile! Why, sometimes he was no farther from home than the castle of Romena, close to where my sister lives, at Poppi, in the Casentino. The motor-bus takes less than two hours to reach Florence, over the pass of the Consuma. I suppose it took longer in Dante's time. But what would he have said if he had been at Kai-feng Fu?'

'You don't seem to mind your exile as much as he did.'

'I mind it, yet I cannot do without it. You know my part of the world. All Englishmen seem to know Vallombrosa, and La Verna, where St. Francis preached to the birds. Can you imagine anything less like the country near the Yellow River? It is not called yellow for nothing. The hills are yellow, at least they are in winter, and the plain is yellow and the water is yellow. And all the people are yellow. The only colour besides yellow is the blue of cotton clothes and the blue of the sky. And it is big. If I want to reach the source of that river it might take me a year, supposing I ever got there at all, which is not likely.

42

Even to reach the sea takes about a week, by train and steamer. Broad spaces, long distances, vast proportions. In comparison, the little countries of Europe seem so small. I wonder people can turn round in them.'

Signor Cante mopped his brow. It was warm in my study and he was a full-blooded man. I offered him a drink, but he refused.

'I was forgetting what I had come for,' he said. 'I want to arrange matters for Renata, if anything should happen to me.'

It was so rarely that I heard Kuniang's real name that when Signor Cante spoke of her as Renata I had to stop and think whom he meant.

'I came to give you the address of my sister in Italy,' he added. 'I think you ought to have it, in case of accidents. And I wished to ask if you still feel that you can keep Kuniang here, knowing that she may be left on your hands in the event of my death.'

'What would you do with her if I could not keep her here?'

'I would probably send her home to Italy, as soon as I found some one whom she could travel with.'

'It might be good for Kuniang – I mean Renata – to go to Italy for a while. But, on the other hand, I think it would be imprudent to face the risks of such a journey if it is not absolutely necessary. And as long as she stays in China I hope you will consider this house as her home.'

'I am more than grateful. But it is a great responsibility. I don't want you to regret your kindness.'

'My trouble with Kuniang is, not that she represents too great a responsibility, but that, as far as she is concerned, you allow me none. She sleeps and eats here, but it is not I who looks after her. She tells me that she has been attending some classes in an American missionary school, but that you have stopped her going to them for some reason.'

Signor Cante chuckled. 'She did not care for them much, and they did not care for her. She took no interest in Abraham Lincoln or President Wilson, and mixed them both up with George Washington.'

'Is she pursuing any other course of studies since she left the missionaries?'

43

'I have asked the wife of my Russian colleague, who lives just down the street, to let Renata come to their house for a few hours every day. They are all very artistic. They sing, and they play, and they paint. I do not suppose that Renata will learn much. But Matushka – that is what they call the mother in that family – can keep an eye on her, as on her own daughter. Both Fédor and Natasha have been Renata's playmates ever since she was quite little.'

It seemed unkind to criticize, especially as Signor Cante appeared so pleased to have found some one who would continue Kuniang's upbringing. But I could not help feeling doubtful as to his choice of an instructress. A lady who handed you the butter in her fingers was not my ideal of a person to whom one's daughter should be confided.

'Are you sure they are not just a bit primitive in that family?' I asked.

'I should say that, in some ways, they are quite primeval,' answered Signor Cante. 'Indeed, I believe that they pride themselves on being Old Russians, whatever that may mean, and in keeping up traditions and customs that in more modern houses have been given up or forgotten. I would not care for Kuniang to live with them all the time. They are far too careless, and untidy, and happy-go-lucky. I am staying with them now, myself, and they are most kind and hospitable. They have some fine bedrooms in the house, but as often as not they do not sleep in them. They pass the night, half-undressed, on a pile of cushions, in any room in which they happen to be. And sometimes, instead of sitting down to meals, they will go and forage in the kitchen, and eat things half-cooked out of the saucepans. But they are fond of Kuniang, and she likes the idea of going to them. She prefers it to being left to loaf about, and I am sure it is better for her, even though their ways may be a bit unusual.'

'Well, in case anything is required of me, I will be here. You may be sure I will do my best.'

Signor Cante thanked me, and gave me his sister's address in Siena before he got up to say good-bye. That same evening he was to take the train to Kai-feng Fu.

Although it was really no business of mine, Signor Cante's decision to send his daughter to the Russian family for the greater part of each day made me feel like Baloo, when Mowgli was carried off by the monkey people. Even Kuniang had to admit that Matushka and her husband, known of course as Patushka, reminded her of the Bandarlog. But she found that life in their company was full of thrills, not always pleasurable, but better than dullness at home.

What she learnt from them, if anything, I never heard. But she would go off to their house in the morning and again in the afternoon, and often she would not come back till bedtime. She looked well and contented and mildly amused, so that on the whole I had to admit that the arrangement appeared to be working smoothly. The only thing I noticed, and which showed that she was not well looked after, was a certain untidiness in her clothes. In the days when she had frequented the convent school the nuns had doubtless exercised a certain surveillance on Kuniang's garments. But this was lacking among people who prided themselves on possessing the artistic temperament.

Once or twice I saw Kuniang puffing at a cigarette, without the appearance of deriving much enjoyment therefrom. As nobody told her that she must not smoke, tobacco never acquired for her the charm of a forbidden fruit, and never became a habit.

Whenever I saw Kuniang, she would have something to tell me about the Russian family, and what she said confirmed my opinion that their mode of living was archaic.

Patushka and Matushka were very religious, according to Kuniang. They were *staravierzi*, or Old Believers, and had ikons all over the house, and images of saints, with metal haloes that stuck out of the picture. In the ecstasy of prayer they would fling themselves full length on the floor, and they made a point of getting drunk at Easter, to show how pleased they were that Christ was reborn.

'They are always talking about their souls, and telling me how depressed they are and what awful troubles they have. But they don't really mind as long as they can talk about it. And everything is an excuse for a feast.'

'And how have they brought up the children?' I asked. 'Do they also hand round the butter in their fingers?'

'No. They are much more civilized than their parents. I suppose it comes from living in China, where every one has good manners. Patushka thinks nothing of throwing a plate at his wife, if he does not like the food. But if he really hits her with it, he flings himself on his knees and sheds tears, and kisses her and begs her forgiveness. Fédor and Natasha get things thrown at them too, but they would never behave like that themselves. They are vague and dreamy and rather lovable. They know an awful lot, and can talk about politics and art, but what they like best is flying kites. They learnt that from the Chinese. They have their kites made at the Loong-fu-ssu – quite plain, and then Fédor paints them. He paints quite well. He has made one kite to look like a huge caricature of his father, and another like his mother. The most awful things! I don't think that Patushka and Matushka have seen the kites near by, and they don't know what they represent. When they find out there will be trouble. They don't like being laughed at.'

I reminded Kuniang how, in the old days, when she still lived with her parents in the pink house, we used to see Fédor and Natasha playing about in the street, all alone, and climbing up the incline on to the Tartar Wall.

I asked: 'Are they still allowed to run wild, as when they were small?'

'Most of the time they go where they like and do what they please. In other ways they are treated very much like the boys and girls in Tom Sawyer's school. There is a birch-rod kept behind the looking-glass in the school-room, and every now and then it is brought out and used, for no reason that really matters. This generally happens when there is a yellow wind. Both Fédor and Natasha take it as a matter of course. I suppose it is filial piety.'

These particulars did not surprise me. I have never read a book about Russian family life in which some one does not get whipped. The hero of one Russian novel was a consumptive hat-maker, who beat his lame wife with a broken umbrella. Kuniang's allusion to the yellow wind was also quite clear. Most people in North China suffer from nerves during the winter months, when the air is so dry that one gets an electric shock every time that one touches metal, or takes off one's furs. The nervous tension becomes greater before a dust-storm, known locally as a 'yellow wind'.

Kuniang added: 'Whenever there is a wind, they all complain of *toska*. I asked them what it meant, and they said it is the same as *cafard*. But I don't know what that is either.'

'In English, we call it spleen,' I said. 'You had better be careful, or some day they will vent it on you.'

'I am sure they will. With the birch-rod. I have had some narrow escapes already. Matushka treats me quite like one of the family, and it is no use being shocked at anything they do.'

'You mean that they are children of nature?'

'You might call them that. Last summer Patushka had a swimming-pool made in the garden. Lots of people have them now in Peking, and it cost him next to nothing. He got all the workmen and the materials from the railway. When it was ready, and full of water, they all went in without any bathing-suits. I took one along with me, but I never wore it. I did not like to be the only one to do so when they were all naked. Afterwards we used to lie on the grass, in the sun. It was lovely. But think how shocked the missionary people would have been, whom Papà used to send me to!'

'The Russian monkey-house may be more amusing, with its bathing-costume like that of Eden before the fall. It is all right as long as no serpent enters into your garden.'

'They are really great fun! Instead of pretending to be good, like the missionaries, they will spend hours in telling you what dreadful sinners they are. And then they will beat their chest and groan and say: *Gospodi pomiloui!*'

'If all you tell me is true, they seem to make as much joss-pidgin as the missionaries.'

'They think themselves very religious, but they are never solemn and superior about it. It's all play to them, really. When they have finished talking about their sins, Matushka will sit down at the piano, and Patushka get out his violin, and they will play and sing and dance, and be thoroughly happy!'

'How utterly childish! I hope, at least, that they sing well.'

'Beautifully! I feel that nothing else matters when they begin to sing. They have not got fine voices, and they stop and quarrel over keeping time. But just to hear the song of the Volga boatmen brings tears to my eyes, though I believe it ought to be sung by a very big chorus, all of men. I do not enjoy really good music half so much. I think there must be something childish in their singing, as in everything else they do. It is as if a baby's hands took my heart and played with it, ever so gently. Then they will sing camp-songs, and war-songs, full of a wild throbbing that stirs your blood: one seems to hear the slap of saddles, and the thunder of hoofs, and the ring of stirrup against stirrup. This kind of music seems to drive them all crazy. When he hears certain tunes, Patushka starts dancing all by himself. He twists round from the waist, so that his body seems to be made in two pieces. And he bends his knees and lowers himself almost to the ground, and he kicks out his feet one after the other. I have tried to do it myself, but it is very difficult.'

Kuniang made an attempt to imitate Patushka in a Russian national dance, lowering herself on bended knees, as if she were doing Swedish exercises. But it ended in her rolling over on the carpet.

'Patushka must be pretty nimble,' I said, smiling. 'It hardly seems to be a dance for a middle-aged man. Do the others join in?'

'No. I think Matushka might, but she has to remain at the piano. And Fédor and Natasha have never learnt it. But Fédor gets wildly excited. He starts kissing me and stroking me, and he pulls me down with him on to the sofa. Nobody pays any attention. But it is awkward if there are visitors; you see, my skirts are so short!'

I did see.

V

I sometimes wonder how Kuniang's character, at this period, would have been analyzed, and her mental and physical development described, by those novelists who, of recent years, have specialized in the sex-psychology of the young, and written about the 'suicidal obsessions of morbid adolescence'. In spite of her abnormal environment, they would have found Kuniang a disappointing subject for any one wishing to produce remunerative prose out of budding manifestations of sexuality.

Kuniang's upbringing left her entirely untrammelled. Nothing was hidden from her. No one attempted to repress her natural instincts or curiosity. She learnt all there was to know before she learnt that anything could be shocking or improper. She had no parents at hand to defend her even, if necessary, against herself, and to guide her along the recognized paths of convention. I doubt if she ever learnt that society's verdict, in these or in other matters, could matter to her. Such knowledge of natural and social phenomena as the family of the Five Virtues possessed was passed on to Kuniang, often through the medium of Little Lu. And the Russian family contributed from its own peculiar store, with characteristic and immodest frankness.

At times, Kuniang found that Fédor was difficult to keep in order. He took liberties, which would have made orthodox people throw up their hands in horror. She accepted or repelled such advances composedly, as manifestations of a young man's fancy that in the springtime of life or of the year turns lightly to thoughts of love.

No one, I am sure, suffered less than Kuniang in the process of sexual development. She offered an example of the advantages of leaving youth to itself, in surroundings that are neither foul nor pharisaical. Hers was a healthy, cheerful outlook on all that was good or bad, and she seldom stopped to think which was good and which was bad. To the pure all things are pure.

Meanwhile she was growing up. One of the first out-ward signs in her of a newly achieved importance was that she acquired a dog. Or perhaps it would be more correct to say that a dog acquired her.

Most well-bred dogs are characteristically represen-tative of their nationality. An Aberdeen terrier has Scotsman written all over him, and a Pekingese is essen-tially a product of the Forbidden City.

The *k'ai-men-ti* at my lodge always seems to have a litter of these little dogs bustling about his premises. A familiar sight at the entrance of my house is a small and supercilious Pekingese sitting on the threshold and enjoying the passing show, while his 'master' squats behind him and hunts for his fleas, with gestures remi-niscent of a monkey-house.

Kuniang has always been the friend of successive families of puppies, but it was only after she left school that one of the *k'ai-men-ti's* dogs definitely attached itself to her. People accuse Pekingese of being snobs. But it should be borne in mind that for many centuries they have been 'palace dogs', used to having their own per-sonal servants and cut off by their superior rank from any social intercourse with underlings. A new air of deference in the attitude of the Five Virtues towards Kuniang may have been manifest to the dogs in the *k'ai-men-ti's* lodge; for the most important and disdainful of them all, who up till then had merely accepted her advances with benevolent condescension, now decided to consider himself *her* dog.

Kuniang, who had been reading *Three Men in a Boat*, called him 'Uncle Podger'. She said he was always bossing everybody and making believe that he ran the whole house. The servants spoke of him as *hsiao-ko* (lit-tle dog), as if he were the only one. His real name was Hwang Feng, meaning Yellow Wind.

Uncle Podger's newly given allegiance was typical of the gradual change in the world's attitude towards Kuniang. She was no longer the child to whom I offered a refuge out of kindness, almost out of charity. She had become a member of my household, with an assured position therein. The Five Virtues realized, I think, that

Kuniang might become an ally of mine in our long campaign over 'squeeze', and they were careful to retain their ancient hold on her affections.

As for the foreign community, they found nothing strange in the fact that there was a young and pretty girl living in my house. Peking is a gossipy place and not unready to think evil. But it will accept the most abnormal situations without censure if they conform to the local mentality. This mentality admits of no illusions, but it is not necessarily malicious.

The Chinese point of view became manifest in the attitude of my landlord, Mr. Yè.

The last time Mr. Yè came to the house, to pay me one of his periodical calls, he inquired privately of Exalted Virtue whether I was bringing Kuniang up to be a wife or a concubine. It was Kuniang herself who told me of this conversation. She added that Exalted Virtue had answered that nothing was decided as yet. Kuniang could not understand why I was so taken aback.

'After all,' she said, 'it was a very natural question. Most Chinese girls are married at my age, or somebody takes them on as concubines.'

'Kuniang, these remarks of yours seem to me premature and not in the best taste. Remember that you are living in a respectable European household and that you were brought up in a convent school! What would the nuns say if they heard you talk like that?'

'It takes more than that to shock a nun in China. All they worried about was my clothes in the hot weather. They would not let me go to school without stockings, and I had to wear a little jacket, to hide my bare arms. One day, in June, they sent me home in disgrace, because I had on a cotton frock and no underclothes. On the other hand, they are quite friendly with the women who live in the white house, opposite the Austrian glacis. One of them would have starved if it had not been for the French nuns; they provided her with coal and with food, and got other people to give her clothes. You see, she could not work, for she had caught some disease from a German.'

'Kuniang,' I said. 'Will you tell me if you yourself are ever shocked by anything?'

'I suppose the truth is,' she said, after a pause, 'that we are all shocked by different things. The nuns used to bother about my bare arms and legs. You are often shocked by things I say. I used to think that the Russian family never got shocked about anything, till Fédor lit a cigarette at the candle which he was to hold in church on Christmas Day. Then there was the most awful row. The Five Virtues are quite easily shocked. They keep a little ivory figure of a naked woman (and even she is not quite naked) to show the doctor, when he comes to visit the Old Lady, or the Mother of Little Lu. When one of them is ill, she points out on the ivory figure the spot where she feels a pain. In this way she does not have to show herself to the doctor without her clothes. They were all horrified when the doctor came last month and felt my tummy, after I had had indigestion.'

'Yes. But what about you? Are you never shocked?'

'Oh, yes. Quite often. But not about things like that. When people are unkind and cruel, then I am shocked. Nothing else seems to matter really.'

'Can you tell me of something that shocked you?'

'There was a French book, called *Aphrodite*. That shocked me very much.'

'I am glad to hear it.'

'The story itself is merely silly. I don't believe any man would prefer to dream about a woman, when he can have her in the flesh. Yet that is what Demetrios is supposed to do. What upset me was the part about the slaves. There is one, a girl, called Aphrodysia, who is crucified. It is too horrible. And then there is one who is made to have a baby every year. Only if it is a girl she is allowed to keep it. But she has three boys, who are killed as soon as they are born, because male slaves are not required in the house of a courtesan. The idea of that poor girl and her babies has haunted me ever since.'

'Well, my dear, you should not read books like that.'

'Matushka says that she was haunted, when she was my age, by the story of a deaf and dumb giant, in a book by Turguenieff. The giant was called Mumu, and his one companion, his one interest in life, was a lady pointer, whom he loved with all his heart. But, one day, Mumu's mistress said that the dog must be destroyed, because its barking disturbed her. Mumu had no choice but to obey. He took his dog to the frozen river and dropped it in, so that it disappeared under the ice. Matushka says that the story of poor deaf and dumb Mumu, standing on a block of ice, with his dog in his arms, the tears running down his face, because he is going to drop it in, was the first nail driven into the coffin of the Old Russia, where the peasants were all serfs.'

'That may be, Kuniang. But most Russian books are morbid, and it is a mistake to torment one's self with the horrors that one reads.'

'I am only telling you what are the things that shock me. And it is not only what I read, but what I see. You know those little restaurants just outside the gates of the Tartar City? The people from the country stop and eat there, before they enter the town. And the dogs who have no master sit at their feet and wait for scraps to fall to the ground. Have you noticed that those dogs never look up and beg, like Uncle Podger does? They know it is no use to ask any man to give them something. No man ever has. So they never even raise their heads. It is only what people drop by mistake, or throw away, that the dogs hope to snap up. When I think of those starving dogs, with the smell of food all around them, looking down, always looking down, I sometimes cry with the misery of it. Has nobody ever taught these people to be kind, just kind?'

I got up and went to my bookshelves to take down a book. It was *The Light of Asia*. Then I answered Kuniang's question:

'Yes. There was one. He was an Indian prince, called Siddartha. He sought a way to deliver mankind from all its cruelty and suffering. For days, and months, and years, he fasted and meditated, and strove to lift his soul to the sublimities, so that he might gain wisdom and teach his fellow-men. At times, his spirit hovered above the transient things of earth, and he knew that he had only to persevere to reach his goal and to achieve the world's salvation. But a shepherd passed by with his flock, carrying in his arms two lambs that could not follow. They were not the only ones:

A ewe with couplets in the flock there was,
Some hurt had lamed one lamb, which toiled behind
Bleeding, while in front its fellow skipped,
And the vexed dam hither and thither ran,
Fearful to lose this little one or that;
Which, when our Lord did mark, full tenderly
He took the limping lamb upon his neck,
Saying: Poor woolly mother, be at peace!
Whither thou goest, I will bear thy care;
'Twere all as good to ease one beast of grief
As sit and watch the sorrows of the world
In yonder caverns, with the priests who pray -'

I put the volume back on its shelf. Kuniang watched me without speaking. Her eyes were very bright and shining: like starlight, on a night in spring.

4 Domestic Troubles

I

My garden and the roofs of the pavilions offer shelter to
a number and variety of birds, such as starlings,
hoopoes, and woodpeckers of various sizes and
plumage. More numerous are the sparrows, crows, and
magpies, who seem to think that the place belongs to
them. They are so sure of being unmolested that they
hardly condescend to get out of my way when I walk
along the paths. In the spring, before the rain comes, the
sparrows follow the gardener about, as he waters the
plants, and they sit watching him prepare the hose and
turn on the tap, barely waiting for him to finish, before
they hop down to drink and bathe in the puddles.

A pair of hawks have their home high up under the
eaves of the guardhouse on the Tartar Wall, and sometimes they hover above my garden, but the crows soon
combine to chase them away. These crows have their
nests in the branches of the pines in the courtyards of
my dwelling, but in the daytime they go out to scavenge. I
sometimes watch them returning to roost in the evening.
When there is a dust-storm, I see them beating up
against the wind, and getting blown back when there
comes a gust stronger than the others.

Some years ago a friend presented me with a tame
heron, which I keep in the garden. Its wings are clipped,
to prevent it flying away. It stalks about stiffly and emits
a raucous cry, expressive of an utter boredom. Indeed,
its only diversion consists in being chased round and
round by Uncle Podger, egged on by Little Lu.

If, instead of chasing the heron, who does nobody any

harm, Uncle Podger would keep my garden free of cats I would be grateful. But he has not always come out well from his encounters with cats, and now he pretends that they do not concern him in any way. Like most Chinese (humans and dogs), Uncle Podger is sensitive about 'losing face'.

I have always felt a certain dislike for the cats in the neighbourhood, because they come into the garden to hunt the birds. One summer day, when I was enjoying an afternoon doze, I was awakened by a tremendous miauling, just beneath my window. Annoyed by so much effrontery, I seized a revolver, which I always keep near the bed, and, opening the shutters, I fired a shot into the bushes, without taking aim and without doing the intruder any injury. He was a black and white cat. I saw him as he made off over the garden wall. But that same evening there he was again, with his eyes fixed on my pigeons, who were strutting about, all unconscious, in the grass.

'Ah, you brute!' I exclaimed, 'I'll teach you to come here after the birds!'

And fetching a gun, I let off a cartridge at him, charged with very small shot. For the second time that day he bounded over the wall and disappeared, though I think, that, this time, he did get a few pellets under his skin.

The matter might have ended there, but it so happened that I had twice awakened the Old Lady from her slumbers. Lao Tai-tai asked her son what was the reason of those repeated shots, and Exalted Virtue answered that the Great Man had fired twice at a black and white cat, who had not suffered any inconvenience therefrom. The Old Lady was much impressed and ventured an opinion that the cat in question had remained unhurt owing to the possession of supernatural powers, which gave it immunity from the action of firearms. It followed that the black and white cat must be (so the Old Lady affirmed) a transcendental being.

Indirectly she paid a fine compliment to my marksmanship, excluding the possibility that my aim had been defective. So much faith is undeserved on my part. On those rare occasions when I go out shooting I make what the Germans call *Löcher in die Natur*. The missiles that

56

leave my gun-barrels make holes in Nature in general, and not always in the individual specimens of her fauna.

The day after the episode of the cat, at about five in the afternoon, I rang for my tea, and nobody answered the bell (this is by no means a rare occurrence; the Five Virtues lead an intense social life in which I have no part). I rang again, and again no one appeared, so I went to see what had happened. I found the entire family of the Virtues collected in front of the bronze incense-burner, consuming incense and making obeisances to a large sheet of gilded paper, on which were written some Chinese characters, placed vertically, one under the other. The characters were 'Mao Chan Chun Uè', and might be translated 'Residence of the Marshal Cat'.

The Old Lady was acting as priestess in this ritual, and the whole family appeared to be far too absorbed to take any notice of me. After gazing on the scene for a few minutes, I returned to my study. I could wait for my tea.

The next time I saw Kuniang, I asked her what it was all about. She told me that the Old Lady had given strict orders to her descendants, when they met the black and white cat, to prostrate themselves before it. The title of Marshal, which appeared on the sheet of gilded paper, had been conferred on the cat by reason of its eminent military qualities.

But this beatification did not end well. The cat returned during the night and ate up two white rabbits, which were supposed to belong to Little Lu, though I suspect that the Old Lady intended, sooner or later, to eat them herself. *Inde irae . . .*

As long as my household limits its activities in the realm of magic to propitiating the belligerent spirits of the cats in my garden I cannot really complain. But unfortunately they bring their experiments in occult science into more personal matters, and substitute them for the more ordinary rules of hygiene.

In the winter of 1915–16 Little Lu fell ill. His parents tried to cure him in the usual way. They paid a visit to the temple of Kuan-ti, the God of War. He is the most popular of the gods: a survival of olden times, when the Manchus were all warriors. The father and mother of

Little Lu made the customary payments and burned incense in front of the image of Kuan-ti. Then they accomplished the ceremony known as the Impetration of the Transcendental Prescription (*chou shen fan*), and procured a remedy which chance, divinely inspired, prescribed as a cure.

But Little Lu did not benefit in any way. Nor did he get better when he was made to drink certain infusions, composed of tea, in which had been dissolved the ashes of little bits of paper, inscribed with the best-known aphorisms of Confucius and of Lao-tze.

The obvious uselessness of these remedies caused a suspicion to arise in the mind of the Old Lady – a suspicion that some malefic influence might be weighing on the Home of the Five Virtues.

It was Kuniang who told me about it. She is always well informed as to the private life of the Five Virtues, and she was much worried about Little Lu's illness.

'He does not seem so bad,' I said to her. 'He looks very thin, but he was playing about in the courtyards this morning.'

'If they left him alone I have no doubt he would get well,' said Kuniang. 'But you never know what the Old Lady will do next. She wants to consult a witch-doctor from the Liu-li-chang. The Five Virtues have a family magician of their own, but he is not easy to get at, for he lives somewhere in the Western Hills, and only comes into Peking occasionally. If they consulted him, I would not be so anxious. He is a clever little man, and sensible. But these common witch-doctors are brutes.'

Kuniang was not far wrong. The witch-doctor came to the house and worked certain charms, which made clear (to him) the cause of Little Lu's troubles. His sister, born a few months before, had entered the family as a bearer of evil. She absorbed the vitality of her elder brother, as a vampire sucks blood. Measures were necessary to guard against her malign influence, otherwise Little Lu would certainly die.

It is at this point that – had it not been for Kuniang – things might well have turned to tragedy. It is only too easy to get rid of a suckling babe: a pot of boiling water, in which to dip its head, and all would have been for the best, according to the dictates of local folk-lore. Luckily Kuniang advised Exalted Virtue (whose heart revolted at the thought of sacrificing his youngest born) to speak to me about it. After several consultations we discovered (as we thought) a way out of the difficulty.

The circumstance which permitted his youngest sister to exert a harmful influence over Little Lu arose from their relationship. Had she not belonged to the same family, it would not have been possible for her to absorb the vitality of her brothers and sisters. Therefore it was enough for somebody to adopt little Miss Lu, for her to cease belonging to the family of the Five Virtues and to bring them harm.

So she was given to a neighbouring family, who adopted her for a consideration.

But, unfortunately, also in that family there was an Old Lady (grandmothers are the curse of China!), who happened to fall ill after the arrangement had been carried out. Here was a new and irrefutable proof of the evil influence exerted by that small being, who cried because she had been separated from her mother!

Kuniang hurried to me with this piece of news, and again I decided to interfere. I told Exalted Virtue that he might give his baby to me. At the same time I insisted that Little Lu should be treated by a European doctor and should follow a diet prescribed by him.

This time the stratagem succeeded admirably. Miss Lu, having returned to her mother and once more taking nourishment, as Mr. Micawber would say, 'at nature's founts', grew fatter day by day, and so did Little Lu, who was no longer doctored with infusions of Confucian aphorisms.

My own health remained what it was. Nothing to complain of.

In gratitude for this fortunate intervention, the family of the Five Virtues offered to make me a present of Little Lu. But I declined. It was enough to be considered, as the Chinese say, 'the dry father' of little Miss Lu.

I felt sure that the cloud that had hung over the Home of

the Five Virtues had passed away, but it was not so. One morning Kuniang came and told me that little Miss Lu was dying.

'Little Miss Lu!' I exclaimed. 'Do you mean the baby? I never knew it was ill.'

'Nor did I. That is the pity of it. She has been ill for some time and nobody told me.'

'Why not?'

'First because we were crossing the year. And then because of the Old Lady's birthday.'

This explanation may not be easy to understand by any one who has not lived in China, but it was quite clear to me. When little Miss Lu had begun to be unwell we were in the midst of the festivities for the Chinese New Year (that year, the first day of the first moon came on the third of February). To fall ill at such a time is contrary to all rules of correct conduct. No one had any time to think about the baby's illness. She might have been saved even after the New Year was over, but, unfortunately, just in those days came the birthday of the Old Lady. After one has reached sixty years each birthday marks an ever greater triumph. The Old Lady is well over seventy, and it almost seemed as if the congratulations and the ceremonial visits would never end. Meanwhile little Miss Lu was dying.

Kuniang suggested that she herself and Exalted Virtue and the Mother of Little Lu should take the baby to the German Hospital, and they started in rickshaws together. I went to see them off at the door. One glance at little Miss Lu made me realize that it must be too late.

After little more than an hour Kuniang came back to my study. I looked up inquiringly, but she shook her head without speaking, and went and sat on the sofa, burying her face in the cushions. Uncle Podger had followed her in. When he saw that she was crying he put up his paws on her knee and whined.

I felt a lump in my throat and my eyes grew misty. Yet it was only one tiny baby who had died of all the millions in China.

5   Donald and the Silks

Clever people, who know all about women, have told me
that one should never speak of a girl's *first* love-affair.
There is no such thing. There was always one before,
some one to whom she gave her heart, perhaps uncon-
sciously, and only for a few seconds, when crowing in
her cradle. Nevertheless, I think I am justified in saying
that in Kuniang's life Donald Parramoor represented
her first love-affair. It lasted about six weeks.

The first I heard of it was when Kuniang began to
receive, by almost every post, a series of illustrated
postcards of the vulgarly sentimental kind that, in Western climes, are sent by amorous soldiers and sailors to
their sweethearts. In Peking you can buy them in Hata
Mên Street, and they cost quite a lot, thirty or even fifty
cents each, having been imported from abroad.

As all the mail for the household was brought to me, I
could not help seeing the letters and postcards that were
addressed to Kuniang. One day three cards arrived for
her by the same post. It will be enough – more than
enough – if I describe one of them. It was a coloured
photograph of a mature, but still attractive-looking,
matron, in a tight-fitting bathing-suit. She held her head
a little on one side and was smirking, while a young man,
also in a bathing-suit, bent over her as if he were going to
kiss her and felt a little nervous about it. The lady held a
parasol, open, in one hand, and a magenta-coloured
handkerchief was tied round her head. The background,
which had obviously been added afterwards by the pho-
tographer, represented a calm sea, with rocks in the

61

foreground and a yellow moon reflected in the water. There was no signature on any of these postcards, but on one of them was written 'For ever', and on another 'In memory of your first love'.

I handed this correspondence to Kuniang and asked who had sent her such awful things. She picked them up and examined them with an expression of shamefaced amusement.

'It's Donald,' she said. 'Silly fool! Did you ever see such horrors in your life?'

'He must have got appalling taste,' I remarked.

'No. He has wonderful taste. That is the joke of it. But he says I have not enough sentiment in my cosmos (whatever that may be!). And these postcards will serve to correct acidity.'

'But who is he, and where did you meet him?'

Kuniang explained. Donald Parramoor was a young American who was touring the world in the company of his two sisters Elsie and Norah. Kuniang had met them in the Clock Store, in Hata Mên Street, buying silk. As they seemed to be in difficulties, she had offered to interpret for them. They had immediately made friends, and she had been to tea with them at the Hôtel des Wagons-lits. It appeared that Donald was an artist, and had expressed a desire to know me, because some one had told him that I possessed a wonderful collection of old Chinese silks, cut velvets, and embroideries. Kuniang asked if she might bring him to the house.

I confess to a fellow-feeling with anybody who loves silks and velvets. Any one who showed an interest in my very modest collection could only be a kindred spirit. So Donald Parramoor and his sisters were invited to lunch for the next day. We met at the door of Kuniang's pavilion. I judged Donald Parramoor to be about twenty-seven years old and his sisters, who were pretty girls, but rather too plump, a little younger. He wore the usual horn-rimmed spectacles that for a time were so much affected by men of his nationality, as by Chinese mandarins of olden days. He talked incessantly and ordered everybody about in a genial way that appeared to be thoroughly successful. He belonged to the type of

Transatlantiques who consider that the world is their playground. I am told that the type is dying out. I hope not. They make for the gaiety of nations.

We proceeded together towards my study, and as always happens when anybody comes to the house for the first time, they stopped to exclaim at Ah-ting-fu's sign over my door. But Donald Parramoor made an entirely original, if ungrammatical, remark.

'Why,' he said, stopping in front of the sign, 'that's me all right.'

I asked him why he would describe himself as a maker of heavenly trousers.

'Because I'm a painter, and my speciality is costume. I am a pupil of Bakst. You know who I mean: the man who designed the costumes for the Russian dances. And I've worked with Benda, who makes masks. My ideal in life is to play with masks and music and moonlight; to dress up all the good-looking men and all the pretty women in lovely costumes, and have them make love against wonderful backgrounds of changing lights and shadows. That is what I call real philanthropy. Do you know why I am in Peking? To study the costumes of the Chinese theatre. They are full of ideas. Yesterday I saw a belt such as I had never seen before: it was made of rectangles of looking-glass. The man who wore it was a traitor, because he had a white face. On the Chinese stage, when you have a white face it means you are a crook. I wish we could arrange things that way where I come from. Life would be much simpler. But they have no pretty girls on the stage here. No beauty chorus. Only Med Lan-fang, and he's a man, though his make-up is wonderful. Now, I may be vulgar, but I like a beauty chorus. Give me a row of pretty girls with nice legs and let me have the dressing of them, and *then* you'll realize that your Uncle Donald is the big noise!'

His sisters confirmed this version of Donald's life-story.

'As to Elsie and I,' said Norah to me a little later, 'we are just his manikins. And woe to us if we don't keep slim! If he had his own way, when we are travelling about, he would drag us into every silk shop in the East and make us take off our frocks, while he drapes rolls of silk and rugs of fur round us. And at home he is worse. He seems to think that it does not matter how much of her clothes a girl takes off, as long as he's there with something pretty to put in its place, even if it's only a silver star or a wisp of gossamer.'

After lunch I opened the big camphor-wood boxes in my study, and we took out the silks: mandarin coats; rolls of damask; hangings and embroideries from the Imperial tombs (looted by marauding soldiers); cut velvets from Nanking; heavy silks from Che-kiang; light silks from Shan-tung; *kosseus* and satins: all the products of the looms that once were sent to Peking as tributes from the Central Provinces to the Court.

Donald Parramoor pored over the single pieces with an absorbed interest which completely won my heart.

'Why is this padded?' he asked, as he spread out a lovely piece of rose-coloured satin. 'Is it meant for a bedspread?'

I answered, speaking rather low, so that his sisters, who were at the other end of the room with Kuniang, might not hear:

'That is what the eunuchs used to wrap round the naked concubine, when they carried her through the courtyards of the palace, to lay her on the Emperor's bed.'

'You don't say so! Now, that's what I call real civilization? Something like Cleopatra in the carpet. But it is a pity that the lady would have a yellow skin. She would have looked much better, when they unwrapped the parcel, if she had been white.'

He dived back into the camphor-wood box, and brought out some Court robes.

'The tailors and dressmakers here,' he said, 'do not seem to think much of the human form divine. Look at this coat: russet brown satin, with great plaques of embroidery, gold and blue, like the wings of those little butterflies that are called "chalk blues". This, by the way, is the "Peking stitch", something like a French knot. One could not produce more beautiful colours,

64

even in these days of aniline dyes. But the shapes! Whoever had shoulders that shape?'

'That coat was made to be worn at the yearly ceremony on the Altar of Heaven,' I explained. 'Probably the person who wore it was a portly old gentleman with a paunch, and gout in his fingers. You don't often find the human form divine in the higher government officials.'

'Perhaps not. But the Chinese Court robes for women were not any better. Here is one: embroidered with sprays of wistaria; perfectly lovely. But what is the use of a woman having a figure, if you drape it in wide trousers and a short jacket with wide sleeves? Now, in Egypt they understood the matter perfectly. Do you remember the cute little straps that the harpists and the flute-players wear in the drawings on Pharaoh's tomb? I once tried to dress the dancing-girls that way for the second act in *Aida*. But the management said the costumes were hardly suitable for the Metropolitan. They suggested the *Folies Bergère*.'

Kuniang had come nearer and was standing in the light of the window. Suddenly Donald seized a roll of green damask (silver peonies on a background of apple-green), and he draped it round her. Then, with a few deft movements of his hands, he undid her hair, and let it fall in a river of gold over the green and silver.

'An emerald on her forehead,' he said, 'and two white aigrettes that fall back behind the ears. Her arms and shoulders bare, with green jade bangles. The side of the dress open, to show one bare leg. Sandals of silver and emeralds. Her lips, geranium red. Her eyes heavy with kohl. And a robber chief in chain armour, to lift her into the saddle of his white horse and lead her over the silken carpets of his war-tent, like Tamerlane showing his bride to the banqueting Emirs!'

II

I could understand why Donald Parramoor was popular with young women. He made up to them through pretty clothes and the fun of dressing up. But I discovered that

65

he could also make himself agreeable to the aged. Kuniang started to show him round the house, while I talked to his sisters. Twenty minutes later, as they had not come back, we went to look for them, and found Donald in animated conversation with the Old Lady. Kuniang and Exalted Virtue were acting as interpreters. The subject of the conversation, this time, was not clothes but coffins. I suppose that Kuniang must have mentioned to Donald that the Old Lady's coffin was stored up against the day of her death. Donald seized upon the idea with delight, and asked the Old Lady to describe her coffin: its size, its weight, its colour.

'Red lacquer and gold!' he exclaimed. 'And the same on the catafalque, with bearers in dark green. Orange and gold and green are the colours of woods in autumn. And then the disks of gold and silver paper that they toss up into the air: spirit money, to be spent in another world; cheques that the dear departed will cash in heaven! How odious, in comparison, are our Western funerals: black hearses, and black horses, and fast-fading flowers. Why should black be the colour of death? Why not the colours of a sunset?'

The Old Lady could not understand a word of all this, and neither Kuniang nor Exalted Virtue could possibly interpret. But they all seemed much pleased with one another, and grateful for the nice things that Donald wished to say. He took his leave of the Old Lady, with many expressions of esteem, and then attached himself to Kuniang again.

'Do you know, Miss Kuniang,' he said, 'that all this reincarnation business that the Chinese believe in is perfectly true. I speak from bitter experience. Two thousand years ago I was born in China. I was a mandarin, with a huge jade ring on my thumb, a ruby button on the top of my hat, and a peacock's feather falling over my left shoulder – so! I had so many wives and concubines that I did not know them by sight: all except one, who was my favourite. Her name was Little Candle Light. Now, isn't that a pretty name? One day I made her dance, with bare feet, on a golden floor encrusted with sapphires. She was lame for weeks afterwards, poor girl! For, you see, I was a great sinner. From the Great Wall to the River of Pearls there was no greater sinner than I. Why, I drowned forty-six of my mothers-in-law in the Yellow River! And that, as any Chinese will tell you, is not filial piety. At the age of fifty-one I died from eating too many sharks' fins cooked in honey, and I was not reincarnated for more than two thousand years. As a punishment, and as an expiation of all the sins I had committed in a former life, I was condemned to be born out of China, in a miserable country that did not even belong to the Son of Heaven. So I turned up at Pittsburg. You have never been to Pittsburg? Then the tragedy of my reincarnated soul means nothing to you! But you *do* know about Mary and her Little Lamb?

'Well, listen to this:

'Mary had a little lamb,
Its fleece was white as snow!
She took it down to Pittsburg,
And now look at the damn thing!'

III

Kuniang would have listened for hours on end to Donald Parramoor's illuminating conversation, and, on his part, he was lost in admiration of her, and was ever imagining new guises in which he would have presented her on the stage. For Donald, as for Shakespeare, all the world was a stage, and all the men and women merely players, to be dressed up. At one time he would visualize Kuniang as Elsa, in *Lohengrin*, with her hair in two long tresses, bound up with ropes of pearls. Another time, as Roxane, in *Cyrano*, and though his French was of the sort that outside a theatre would not take you much farther than the shops in the Rue de la Paix, he quoted, with a strong American accent, the verses from the balcony scene:

'Comme, lorsqu'on a trop fixé le soleil,
On voit, sur toute chose ensuite, un rond vermeil,
Sur tout, quand j'ai quitté les feux dont tu m'inondes,
Mon regard ebloui pose des taches blondes!'

Strange to say, when he talked of Kuniang's hair, Donald dropped his slangy phraseology. The scenic artist that he was felt the inspiration of those marvellous tresses.

Once we were standing together at the door of my house. The young people had been riding, and had just dismounted. Kuniang was giving the pony carrots. She had taken off her hat. Her hair was not put up, but tied with a brown ribbon, so that it fell on her shoulders.

Donald Parramoor gazed at her with a rapt expression on his face, and he exclaimed, almost as if he were talking to himself:

'Like the crown of Montezuma!'

'What is like the crown of Montezuma?' I asked.

'Kuniang's hair.'

'But why especially of Montezuma?'

'Because the crown of Montezuma is the most beautiful ornament that has ever been designed to lend magnificence to the brow of a king. It is made of the tail feathers of a bird of paradise, feathers like ribbons, four or five feet long, and their colour is a shiny golden yellow, with green shadows. The original crown can be seen in Vienna, in the Natural History Museum, but one cannot appreciate its loveliness, because it is spread out like a fan, and hung on a wall, in a dark corner. Besides, it is very old; the feathers are worn and dusty. They have lost their colour and their sheen. But once I had a similar dress made for a costume ball. You have no idea what wonderful effects can be produced by a crown of feathers.'

I looked again at Kuniang. The evening sun shone in her hair. I thought to myself that no crown could ever equal beauty such as that.

A few days later Kuniang informed me that she had just been to the station to see her friends off. They were starting for Europe. Before leaving, Donald had promised her to have a costume made, with a crown of feathers, like that of Montezuma, and to send it to her. But for some months nothing more was heard of the matter.

6 Elisalex

I

Every now and then I go for a walk on the path that runs
along the top of the Tartar Wall. Once, one could walk
all around the city by that path, but recently it has been
closed with barbed-wire entanglements at the Hata Mên
and the Ch'ien Mên, so that my old walk is now much
curtailed.

One Sunday morning I was surprised to meet Kuniang
and Uncle Podger on the Wall, in company with a lady
whom I had never seen before. I took off my hat, Kuniang
smiled, and the lady bowed. We might have passed each
other without stopping, if Uncle Podger had not complicated matters by standing in the middle of the path and
gazing alternately after Kuniang and myself, as if hesitating which of us to follow. Before he could make up his
mind we had entered into conversation, and Kuniang
went through a somewhat inefficient form of introduc-
tion, in which I did not catch the lady's name, and I doubt
if she learnt mine.

We talked for a few minutes and then walked back
together to where our rickshaws were waiting, at the
foot of the incline, near the American Legation Guard.
The usual questions that one puts to any one whom one
meets in Peking for the first time revealed the fact that
the lady was Russian (though she spoke English perfectly), and that she had arrived three weeks before
from Harbin.

I was much struck with her appearance, which was
singularly attractive, and with the charm of her voice
and manner. A real society woman is a *rara avis* in

69

Peking, and Kuniang's new friend was obviously a *femme du monde*. She was extremely well dressed, in black, with black furs, which were wrapped round her so as almost to hide her face, for it was a bitterly cold day, just after the New Year.

As we drew near to the tower that rises over the Ch'ien Mên, I pointed out the roofs of the Forbidden City, with the sunlight flashing on the yellow tiles, the distant view of the Western Hills, and, to the south, the triple roof of the Temple of Heaven. The lady regarded these objects of interest with mild curiosity and without any expressions of enthusiasm. She was in no way 'thrilled', as so many foreign tourists profess themselves to be. Possibly she found humanity more interesting than buildings or views of distant mountains.

When we left the wall and got into our respective rickshaws, I was surprised to discover that our ways home lay in the same westerly direction. The lady was staying with the Russian family! She did not look the sort of person who would be intimate with Patushka and Matushka. They were rough diamonds: she was a polished stone, in a setting by Cartier. She looked as if she might belong to that class of Russians who, before the war, passed their winters in expensive hotels on the Riviera, and in summer gave picnics on the islands near St. Petersburg, with servants in livery serving iced champagne, lace-bordered table-cloths spread out on the grass, and gold plate among the crocuses.

As we neared Patushka's door I took leave of my companions and made a sign to the rickshaw coolie to continue on his way. But the lady asked me if I would not come in and have some tea, to warm me after the drive through the cold.

I had never set foot in the house of the Russian family, and therefore I hesitated a moment before accepting an invitation that did not come from them. But there was something so fascinating about their guest that I could not resist the idea of seeing a little more of her. So I got out of my rickshaw and followed her and Kuniang into the house. As soon as I got in I drew Kuniang aside and asked her hurriedly who her friend was.

'They call her Elisalex,' said Kuniang. 'I have never heard her surname. I think she does not like it to be mentioned.'

'Elisalex,' I repeated. 'What a strange name!'

'It is short for Elisabeth Alexandra.'

Kuniang pronounced the *i* in Elisalex as in Elizabeth, but rather more accentuated and drawn out.

'What is she doing here?' I asked.

'She was a great lady in Russia. But something happened. I don't know what. And she got into trouble. People say that she has become a communist and that she is waiting for a revolution to break out in Russia. Then she will go home.'

I was about to answer that I had never seen any one look less like a communist. More probably she was one of the wrecks of good society. Not a hopeless wreck: just a good ship temporarily aground at low tide.

At this moment the lady named Elisalex, having taken off her hat and her furs, came up to us again and we had to stop talking about her.

I was not sorry to hear that neither Patushka nor Matushka was at home, but only Fédor and Natasha. They bade us welcome very politely. The former was dressed, Russian fashion, in dark trousers and a linen tunic, belted in at the waist and embroidered at the collar and cuffs. Natasha was a lump of a girl at the ungainly age, wearing a plain frock of Shantung silk, cut like a night-dress. Both brother and sister had lank fair hair without any lights in it, and dreamy grey eyes.

Though Chinese houses are all much alike, foreign occupants bring to them a touch of their own nationality. In the entrance hall of Patushka's house was an enormous brick stove, built into the wall, which gave out an almost tropical heat. From the hall we passed into the sitting-room, which opened into a big corner room: this was evidently what Kuniang had once mentioned to me as 'the schoolroom'.

The sitting-room was furnished with an enormous divan and some arm-chairs, hideously upholstered with a shiny horsechair cloth, on which some really fine cushions of old Chinese brocade looked strangely incongruous.

Two cast-iron-expressioned portraits of Patushka in uniform, and Matushka in evening dress, added a note of gloom to that already cast by the horsehair furniture. Kuniang and Elisalex went at once and sat on the divan, and Fédor remained with them. I followed Natasha into the schoolroom, where she began to make tea at a lighted samovar which stood in the corner. I always like to see a work-room. It serves so well to reveal the character and the habits of the people who inhabit it.

The Russian family's schoolroom was a pleasanter place than the sitting-room, and probably more lived in. What struck me first was a row of shelves on the wall between two windows. The shelves were full of specimens in glass jars or bottles. On closer inspection they proved to be a collection of spiders preserved in alcohol. I asked why they were there, and Natasha explained that her father had painstakingly collected them from all over China, during many years, on behalf of a Rumanian prince who specialized in spiders. Patushka had been promised large sums for his collection, but when it was almost completed the Rumanian prince had died, and nobody wanted the spiders any more. Spiders had been a very sore subject in the family ever since. It was hardly safe to mention them. They represented a wasted effort, a labour come to nothing.

On the side of the room opposite to the wall with the spiders an upright piano stood against the wall. It was open, and a bow and fiddle lay on the top among the music-books. I glanced at an open score on the music rest. It was a sonata of Grieg's, for piano and violin. When Russians take the trouble to play at all, they generally play well. I doubt if that schoolroom ever knew the horrors of similar sanctums in England: the five-finger exercises, haltingly repeated *ad infinitum*, or the latest song from musical comedy, strummed with one finger by boys and girls picking out the tune.

The room was heated by an American stove, with rusty metal tubing which meandered round and about, suspended by wires from promiscuous nails in the cornice, till it found an exit over a glass door that opened out on to a veranda. The length of the tube may have added to the calorific properties of the stove, but it also permitted the escape of a considerable amount of fumes from the burning coal. The stove stood in front of an open fireplace, which had evidently been put in, at some time, to satisfy the foreigners' craving for open fires. But it looked as if it had never been used.

A large looking-glass in a gilt frame had its base resting on the mantelpiece and leant outwards, giving a distorted reflection of a table in the middle of the room and of a powerful lamp in a green shade, which hung just above it. The table had a rust-coloured cloth on it, with a fringe of yellow tassels. It was covered with books, newspapers, sheets of drawing-paper, tubes of paint, and boxes of cigarettes.

On the wall, above the piano, was an original study, by the artist, for Vereschagin's picture 'Left Behind', representing a dying soldier abandoned by his comrades. Some prints of the '1812' series of pictures by the same artist, of Napoleon's Russian campaign, were no less harrowing. Only the characteristic mental detachment of Russians, and their habit of separating theory from practice, could have made it possible for anybody to keep such pictures continually before their eyes, in time of war.

While I was looking at the pictures Natasha brought me a cup of tea. She told me that Vereschagin had been a friend of her father's.

'He was blown up, you know, in the *Petropavlosk*, in 1904.'

I did not know. But the friendship with Patushka explained the morbid taste in mural decoration.

'Your brother also paints, does he not?' I asked conversationally.

'Yes. He is beginning to get quite good at it. There is nothing in this room by him, except that head on the door.'

She pointed to the door by which we had entered. On one of the upper panels was a rough portrait of Natasha herself in oils; a head and shoulders, unfinished, but strangely alive and vivid.

73

'Why did he paint it there?' I asked. 'Is he going to decorate all the room in that way?'

'No. It was only because he had run out of canvas. Patushka was in an awful rage and half skinned him for spoiling the door.'

I remembered Kuniang's information concerning the birch-rod that was kept behind the looking-glass. That also might be considered as part of the characteristic furnishings of the room.

Yet, on the whole, the schoolroom gave me a not unpleasant impression of the family which used it: unaffected, clever, careless people, indifferent to appearances and to the refinements of civilized life, but sensitive to beauty and easily receptive of culture. For a moment I almost persuaded myself that Signor Cante had not made a bad choice.

But what of the newcomer? What of Elisalex?

She was obviously of a very different type: the type (so I guessed) that varies little throughout the ages. The eternal courtesan; the immortal Circe, wielding the ever-delightful magic of perdition.

II

I went back to the sitting-room and took one of the arm-chairs.

Fédor was talking with considerable animation. He was full of a great piece of news: Rasputin had been murdered in St. Petersburg. Fédor said that most of the Russians in Peking were delighted and had lit candles in their church in honour of the event.

'You must be pleased,' he said to Elisalex. 'Now that Grigori Efimovitch is dead, you may be able to go home.'

Elisalex appeared reluctant to discuss the matter in the presence of a stranger. She answered that Rasputin's death had come too late to make any difference to her, but it might hasten the fall of the Empire.

Fédor made some indignant exclamation, which I did not understand.

'Do you think the Empire will fall?' I asked. The idea

filled me with apprehension for its possible effects on the war.

Elisalex answered quietly: 'Grigori Efimovitch, or Grishka, as we called him, predicted that he would be murdered and that, six months afterwards, the Tsar would lose his throne and his son. The first part of the prophecy has come true.'

'I did not know he prophesied. I thought he was only a shady mesmerist and charlatan.'

'He was not wholly a charlatan. Indeed, he struck one as being sincere, and he certainly had the prophetic instinct. It was not a happy gift. Except where the health of the Grand Duke Alexis was concerned, all Grishka's visions of the future were dark and gloomy. He prophesied that the Germans would be beaten, but that Russia would be subjected to such a martyrdom as never has been recorded in history.'

'Let us hope that he was a false prophet, at least as far as Russia is concerned.'

Fédor agreed with me in this pious hope. He spoke of Grigori Efimovitch as the ruin of his country, and said that after his death all would be well with Russia. I liked the tone of *saeva indignatio* in the boy's voice. He had all the fire and assurance of youth, despite the dreamy eyes. Elisalex let him talk and did not say anything more, until I asked her:

'How was it that such a man acquired so much power in Russia?'

'His power over the Empress, as you probably have heard, was based on her belief that he could arrest the attacks of haemorrhage that threatened her son's life. But Grishka's power over the *Rasputiniztky*, as his followers were called, came from the fascination of his doctrines. He taught that salvation lies in repentance and in forgiveness. In order to repent and to be forgiven, one must have sinned. Sin is a first step towards salvation. As you can imagine, he did not lack disciples.'

'You were one of them yourself, were you not?' asked Fédor.

It was a tactless question, which only a boy would have put so crudely. Elisalex did not appear to resent it, but she changed the subject.

'Grishka,' she said, 'did me a lot of harm. But now he is dead. Let him rest in peace. Why do you not show us your drawings, Fédor? I am sure our new friend would like to see them.'

Fédor went off to get his drawings. While he was out of the room the conversation flagged, but I took the opportunity of looking more closely at Elisalex. She was dressed in a tight-fitting frock of black satin. Her figure was perfect: tall and lissom and strong; the curves full, but not accentuated. She was what the French call *une fausse maigre*. Her eyes were brown, with grey light in them, like agates. Her face reminded me of a famous beauty of the last century, Cléo de Mérode. I had never seen this lady in the flesh, but had admired her photographs in shop windows when I was still in my teens. Like her, Elisalex wore her hair parted in the middle and drawn down on either side, so as to hide most of her forehead and to cover her ears. It is a mode of hairdressing that has long gone out of fashion; it used to be called *à la vierge*. I was surprised that any young woman should still do her hair that way in the year 1917. But it suited Elisalex, and, as I looked at her, I was reminded of an Italian saying which I had learnt from my mother: *'Donna slava, tre volte donna'* ('The fascinations of a woman multiplied by three').

I was also a little astonished at the extraordinary sympathy that seemed to exist between Elisalex and Kuniang. It was manifest, not so much in what they said, as in their attitude towards one another. There was a melting tenderness in the way that Elisalex looked at Kuniang, and the latter showed an almost schoolgirlish adoration for the elder woman. Natasha looked, and perhaps felt, left out in the cold.

After a few minutes Fédor came back with a portfolio full of drawings and laid them down on a small table, which he brought up and placed at my elbow. I picked up the drawings and examined them, one by one. They showed no little talent, with an occasional weakness, or a touch of exaggeration, which gave to some of the portraits almost the form of caricatures. There were figures: Chinese servants, old men and children, and a whole series of boys occupied in Fédor's favourite sport (as Kuniang had once explained to me) of flying kites; the young bodies showed both movement and tension, despite the enveloping drapery of loose-fitting clothes. Fédor evidently had a good knowledge of anatomy. There was a sketch of Kuniang, pretty but not very like her. Some Mongols in the Llama mantle and head-dress. A group of ponies in water-colour. One of the ponies was painted a bright yellow, and another a deep violet colour. I like an artist to have the courage of his opinions, and to paint things as he sees them, or imagines that he sees them.

I picked up the next drawing. It was a *sanguigno*, the colour of rust, and represented a young woman, undraped, seated on a balustrade, clasping her knees with her hands and turning her face to look at the painter. The nude figure was full of seductive grace. Her long hair was parted in the middle and covered her forehead and her ears. The likeness was unmistakable: no need to read the words written underneath, *Elisalex – December* 1916. Fédor had done full justice to her lovely shape, and she had posed for him in all the dizzy charm of beauty unadorned.

7 'Love-Love Pidgin'

I

A week after I met Elisalex for the first time the early morning post brought me an anonymous letter concerning her. The envelope bore the Peking postmark.

The letter was written in pidgin-English, and, judging by the handwriting, the author must have been a Chinese, having more familiarity with the paint-brush with which one designs ideograms than with the pen. It began by saying that there was a virgin living in my house who every day went to a Russian family (it gave their Chinese name):

> 'This family velly bad family. No can teach. No behave plopa. Young master makee love pidgin. *Tai-tai* (lady) makee thump.
>
> 'Chin-tien (to-day, now) new piecee *tai-tai* come China-side. Go lib in same house. This *tai-tai* makee love-love pidgin. In tea house outside Ch'ien Mên muchee talkee about this *tai-tai*. She no good flin for Missee. What for she come China-side? Makee play pidgin. Soon she wailo way. Makee big bobbely.
>
> 'You talkee Missee this *tai-tai* no can do.'

I never had any doubt as to who had written this letter. The author could only be my late *tingchai*, the one who had left my service, to take up the writing of anonymous letters as a profession. His pidgin-English was not very pure (only the Cantonese speak this strange language in its original form). But I noticed the subtle distinction between 'love pidgin' and 'love-love pidgin'. The first of these expressions means simply to make love (love business). But love-love pidgin means something different. It corresponds to voluptuousness or sensuality. The expression was applied to the newly arrived *tai-tai*.

It seemed to me almost certain that the Five Virtues had inspired the letter, and probably paid to have it written. They included Elisalex in the feud that they had always kept up with the Russian family since Fédor had pulled Little Lu's pigtail and had been disrespectful to the Old Lady.

'Play pidgin' is a sham, or humbug. And the lady would soon go away and make 'big bobbely' somewhere. In other words, she would stir up a revolution. This showed that the Five Virtues were aware of her reputation as a communist. I wondered if the Chinese servants in the Russian family's house were related to the Five Virtues and furnished them with 'inside information'.

Of late I had become almost reconciled to the idea of Kuniang being entrusted to the Russian family, even though I might consider their *milieu* unsuitable for a young girl who was not herself a Russian of Matushka's own class. As to the newly arrived *tai-tai*, I felt inclined to agree that she was not a very desirable friend (*flin*) for Kuniang. But what could I do about it? Kuniang seemed enthusiastic over Elisalex and perfectly contented with the arrangements made for her by her father. Yet it was more than likely that Matushka was now in the habit of extending to her such corporal punishments (described in the letter as 'makee thump') as Fédor and Natasha were occasionally subjected to.

I do not know what object, if any, the authors of the letter hoped to attain. But the result of their anonymous communication was to make me realize, not that I must immediately put a stop to Kuniang's companionship with Elisalex and her hosts, but that I, myself, ought to do much more for Kuniang than I had done up till then. Even if I had no other responsibility than to offer her food and shelter, I should take a greater interest in the matter. Also I had noticed that Kuniang's clothes were often shabby and unsuitable for her age. Was it merely a question of money? Chinese railways often keep their employees waiting for their pay. Could I do anything about it?

I decided that, in future, Kuniang must take her meals with me. If we saw each other often and regularly, I might find some way of making things easier for her. So I took the first opportunity of mentioning to Kuniang that I felt lonely and in need of company. Would she come and cheer me up at meal-times? She accepted with evident pleasure, and we sat down together that same evening. It was the first meal we had taken together in all the years that she had been in my house. Uncle Podger was also of the party.

Kuniang made her appearance in my study just before eight o'clock, arrayed in what had once been a 'party frock'. The sleeves had been long but now only reached her elbow, and the skirt was ridiculously skimpy, both in length and width. Yet it had obviously been let down and let out. The material (it was made of blue morocain) showed the alterations in the difference between the parts that were faded and those which were not.

Kuniang had never been timid with me, even as a child. That evening she was pleasantly excited. Her eyes sparkled; her hair caught the light of the lamps; the half-moon on her forehead glowed and faded and glowed again, while Exalted Virtue and his acolytes served us with their usual quiet dignity. I would not have been surprised if Kuniang had eaten the peas off her knife and drunk the water out of her finger-bowl. But despite her familiarity with the Russian family and frequent meals with chopsticks in company with Little Lu, her table manners were excellent. It was pure joy to see her opposite me and to know that, in future, she might always be there.

We talked, I suppose inevitably, of Elisalex.

'I have never had a real friend: some one to whom I can say anything I like and ask questions of. Elisalex is so kind and understanding. I tell her any silly thing that comes into my head. But Natasha is awfully jealous. In fact, they are all angry because Elisalex is fonder of me than she is of them. The only one who isn't jealous is Fédor.'

'She is kind enough to him. She has let him do a portrait of her with nothing on.'

'Yes. And now he wants to do a portrait of me in the same costume.'

'The devil!'

'I would much rather he didn't. But it is difficult to refuse, after Elisalex has consented. They have all seen me without my clothes, when we took baths, in the swimming-pool, last summer.'

'It is not quite the same thing, and I think you ought to be treated differently from Elisalex.'

'It is not possible to live with people and expect them to treat you differently. It only leads to trouble. Elisalex treats me differently from the others, and it makes them angry. But she can't help it. You see, they are afraid of her, and I am not!'

'Afraid of her? When she is their guest! Why should that be?'

'I can't think! But when she gets annoyed even Fédor hardly dares look her in the face.'

'Are you sure all this is not your imagination?'

'Oh, no! Yesterday Patushka threw a teapot at Natasha and hit Elisalex by mistake. She sprang up, her eyes blazing and her nostrils quivering with rage. She did not say a word, but the next moment all the Russian family were grovelling at her feet. I don't know what they said, but it sounded as if they were begging for mercy.'

'I am inclined to think that you are making all this up.'

'I could never make up such nonsense. I think they were all much annoyed that I should have been in the room when it happened. The Chinese Boy was also there, but he took it all as a matter of course, as they always do. He was waiting to serve some pancakes to Matushka, keeping them warm in a dirty napkin.'

'How long did they remain on the floor?'

'Well, Elisalex caught my eye, and saw that I was trying not to laugh. And then she tried not to laugh either. But we could not help it. And while we were nearly choking, the Russian family all sprang up, and Patushka kissed our hands and behaved as if his life had been spared. I never saw anything so ridiculous in my life. But later on Matushka took it out of me for laughing at them when they were all shivering with fright on the floor.'

At this moment our conversation was interrupted by Uncle Podger's dinner being brought in: a bowl of rice and liver. For what he receives Uncle Podger is not truly thankful. He expects to be cajoled into eating his dinner, as if thereby he were conferring a boon upon humanity. Kuniang had to go down on her knees and stir it up for him before he would look at it.

II

When we had finished dinner Kuniang made an unexpected proposal. She asked me if I would like to see her room.

'With pleasure. But I know your room well, unless you have done something new to it.'

'I have done it up with a floor of Japanese matting. It makes it so much prettier, if you don't mind sitting on the mats. Papà gave me the money. He really meant me to buy some new clothes with it, but when the bill came in for my room I had only twelve dollars left. So all the clothes I have been able to buy is a little Japanese kimono: the short kind, that you wear without an *obi*. I had quite given up wearing this frock, but now I have been obliged to get it out again. It is so tight I can hardly get into it, and I have to call the Mother of Little Lu when I want to get it off.'

'What will your father say when he hears that you have spent all your money in decorating my house with Japanese mats?'

'Poor Papà! He is used to my doing silly things like that. Yet I hate to trouble him. My room is much nicer now. But I must try and do without new clothes for a bit longer. The worst are my underclothes. I have no nighties left at all, and I sleep in my skin. It feels quite funny till you get used to it. For the day I have some old silk petticoats that I bought two years ago. The woman in the shop called them *Princesses*. I don't think it would be a good name for them now.'

So this was the explanation of the shabbiness and inadequacy of Kuniang's garments! She certainly needed some one to look after her. The Russian family and I, between us, did not seem to be making a good job of it.

I accepted the invitation to see the improvements which Kuniang had made to her room, and we crossed the courtyards together, hurrying because of the cold. Only one end of the pavilion had been done up in Japanese style. Six cushioned mats covered the floor and were held in place by a light wooden frame. Against the side of the room were two tiny bookcases and on the mats themselves were two vases, one of which contained some long grasses and the other a lamp and shade. On the walls were pictures of birds painted on hanging panels of silk.

I understood Kuniang's reasons for choosing that particular style. In a Japanese house, once you have laid down the mats you have practically furnished a room. You need not buy sofas or chairs and tables. The medley of cheap and old-fashioned furniture which had been brought from Signor Cante's apartment and dumped into my lumber-room for Kuniang's use was not calculated to make 'the home beautiful'. I admired her taste in trying to improve her surroundings at a very small cost. The little room might not be comfortable for people unused to sitting on the floor, but it was pretty.

The opposite end of the pavilion was furnished as before, and could be cut off by a curtain. Kuniang's bed had been covered with a piece of green damask and had some blue and green cushions on it. The new Japanese kimono was hanging conspicuously on a peg.

When we took off our shoes, in conformity with Japanese custom, I noticed that Kuniang's stockings offered some wonderful examples of artistic darning, as practised by the Mother of Little Lu. The feet resembled those mosaics of silk, called *kosseus*, that are so highly prized by collectors of Chinese antiques.

Uncle Podger did not join us in the Japanese room. He went to lie on Kuniang's bed.

'Uncle Podger does not approve of there being no

sofas and chairs for him,' said Kuniang. 'When I can afford it, I must get him a basket.'

To tell the truth, I felt rather inclined to agree with Uncle Podger, though, to please Kuniang, I hastened to spread myself out on the floor. But Kuniang herself was not dressed for reclining at ease in Oriental surroundings. Her frock was too tight for comfort and too short for propriety. She kept fidgeting and pulling down her skirt, till I suggested that she should put on her new Japanese kimono. She seemed to think that this was a good idea, and retired to the other end of the pavilion to effect the change.

After a few moments I heard a gurgle and a stifled voice calling out:

'Oh, *do* come and help me out of this.'

I went to see what had happened.

Kuniang was standing, quite helpless, with the blue marocain over her head, imprisoning her arms as surely as if they had been tied with rope. Her single under-garment had been pulled up in the wake of the tight old frock. Modesty forbids my telling how much girlish anatomy was left bare by this unfortunate disarray, but it was enough to show an angry redness that could only have been produced by a liberal application of the birch.

I went to her aid, somewhat inefficiently. I found the circumstances a little trying.

Kuniang emerged from her frock, breathless and dishevelled. Not until she had put on her kimono and we had gone back to the Japanese mats did I ask her:

'Is it not time you brought me your half of the crystal seal?'

She did not realize, at first, what I meant. When she understood, she grew red, but answered quietly:

'I can put up with it, once in a while. They are a bit difficult, in these days, in the Russian family. This afternoon there was an awful row, all about the spiders.'

'Do you mean those bottled spiders that they keep on the shelves?'

'Yes. We were ragging in the schoolroom, and knocked over a whole line of bottles with spiders in them. Six of the bottles were broken.'

'*Araignée du matin, chagrin!* But I thought nobody wanted them any more, now that the Rumanian prince is dead?'

'Nobody does, really, though Patushka thinks that he may be able to sell them to some museum in Petrograd. The spiders were just an excuse. Matushka took it out of me for having laughed at them when they were all begging for mercy from Elisalex. I thought she was never going to stop.'

Kuniang rubbed herself pensively through the kimono, and asked:

'Do you think Pond's Extract would be any good?'

My first impression of the Russian family had been correct. Signor Cante was a fool to have entrusted his daughter to such people. It was obvious that I ought to interfere. But before flying to the rescue of a damsel in distress one must be sure that the damsel is willing to be rescued.

Except to ask about the Pond's Extract, Kuniang had not expressed any desire for my support and assistance. She had not complained. She never did complain. Her father must not know that, with her, all might not be for the best in the best of worlds. I must not be bothered. She could put up with being birched now and then by Matushka. And in the end she would doubtless accede to Fédor's request and pose for him in the altogether. Had they not all bathed, naked, in the swimming-pool last summer?

But my impression was that the coming of Elisalex had brought a change of atmosphere into the Russian family. Children of nature they had always been, with the healthy shamelessness of savages. But Elisalex was no child of nature. Hers was the shamelessness of Phryne. Might not the writer of anonymous letters be right when he spoke of her making 'love-love pidgin'?

We sat there for some little time while I wondered what I should do. I could not decide at once: it was a matter that needed thinking over. *La nuit porte conseil.* At length I said:

'Will you come to my study to-morrow morning, before you go to the Russian family?'

Kuniang looked surprised, so I added: 'I need your help.'

'You need *my* help? A few minutes ago you were asking me why I did not bring you my half of the crystal seal?'

'Now it is the other way round.'

Kuniang looked at me suspiciously, but I only smiled. In the end she said she would do anything I wished.

A few minutes later I got up to go to my room. Kuniang came to the door of her pavilion, to say good night. As I passed out, I stopped for a moment and kissed her lightly on the cheek. In my kiss there was a little of the sadness of a farewell. I was saying good-bye to the old Kuniang, who had grown dear to me as a child.

I ran down the steps into the open air. The sloping roofs of the pavilions loomed darkly against a frosty, starlit sky. And high up above the roofs the tops of the pines whispered to each other as if telling secrets about what went on below. I looked back. Kuniang was standing by the half-opened door, her slim figure in the Japanese kimono silhouetted against the faintly lighted room, like a scene in *Madame Butterfly*.

From somewhere inside Uncle Podger barked reassuringly. He was not oblivious of his responsibilities.

III

Next morning, when Kuniang, followed by Uncle Podger, came to my study, a little before ten, I said to her very seriously:

'I hope you will consider this as a business interview. Please take a chair.'

'Mayn't I sit on the floor?'

'How can I talk of business matters to a person sitting on the floor? However, have it your own way.'

Kuniang subsided contentedly on the carpet, close to my feet, while Uncle Podger curled himself up on my best arm-chair.

'And now,' said Kuniang, 'what can I do to help you?'

I cleared my throat and tried to look important. I wanted Kuniang to have the impression that she was at a committee meeting, with Uncle Podger asleep in the Chair, so I began:

'I am badly in need of a secretary-typist, especially one who can speak more than one language, as you can. You have had plenty of practice on my old typewriter. All you will have to learn is to keep my papers in order, and the ordinary rules and forms of business correspondence. So I would be pleased if you will take on the job. For the first three months I won't pay you anything. Later on I will give you one hundred dollars a month, and a rise after one year, if satisfactory. You won't be able to pass so much time with the Russian family, nor will Matushka be responsible for you in any way. I will arrange all that with your father. But, of course, you can go and see them, as a friend, whenever you like. And you could ask them to come and see you here.'

Kuniang was staring at me, from the floor, with concentrated attention.

'I don't believe,' she said, 'that you need a typist at all – at least, not such a rotten one as I am.'

'If you are as rotten as all that,' I said, 'I won't pay you. That is all.'

But Kuniang was unconvinced.

'Why are you doing this?' she asked, looking up into my eyes.

I stared back at her, without quite knowing what to say. Then I asked her, in my turn:

'Why do you suppose I am doing it?'

The answer was unexpected:

'I suppose it is because you are so kind – always so kind. There is nowhere for me to go, and Papà is poor, so you let me live here. And now . . .'

She was still looking up at me, and trying to smile, but suddenly her eyes brimmed with tears, and she bent her head down on her arms to hide her face.

I stroked her hair gently and answered:

'You are quite wrong. If anything, I am doing this because I want to make amends, now that I realize how badly I have been treating you.'

Kuniang lifted her face, all wet with tears, and echoed:
'Treating me badly! *You?*'

'Yes. This house is all the home you've got. Yet nobody in it, except the Five Virtues, gave a thought to your food or to your clothes. For the first time, yesterday evening, I asked you to dine with me. I feel ashamed when I think of your scrappy, solitary meals, taken anyhow, in the kitchen or in your room, during all these years. I paid so little attention to you that I did not even know you had refurnished part of your pavilion, at your father's expense. I noticed that you had grown out of your frocks, but I took no trouble. I merely wondered why you were not suitably dressed.'

Kuniang interrupted:

'It was all my fault. Papà gave me the money for new clothes.'

'I know. But there was nobody to advise you how to spend it. You have always had to fend for yourself. It is a wonder you have not done more silly things than you have. But now I want you to take up a definite position in my household, and then you will find that your position in the Russian family will become quite different. As my secretary you will be entitled to respect from Matushka and everybody else. If you accept my offer, the first thing you had better do is to write a note to Matushka, telling her of your new status in the Home of the Five Virtues, and excusing yourself from going there this morning as usual. That will give them something to talk about till you go and see them.'

Kuniang remained buried in thought for some moments, and then she asked:

'You are sure you would not mind my seeing Elisalex?'

'I don't mind who you see. Ask them all here to tea, if you like, and as often as you like. And go to them when you want to. All I ask is that you should give me some of the time that you used to pass with them.'

Kuniang looked relieved, and rather pleased.

'I do not know how to thank you,' she said. 'But I am not ungrateful.'

'That's one thing settled. Now there is something else I want to tell you.'

'What is that?'

'It is a logical consequence of the proposition which has just met with your approval. As my secretary, I cannot have you going about like that. You must have some new clothes. I may also add: some new underclothes. Since you have spent your father's money on improving my house, it is only fair that I should contribute towards the refurnishing of your wardrobe. We might go this morning to Morrison Street, or to the Legation Quarter, and see what can be done. I believe there is a new Japanese shop where you can buy the most lovely undies.'

Kuniang gave a little jump of delight. She scrambled up and flung her arms round my neck.

'Oh, you darling,' she said disrespectfully. 'I am just dying for some new pants!'

An hour later, after having sent a note to Matushka, by means of the *tingchai*, Kuniang and I sallied forth on our first shopping expedition. That day we went no farther than the Japanese emporium, where Kuniang bought some new stockings and some ready-made undies, while ordering some more to be made for her in Japan.

We did not immediately let ourselves loose on the town for the acquisition of other garments. I was afraid that the Peking dressmakers, if they saw the weals on Kuniang's skin, might think it was my doing! But in due course I gave Kuniang her head, and merely stood by to see what she would do. I have always believed that, with women, most problems can be reduced to a question of clothes. I was sure that they would treat Kuniang very differently in the Russian family if she were well dressed. And Kuniang herself fully realized how much moral support is given to the feminine mind by a few feet of flimsy material in the right place.

I had seldom enjoyed anything so much as those expeditions in search of feminine apparel, even though Kuniang embarrassed me sometimes by insisting that I should be present during all the changes and tryings on. My love of silks and chiffons and velvets found a much more satisfactory outlet in choosing frocks for her than in the acquisition of old court-robes, and embroideries, and hangings from Imperial tombs. Only once did I raise any objections. It was when she appeared to be contemplating the purchase of a Paris model: a ball-dress in black velvet and *diamanté*, very suitable for a matron on the wrong side of forty.

What the shopkeepers thought of us I do not know. They were glad of our custom anyway.

Besides frocks, Kuniang required riding-breeches, and for these we went to Ah-ting-fu's new shop in the Hata Mên. I said I would wait outside with Uncle Podger, but Kuniang had hardly entered the shop when she appeared once more at the door and beckoned to me.

'You must see this,' she said. 'It is as good as the Heavenly Trousers.'

I was puzzled, but followed her indoors. A rickety wooden staircase led to an upper floor, and on the wall above the steps was a notice in English:

LADIES HAVE FITS UPSTAIRS

Kuniang laughed delightedly.

'You cannot possibly leave me to have a fit all by myself,' she said. 'Please come too.'

So I followed her up the staircase.

8 The Mandarin Coat

I

In justice to Kuniang, I ought to tell, at this point, how she became quite an efficient secretary-typist: how, when copying out my stories, she learnt to leave one space after a comma and two after a full stop; to indent, when beginning a new paragraph, and to supply the missing parts (address, date, and suitably graded salutations) in the letters I dictated.

I learnt from her as much as she from me, if not more. And it had nothing to do with the American system of filing. Together we travelled in the realms of gold. A simile of mine, a quotation, an allusion, would provoke some question from her, and then we would turn to the bookshelves and seek the source. I felt like an enthusiastic native, showing a no less enthusiastic tourist over a lovely countryside, opening vistas as I opened pages. To guide a young thing through a library is like training the wings of the mind. And the teacher learns by teaching.

Some of my Chinese stories I owe entirely to Kuniang, for without her I could never have written them. It was she who unearthed the local superstition from under the commonplaces of very ordinary events.

It was she who lured me from the dusty annals of long-forgotten dynasties and taught me to contemplate and to describe the world within my own courtyards and that which lay beyond the outer wall of the Shuang Liè Ssè. She brought me fragments of folk-lore and gave me new ideas in the shape of delightful Chinese names. What writer, worthy of the name, could resist making up a story about: *The Temple of Costly Experience, The Hill*

91

of the Seven Splendours, or *The Inn of Perpetual Misfortune?*

It was Kuniang who discovered a legend concerning an Emperor's robe which I had bought in the Chinese City. What no one would tell *me,* some one (possibly Little Lu) told *her.*

Here is the story, just as Kuniang herself typed it out for me. It is called:

THE MANDARIN COAT

There is a little street in the Chinese town, which for me holds great temptations. It is a narrow, unpretentious thoroughfare, but there you can buy the very splendour of the East, in a cut velvet, in an embroidered flower. It is called the Street of the Silks.

Two thousand six hundred years before our era the Lady of Si-Ling, wife of the Emperor Huang-ti, tended with her own hands the mulberry-feeding moth, warmed it and guarded it from all harsh sounds. She it was who invented the loom. And in her country the art of embroidery reached perfection in times to us prehistoric.

Fifty patterns for brocades and embroideries were laid down at the time of the Sung dynasty: the Taoist paradise, with its genii; the Dragon and Phoenix (symbols of the Emperor and the Empress); peacocks, pheasants, storks, and bats; lotus flowers and cherry blossom; peonies and roses; tortoises and serpents; clouds and Buddhist symbols; water-weeds and playing fish; wild geese flying in the clouds. . . .

Even I remember the days on which sacrifices were made to the God of Silk-worms, in a temple within the Palace grounds. Those sacrifices had to be offered up by an Empress. When the Empire fell, the cult of the silk-worm disappeared, and with it the old prestige of the weaver and the embroiderer. To-day the splendour of an ancient art and the glamour of the Imperial tradition have found their last refuge in a narrow street of little shops, on the southern side of the Tartar Wall, not far from the Home of the Five Virtues.

92

There are only twenty shops in the Street of the Silks. The one that I prefer is so tiny you would never believe that it could contain valuables for more than a few hundred dollars. You enter by a long, narrow corridor, where there is always a big, sleepy dog, who wakes up and precedes you into the house, growling to warn his master of a customer's arrival. The shop consists of two rooms, the size of cabins on an old-fashioned steamer, with curtained shelves, very much like berths. There is just room enough to sit down and drink tea, while the shop-boys (all relations of the proprietor) pull the silks down from the shelves or out of two red lacquered cupboards. Here are velvets and brocades from Nanking, raw silk from Shantung and flowered silk from Canton, embroidered petticoats and mantles, rolls of damask for panels or for screens, Buddhist vestments, veils and ribbons for Tartar or Chinese hats. All these materials heaped up in the dingy little room dazzle the eye and tire the senses with the richness of their colour and design.

The proprietor's name is Little Li (pronounced *lee*). He looks as if he might be twenty-five years old, but he is already a grandfather. We talk in a mixture of pidgin-English and Chinese, without always catching each other's meaning, except in the essential matter of the price. We have known each other for many years, and I think that my appreciation of what is beautiful in the art of the silk has gained for me his goodwill, even apart from our dealings in bank-notes and brocades.

When I pay a visit to his shop, we sit at a table and partake of tea together, while his assistants get down from the shelves anything that is new since my last visit, as well as those pieces of silk and embroidery for which I have already made an offer, without reaching an agreement as to the price. By this time Little Li knows my tastes and just how he can tempt me to buy. If he has anything especially beautiful to sell, he begins by saying that it is not his, but his brother's (the brother being absent on a journey). He then adds that his brother is asking a big sum. Thus he disarms my protests against an exorbitant price, and justifies his own reluctance to reduce it.

93

The elder brother, who is called Big Li, travels about in the interior, buying silks from provincial merchants, and court-dresses from impoverished Manchu families; I have no doubt that he also buys the loot of marauding soldiers.

My collection of silks is the cause of a silent feud between the Five Virtues and myself. They consider that every article purchased by me should pay duty to the *K'ai-men-ti* when it enters the house. This duty varies from 10 to 50 per cent *ad valorem*, and the proceeds are divided up among the family. My point of view is that a bargain struck between myself and a dealer in the Chinese City is no concern of any one but our two selves. Therefore I feel justified in avoiding the payment of any tax that might be levied at my door. So it happens that every purchase from Little Li is accompanied, on my part, by a small intrigue, intended to avoid the payment of 'squeeze' to my own servants. If the Five Virtues knew for certain in which shop I had bought each piece of embroidery they would go there and demand a percentage on the sum paid, and the shopkeeper would not dare to refuse. As the payment of 'squeeze' greatly affects the price, I can generally obtain a considerable reduction by assuring Little Li that in the bargain struck between him and me no one shall claim a commission.

Various are the expedients to which I have recourse, in order not to reveal the identity of the person who sold me the object that I carry home. I must needs reach the shop on foot, and leave again on foot, lest a rickshaw coolie spy upon my movements. Payment must be made in cash, or at least it must not be specified on the counterfoil of my cheque-book, which the Boys might examine. All this mystery lends an added attraction to every purchase. Besides the pleasure of a newly acquired possession, there is an agreeable feeling of having bought it *sub rosa*. Thus the ordinary business deal takes on a glamour of romance, as if it were an adultery.

On one occasion, however, Little Li himself gave the show away, and revealed to the Five Virtues the fact that I had bought from him a Mandarin Coat. This is the name given, by foreigners in China, to the gala dress of the old Chinese officials, as also to the robes worn at Court on ceremonial occasions. I have many of these coats, but the one to which I allude has a dazzling magnificence which has never been surpassed. It is of yellow satin, embroidered with the twelve symbols which only the Son of Heaven might wear in the complete series. On the breast is the usual gold embroidered dragon, with the scales in relief. He reaches out, with silver talons, towards the flaming jewel, symbol of omnipotence. Round the hem are the waves of the sea, breaking against a mountain with three peaks. On the right shoulder is the three-legged cock, crowing in the sun (a sort of Oriental *chantecler*); on the left shoulder is the white rabbit who lives in the moon, working with mortar and pestle to make the *elixir vitae*, which confers immortality; and here and there, among floating clouds and coloured bats, are all the other symbols of authority.

I came upon this mantle by chance one day, when Little Li was absent and there was no one in the shop to serve me except the young men and boys who act as his assistants and are probably his sons and nephews. I had not found anything of interest and was on the point of leaving the shop when something glittered in the darkness of a half-open cupboard. A wisp of gold caught the light from without. I stretched out a hand and lifted a bundle, which fell open by reason of its own weight. A corner of embroidery escaped from the folds so full of light and colour that it seemed almost alive. I took it into the open and spread it out on a table in the courtyard, which was all lighted up by its splendour. The young assistants watched me anxiously.

'How much does it cost?' I asked.

One of the boys examined the sleeve, to which was attached a little piece of cloth, marked with numbers in Chinese ink. He deciphered the writing and then called his companions in to consultation. After conversing together in a jargon all their own, they informed me that they thought the price was one hundred and fifty dollars.

I was astonished. It was a small sum to ask for such a

work of art. There was a world of difference between the robe that I was examining and the Mandarin Coats that are commonly sold to foreigners and that ladies sometimes transform into evening cloaks. It was enough to look at the golden lights on the waves, round the hem, and to note the perfect harmony of the gorgeous colours, in order to realize that this was indeed a museum piece.

I made a sign that I would buy it and told them to wrap it up for me to carry away. But the shop-assistants hesitated to conclude the bargain without the consent of their master. I reassured them, saying that, if there were any mistake in the price, they might let me know and we would talk it over again. I paid the hundred and fifty dollars and departed with the parcel under my arm.

Two hours later Little Li appeared at my house, asking urgently to see me. He seemed to have forgotten the advisability of keeping our business relations secret. Exalted Virtue showed him into my study with a faintly amused smile on his usually impassive face. Little Li immediately inquired after the mantle.

'It is in there,' I said, pointing to a large camphor-wood chest. 'Does it cost more than I paid?'

'No. Plice can do. My no wantchee selly you. My wantchee selly to Fan Kwei, who wai-lo kwi kwi.'

From this jargon I understood that Little Li did not want me to buy the coat. He wanted to sell it to some 'foreign devil' who would be leaving Peking at once. I asked the reason for this preference.

'That Mandalin coat, he blingee muchee tlouble.'

'You mean that it brings ill luck? But you need not fear. I do not mean to wear it.'

After some discussion Little Li consented to leave me my purchase. He had done his duty by warning me, but if I was not afraid there was no more to be said. And then, the coat would not bring ill luck unless to the wearer. Shut up in a box, it could do no harm.

And indeed, since I bought that Mandarin Coat, things have gone on much as before. But meanwhile I have learnt why so beautiful a robe has acquired such an evil fame. In the world of silks that coat was supposed to be unsaleable. Around it there centres a legend, which has now been told me:

In the reign of Tchouang-li-ti, last of the Ming dynasty, there lived in Peking a maiden whose name was Yu, which means 'jade'. She was sixteen years old when her parents were called upon to send her to the Forbidden City for the selection of concubines for the Son of Heaven. Yu succeeded in passing all the tests, and was chosen as a concubine of the second grade. Her name was engraved upon a tablet of jade, which was placed, with other similar tablets, upon an ivory table in the apartments of the Emperor. When the Son of Heaven desired Yu's presence, he turned over the tablet which bore her name. Then one of the eunuchs would wrap her up in a cover of scarlet silk, and carry her through the courtyards to the Emperor's apartment.

Yu was pretty, and the Emperor often turned over her name-tablet on the ivory table.

Among the other concubines there was one, called Ye (which means 'leaf'), who in the past had been the Emperor's favourite. But since the coming of Yu all other tablets had remained untouched. And Ye was jealous.

One day Ye obtained permission to go out of the Forbidden City, to a Taoist temple, where they worship the Three Pure Ones. From one of the temple priests she bought a thread of white silk, in which was embodied a malevolent spirit of great power. When she got home again she expressed the desire to embroider, with her own hands, a state robe for the Son of Heaven. So the Chief Eunuch gave orders that she should be given yellow satin, heavy and soft, silken threads of every colour, and threads of gold and silver.

So Ye sat down to her task and, during two long years, she sewed and sewed and sewed. The white thread of misfortune passed into one of the symbols that only the Emperor might wear. But into which symbol no one ever knew.

When the state robe was ready, the concubine Ye was allowed to offer it in person to the Son of Heaven, who admired it and put it on. Once again the name-tablet of Ye was turned over on the ivory table.

But meanwhile the spell was working.

That night, from Shan-hai-kwàn, on the Great Wall, came bearers of ill tidings. After thirty years of war the Manchus had broken through. Their cavalry was pouring into China. The smoke of burning towns marked the road they took.

On the hill called *Mei-shan*, within the Palace walls, the Emperor wandered alone, abandoned by his Court. He wore a robe of yellow satin, splendidly embroidered. From the highest of the three pavilions that mark the summit of the hill he watched the flames mount up from the eastern towers, where the enemy was attacking.

An hour later a eunuch passed out of the Palace with his burden of loot, and crossed the *Mei-shan* garden. As he skirted the hillside, he almost blundered into a grim figure, dangling from the branch of a twisted pine. He recoiled, struck by the sudden horror, and almost instinctively dropped on one knee, spellbound by his habitual reverence for the wearer of that splendid robe. But all around was silence, and the hot wind brought the smoke of burning houses. The eunuch plucked up courage and drew near. From the hand of the Son of Heaven, not yet chilled in death, he tore off the green jade *pang-dze*, or 'archer's ring'.

Such is the legend attached to my Mandarin coat. It explains how I bought it so cheap!

But I wonder how much 'squeeze' Exalted Virtue got out of Little Li?

9 The Satyr and the Nymph

I

It was just after the Russian New Year that Kuniang invited Elisalex to the house for the first time. She came, escorted by Fédor and Natasha, and they were shown into the Japanese room. But whereas Fédor and his sister were delighted with the idea of sitting on the floor, Elisalex preferred the arm-chairs in my study. So, after tea, we retired there, she and I leaving the younger members of the party on the Japanese mats. I was glad of the opportunity of getting to know the lady better, and I discovered that she also had reasons for wishing to see me alone.

As soon as we had got seated and she had lit a cigarette (I cannot ever remember having seen her without one), she said:

'May I ask you a question?'

'Of course, though I do not guarantee that I can answer it.'

'I have an idea that your offer to take Kuniang as a secretary was caused by your desire that she should see less of us. Am I right?'

'May I answer your question with another? Do you really think that Matushka's house is a suitable one for a young girl to be sent to for a finishing course?'

Elisalex laughed. 'To tell the truth,' she said, 'I had never thought of it in that light. I understood that her father did not want her to loaf about all day. He sent her to Matushka so that she might be looked after and given some occupation. She has been going there for some time, and you never objected. Only since my arrival have you grown suspicious. It is natural that you should. There are many strange stories about me going the round of Peking. Some of them may be true.'

'You express yourself very frankly,' I answered. 'I will be equally frank with you. It is a fact that I am suspicious of you. It is also true – I am telling you this in confidence – that I received an anonymous letter concerning you. But it told me nothing of your past, and anyhow I don't pay attention to anonymous letters. I have also been wishing that Kuniang's father could have found something for her more suitable than Matushka's household. They are rather too primitive in their habits, and treat her too much like one of the family, especially when Matushka gets annoyed.'

Elisalex looked about for an ashtray. I put one near her, as well as the box of cigarettes.

'I am inclined to agree with you,' she said, 'and to approve of what you have done. But, as I am fond of Kuniang, I wanted to be sure that you will not make difficulties about her seeing me.'

'None whatever. Even if I wished to, which I don't, I have no authority over Kuniang.'

'It is not a question of authority, but of friendliness. Would it be a relief to you, if you knew something more about me?'

'You do not represent an anxiety, so there can be no question of relief. But I would like to know more about you, certainly. I have often wondered what you were doing, all alone in Peking.'

'Why do you say *all alone*? I am staying with your neighbours. I even feel that I am part of the family. Patushka's grandfather was a serf on our estates in the days when a landowner's wealth was counted in so many thousand souls. Though I let Fédor use me as a model they cannot help thinking of me as a great lady, who could send them to Siberia for any little misdemeanour, as in my grandfather's day. Instead of which it is I who am in exile. And, since you asked me, I can tell you that I am in Peking because I got into trouble at home: trouble and disgrace.'

'It is true, then, that you are a communist, and are

waiting for a revolution to break out in Russia before you go back?'

'In a sense it is true, because I could not go back until there comes a change. I do not think I will have to wait long. But a communist revolution would not help me much. Russia can only be held together by an autocrat. It is falling to pieces because the Tsar does not know how to lead, or how to command. Poincaré and Clemenceau are far more autocrats than he is. And the Empress is a super-stitious, hysterical, interfering woman, with a sickly son. As long as Grigori Efimovitch was alive, he galvanized them into a sort of mystic energy. Now that he is dead you will see that the Empire will fall to pieces, like a pack of cards.'

'I have not yet understood,' I said, 'if you are an admirer of Rasputin, or the contrary. But you are the first person whom I have ever heard say a good word for him.'

'Grishka ruined me, and in doing so almost brought dis-aster on himself. I was never his dupe. But I was fasci-nated by him and drawn into the circle of his intimates. Other women gave themselves to Grishka because he told them that a particle of the Supreme Being was incar-nated in him, and that salvation lay in uniting themselves with him. All this made no impression on me, and in some ways I was less attracted by him than repelled. He even had a disagreeable smell, which I never got used to. Yet I could not keep away from him. His was a contagious madness, which found a counterpart in me. His eyes used to blaze with what some people called religious fervour. They were blue eyes, of an almost incredible blueness, like cornflowers in a field of grain. And he had extraordi-nary physical strength. He was violent with me, and rough and indecent. But his brutality excited me. He used to leave me sore and dishevelled and ashamed. But I would always go back for more.

'I met him for the first time when I was feeling lonely and miserable. The man I loved had just left St. Petersburg. Grishka could not console me, but he offered distraction. He was a religious satyr. I was a pagan nymph. And extremes met.'

'I have no doubt you got on very nicely together.'

Elisalex smiled. 'You see, I am being very frank with you,' she said. 'Shall I go on?'

'By all means. It sounds like something out of an unexpurgated edition of *The Arabian Nights*.'

'I have never read *The Arabian Nights*, though I have seen Nijinsky in *Scheherazade*. But the strange part of my story is that it is true, and that some day it may be written as history. I do not doubt that they will describe me as a wanton, a lost woman, in the fullest meaning of the term. And then they will go on to say that the highest commands in the Army, the highest posts in the Government, even ecclesiastical nominations in the Church were discussed and decided in my house by Grishka and his friends. Later on these nominations were suggested to the Empress, who saw to it that they were carried through.

'As long as I was at his side I took care that Grishka should do nothing foolish. He was an ignorant peasant, with no political sense; an instrument in the hands of others. I had good advisers, and I passed on their advice to him. To keep my influence over him I had to submit to all his excesses. I did things that put me utterly beyond the pale. But it was not in vain. Thanks to his influence with the Empress, Grishka was the power behind the throne, and behind Grishka stood I, naked and unashamed.

'His enemies did their best to ruin him. They only succeeded in ruining me. I was the scapegoat. Grishka remained at the Empress's side, with no one to advise him but pro-German agents. By his advice the Tsar took over the command of his armies, and proceeded to the front, replacing the Grand Duke Nicholas. And that was the beginning of the end.'

II

Robert Louis Stevenson, in his essay *Some Portraits by Raeburn*, concludes that Raeburn could paint men and old women, but failed when it came to 'young ladies'. It was perhaps because he could not look into their eyes without trouble.

I had much the same feeling with Elisalex, and for this reason I doubt whether, in describing her, or even in repeating what she told me, I can really do her justice. There was something very disturbing about Elisalex. I suppose it is so with most women who, besides being physically attractive, have a personality which is concentrated on sex.

Her story had carried me very far from the Russian family in Peking, from Kuniang and from the Home of the Five Virtues. Elisalex had spoken of herself as a wanton, as one who had done things which put her beyond the pale. I had no reason to doubt her word, or to suppose that she exaggerated her own influence and her own disgrace. But her part had been played on a greater stage than I had imagined. Some day her story might be quoted in learned volumes on the Decline and Fall of the Russian Empire.

I thought a little over what she had said, and then asked:

'What occurred in the end to bring about your exile? It did not happen often to Rasputin's favourites.'

'No. It was generally his enemies who got into trouble. But I had the misfortune to arouse the suspicion of Grishka's protectors. It began when he forgot to go to a Christmas-tree which the Tsarina had prepared in the Winter Palace. The secret police hunted feverishly for Grishka all over St. Petersburg, and finally found him in my house.

'Then came the famous episode of the Yar restaurant in Moscow. I don't know if the story reached Peking. It was a mere drunken orgy, such as occurred every night, even in war-time. That was the spring of 1915. Grishka and I were asked to dine in the Petrowsky Park. There were the usual players of the balalaika and some Tziganes. Grishka was utterly impossible that night. He started boasting of his conquests among the ladies of St. Petersburg, mentioning each one by name and describing all her most intimate physical characteristics. Then he began to speak of the Empress, whom he called *staraja jenscina* ('the old woman'). He showed us an embroidered waistcoat, under his kaftan, and told us that the old woman had embroidered it especially for him, and that he could do with her what he wished. The other guests began to get nervous and restless. Grishka had lost all control over himself. There were some pretty women among the Tziganes. He dragged one of them out of the group and began to make love to her, but the others interfered and separated them. Then he seized hold of me and stood me up on the table, among the plates and glasses, and started pulling off my clothes. He said that if 'the old woman' were younger, that is what he would do to her. Some of the other guests tried to interfere, but Grishka seemed possessed of the devil. He took off his leather belt and began striking them with it. Our hostess flung down a bundle of notes on the table to pay for the supper, and left hurriedly. The others followed her example. Even the Tziganes had disappeared.

'The affair provoked a terrible scandal. To have coupled the name of the Empress with such an orgy was sacrilege. Grishka's enemies saw their chance to overthrow him, and his friends gathered round in his defence. The Prefect of Police went on purpose to Tsarskoe Selo, to make his report to the Tsar. But the Commander of the Imperial Palaces refused him admittance. It was only by indirect means that the story was brought to the knowledge of the Emperor. After which an official inquiry confirmed all the facts reported. But Grishka's power over the Empress was proof even against such damning evidence. She declared that the holy man had been tempted by the devil and had barely escaped by the aid of divine help. I had been the temptress, the agent of the infernal powers. So I was made to bear the blame. As a rule, aristocrats who get into trouble are merely exiled to their estates. But only with the help of powerful friends did I escape falling into the hands of the *Okhrana*. Fortunately, amid the anxieties of the war, my case was soon forgotten. I crossed Siberia and reached Harbin. Later on I came here and took refuge with Patushka and Matushka.'

'What an Odyssey! And now you go sightseeing with Kuniang.'

'Yes, if you will let me. You can imagine what a joy Kuniang is to a woman like myself. She represents all that I have lost. Indeed, she reminds me very much of what I was at her age.'

'Good Lord!'

'Does that alarm you?'

'I confess it startled me. But surely you were not brought up in the same disorderly way?'

'No, but as a child I was lonely. And it is easy to see that Kuniang has been lonely too. She literally flung herself into my arms when I showed her some little kindness. She tells me that she never had a real friend, a woman friend, to whom she could tell everything and anything. It was just the same with me.'

'Were you not brought up in St. Petersburg?'

'No. In the country, near Jaroslav. I was an only child, and my mother died, as Kuniang's died, when I was quite small. My father was a recluse. He passed most of his time in his library and only troubled about me when I went to see him there. Then he was most kind, and did his best to teach me something, and showed me his favourite books. His idea of heaven was one great library, where you need only take down a book from a shelf to know the answer to any question, and to learn about anything you liked in a few hours of pleasant reading. But, as with most young people, I preferred to learn by experience: my own experience. Most of the time I did what I pleased. I was heiress to big estates and everybody treated me as such. But I was lonely all the same. It is bad for a young girl to be lonely. When you reach my age it does not matter so much.'

I wondered what she meant by 'my age'. Elisalex could not have been more than twenty-five or twenty-six.

'It is still a mystery to me,' I said, 'why you should be so fond of Kuniang. Even if she does remind you of what you were at her age, you must have very little in common with an Italian girl brought up in China.'

'Two people may have nothing in common, and yet love one another. And, as a rule, we love our opposites. What draws me to Kuniang is that she ignores all evil. I

105

do not mean that she is innocent, but that she is kind, with the kindness that sees no harm in anything or in anybody. Such is the kindness of children. Of such is the Kingdom of Heaven.'

I looked at Elisalex in surprise. Her expression had in it all the mystical tenderness that is the birthright of the Slav.

Her next remark surprised me even more.

'Have you ever asked yourself,' she said, 'why I do my hair in this absurd way?'

'I supposed it was because you liked to.'

Elisalex took off her hat and laid it on a small table beside her. Then, to my astonishment, she came and knelt down beside me on the floor, and leant her elbows on the arm of my chair, so that her face was quite close to mine.

'Lift up my hair,' she said, 'and look at my forehead.'

I did as she suggested, and I felt the most pleasurable thrill as I touched her. The next moment I cried out in real astonishment. A little above the left eyebrow was a birthmark, dull red in colour, in the form of a half-moon. In position and in shape it was exactly similar to the birthmark on Kuniang's forehead.

'Do you not think,' said Elisalex, 'that two people so similarly marked must have something in common? Perhaps even a common fate that links them together?'

I did not answer. Indeed, I hardly heard what she said. My hand still held back the dark hair from her forehead. I could feel her breath upon my cheek, and her eyes gazed into mine. Oh, those eyes, those eyes! What did men see in them? What did I see in them, that drew and held me, as with the enchantment of some magic spell? All the haunting beauty of never-ending plains; all the flowers of the *tundra*, all the dazzling splendour of winter's snow; all the lure of nature and all the love of woman shone through the windows of a soul seeking its mate.

I felt giddy, and the room swam round me, as Elisalex encircled my neck with her arms and pressed her face against mine. So did Vivien press her face against that of Merlin, in the wild woods of Broceliande.

106

The next moment Elisalex sprang lightly to her feet and stood looking down at me smiling.

'I too can prophecy,' she said, 'like Grigori Efimovitch. But my prophecies are all of love and happiness ever after. Some day soon you shall kiss Kuniang, as you have kissed me, on the lips and on the eyes. Her face will be warm and tender and sweet. Sweeter than mine!'

She lifted her hand in a little gesture of benediction:

'God bless you, my children!'

10 The Family Magician

The morning after her tea-party Kuniang came to me, carrying a small enamel box in her hand and looking anxious and worried. I asked her what was the matter.

'I don't know that anything is the matter, really. But the Five Virtues have been playing a trick on Elisalex.'

'Another of these?' I asked. And, opening the middle drawer of my desk, I took out the anonymous letter and handed it to Kuniang.

She took the letter and read it through. She did not seem much impressed.

'Did the Five Virtues write this?' she asked.

'They must have dictated it. Probably our old *tingchai* was the actual scribe. What have they been doing now?'

Kuniang laid the little enamel box on my desk. I picked it up and opened it. For a moment I thought that she might be bringing me her half of the crystal seal. But the box was empty. I looked at her inquiringly.

'There is nothing here,' I said.

'That is what is worrying me. Yesterday there was something.'

'What was there?'

'A tiny strip of paper, with some Chinese characters written on it. The Old Lady sent it to me by Little Lu and said that I should burn the paper and make Elisalex drink the ashes in a cup of tea.'

'That is what they call the transcendental prescription. You get them at the Temple of Kuang-ti, in the Eastern City.'

'I think it was the family magician who gave this to the Old Lady.'

'But why put the ashes in your friend's tea? What effect were they intended to produce?'

'I don't know, and of course I did nothing about it. But the Five Virtues are suspicious of Elisalex. They want her to leave Peking.'

'What was written on the paper? Do you know?'

'Yes. Little Lu told me. It said: *Who rides the tiger cannot dismount.*'

'That must be a Chinese version of

There was a young lady of Niger
Who smiled when she rode on a tiger.
They came back from their ride
With the lady inside
And the smile on the face of the tiger.'

Kuniang laughed.

'But what has that got to do with Elisalex?' she asked. 'And what is the tiger she is supposed to be riding?'

'A year ago I might have said it was Rasputin. But he is dead. I don't know who it could be now. The Chinese use that proverb in the sense that it is sometimes dangerous to abdicate from power. But you have not told me why all this should make you anxious. What has happened exactly?'

'Simply that, as I did nothing about it, Exalted Virtue must have burnt the paper himself, and put the ashes into the tea when he served Elisalex yesterday afternoon.'

'And she drank them up?'

'I suppose so. I have not spoken to Exalted Virtue about it. I decided I would tell you first.'

I thought the matter over before giving an opinion. Had the strange scene between Elisalex and myself, the evening before, been a manifestation of some Chinese spell? It did not seem likely. But Kuniang was stil looking anxious, so I tried to reassure her:

'An infusion of Chinese proverbs would not really do Elisalex any harm, unless she choked on the ashes, which she does not seem to have done.'

'Then you don't think that I need take any notice?'

'You might tell Exalted Virtue that you prefer your guests to have their tea served without ashes in it. But I should not take the matter too seriously. It is not as if they had put arsenic in the tea.'

Kuniang went off to give a piece of her mind to Exalted Virtue, and left me wondering why the family of the Five Virtues should be so antagonistic to Elisalex. And what was the meaning of it all?

One afternoon, a week later, I stood at the door of my study, looking up at the sky to see if we might expect a dust-storm, or hope for rain. I saw Kuniang on the flagged path, approaching me in the company of a respectable-looking Chinese, smartly dressed in grey silk, with a black sleeveless jacket, lined with fur. She introduced him as 'the family magician', from which I gathered that he was the person whom the Five Virtues consulted about their family affairs, and from whom they had doubtless procured the transcendental prescription with which to cast a spell over Elisalex.

As Kinglake points out in *Eothen*, you cannot live for any length of time in Eastern surroundings without coming into contact with magic in some form, and being influenced by it, often against your better judgment. For my part, I had no objection to the Five Virtues putting the ashes of Chinese proverbs into the tea, as long as I did not have to drink it myself. But I do object to being mixed up in experiments in the supernatural. And I was not over-pleased when Kuniang brought the family magician to me. She explained that she wanted her fortune told, and added:

'I cannot understand what he says. He speaks the Chinese of the literati. I would rather not ask Little Lu to help, so I thought that perhaps you would.'

I muttered something about being an unworthy substitute for Little Lu, and very reluctantly invited the magician into my study. I offered him a chair and a cigarette and asked him what was his honourable name.

He told me that his name was Wang (I wonder how many million Wangs there are in China!) and that he lived in the Western Hills. He was a specialist in *Feng Shui*; that is to say, he was consulted as to the correct ubication and orientation of houses and temples, in relation to the spirits of wind and water. But people also asked him for advice on personal matters connected with their own lives.

I remembered then having heard a story about 'Magician Wang of the Western Hills'. He had caused a sensation at a political dinner to which he had been asked in the quality of entertainer. At that time the Northern Provinces were just recovering from the shock caused by the murder, in mysterious circumstances, of a famous general. One of the guests at the dinner-party, who appeared to have taken too much wine, asked the magician, in a rather mocking tone of voice, if he could tell them anything about the recent event. Mr. Wang answered:

'To some of the guests at this banquet I could give no information, as to the death of the late general, which they do not already possess.'

The ambiguous phrase had a sinister sound, and shortly afterwards two of the guests had taken their leave. The magician was not invited to any more political dinners. But Kuniang, apparently, wished to consult him.

We had been seated only a few minutes when Exalted Virtue appeared, as he always did when I had visitors, bringing cups of tea, which he put down on a little table in front of Mr. Wang. At first, Kuniang did not ask me to interpret, and indeed there was no need. The magician took her hands in his and examined them carefully, turning them over in his own slim fingers. He did not study their lines, as a palmist does. He looked at Kuniang's face and seemed to be making some mental calculation. But when he had studied her hands and her face and her general aspect for some time he shook his head and remarked that there was nothing particular to say about her. It was a tactless beginning, and Kuniang was naturally disappointed.

'But what sort of a life am I going to have?' asked Kuniang.

111

Mr. Wang considered the question and then answered:

'I see laughter, and I see tears, and in the end peace.'

I pointed out that most lives were a mixture of laughter and tears, and that to all of us, in the end, came peace. Mr. Wang admitted that this was so. But he did not offer to add anything more. I never saw a man who had less the tricks of his trade.

'And is nothing interesting going to happen to me, ever?' asked Kuniang.

I don't know what exact meaning Mr. Wang may have attributed to the word 'interesting', but he answered quite confidently: 'No'.

It was with some difficulty that I suppressed a laugh. The séance was falling flat.

'Won't I get married?' asked Kuniang.

'Oh, yes. You will get married.'

Mr. Wang did not seem to think that getting married was a matter of much interest, one way or the other.

'And do you think I might become a cinema star?'

Mr. Wang had no idea what a cinema star was. I explained that it meant a lady who was very much appreciated by the public in the 'shadow-pictures', such as were to be seen at the Shen Kwan theatre, or at the Peking Pavilion. I do not know whether he understood the question any better for my explanation, but he remained wrapped in thought for a few moments and then said:

'One's own life is always the best.'

I asked him what he meant.

'At the Shen Kwan,' he said, 'we see the shadows of other people's lives. Better to live out one's own.'

After that we stuck badly for a considerable time, until I had a brain-wave. I would ask him about Elisalex.

'Tell me,' I said, pointing at Kuniang (this was bad manners, but I wanted to make myself clear at all costs). 'This Kuniang has a friend, a Russian *tai-tai*, who is now living close by. The Five Virtues do not like this *tai-tai*. They want her to go away from Pei-ching, and have put a transcendental prescription into her tea. Do you know anything about her?'

112

The magician nodded and smiled, to show that he had understood. Probably Kuniang had been right in supposing that the prescription had been obtained from him. Strangely enough, he seemed to consider the matter as a great joke, and chuckled to himself over it.

He touched Kuniang's forehead with his finger, on the mark of the half-moon, and said that the Russian *tai-tai* had a similar mark under her hair (how could he have known that?). And then he said a strange thing:

'If you are a friend of that *tai-tai* many things may happen. But they will not be part of your own life. They will be like shadow-pictures of a life that is not yours.'

'That might be very interesting,' said Kuniang.

Mr. Wang did not agree.

'Better your own life,' he said. 'Your own laughter. Your own tears.'

At this point Mr. Wang took up his tea and drank it all, a sign that his visit was at an end. Then he bade a smiling farewell to Kuniang and bustled out, with an air of having no time to waste. I accompanied him to the second of the courtyards, and as I did so I noticed that the dust-storm, which had been brewing all the afternoon, was drawing near. A great yellowish cloud hid the setting sun, and the air was dry and choking. At such moments one's nerves are drawn taut, like violin strings.

When I got back to my study I found Kuniang still there, curled up on the sofa, her long, slim legs very much on view. She seemed absorbed in thought and oblivious of her surroundings.

'Well,' I said, 'are you satisfied with what the magician told you?'

I sat down beside her on the sofa.

'In all the foreign novels,' she said, 'that I have read about China, there is always a fortune-teller of some sort who says mysterious things which always come true.'

'And in all the foreign novels about China,' I said, 'there is always a wonderful dust-storm, that half chokes all the principal characters. The dust-storm is here all right, and looks as if it might be a bad one. And the family magician has told you that you are going to get married some day. What more do you want?'

'But he said that there would never be anything interesting in my life, unless I got mixed up with Elisalex! And even then it would be to her that it would happen, and not to me.'

I thought to myself that this was just as well, but I did not say so.

For some time we sat there in silence. The room was growing dark. Outside, the wind blustered in the courtyards and whined over the roofs, while the air grew thick with the sand of Mongolian deserts.

Somebody was scratching at the door. It was Uncle Podger, asking to be let in.

11   The Crown of Montezuma

I forget the exact date, but it was towards the end of winter, that a notice arrived from the Post Office in the American Legation Guard, to the effect that a parcel had arrived for Miss Renata de' Tolomei, and would be delivered to her, or to any authorized person who might be sent to withdraw it. The notice mentioned that the parcel had been sent off by Mr. Donald Parramoor.

At Kuniang's request the *tingchai* was sent off to retrieve the parcel.

That evening I dined at a Chinese restaurant with some friends, and returned home about half-past ten. I went to my study and began to read. The book I picked up was Leland's *Pidgin English Sing Song*, and I read (for the hundreth time) the poem entitled *The Princess in Tartary*, which tells of a Chinese Emperor's daughter (the word used for 'daughter' is *kai*), who has married a Tartar king. But she is cold and miserable in the northern land, and does not like the Tartar huts, which she is expected to live in. She does nothing but weep ('cly, cly') all day. So she makes up a song, for the birds and the wind to carry to her father.

When the Emperor hears of his daughter's distress, he has a Chinese town, with palace all complete, built for her in the cold Tartar land, so that she may feel more at home:

He sendee muchee coolie,
   He sendee smartee man,
He makee China city
   In-i-sy t'hat Tartar lan'.

He kai catch plopa palace
    An coachee galantee,
No more hab makee cly cly.
    My sing-song finishee.

Ai! Wind he wailo 'way,
    Ai! Wind he wailo long,
An' bleeze blow ovely almon'-tlee,
    An cally a birdo song.'

There is an open fireplace in my study, and the fire was lit. While the intense cold lasts the house has to be heated with stoves, but for the end of the winter an open fire is enough, and is pleasant to look at.

I knew the verses by heart, and I was beginning to feel sleepy. Putting down my book, I remained for some moments staring into the fire, my thoughts far away. And then, although I heard no sound, I had the feeling that I was no longer alone.

My study takes up the whole length of the pavilion, and consists of one big room, which, however, can be divided into three, by closing up the central spaces within the two incomplete partitions (such as are to be found in most Chinese houses), made of sandalwood and little panels of painted silk. When I am alone the room is lighted only by my reading-lamp and by the glow of the fire.

I looked round to see if some one had entered without my hearing the opening and shutting of the door, and then I saw a figure standing only a few yards from my chair, motionless against a background of dark shadows. The figure stood under one of the semi-partitions that divided up the room, so that it appeared to be framed by the painted silk panels in their sandalwood supports.

For several seconds I remained staring, struck dumb by sheer amazement. Was it a human figure that stood among the shadows, or was it an Oriental god?

The face was of a deep violet colour, with circles of white round the eyes. The nose was shaped like a vulture's beak, under which was a large mouth, with closed lips curved upwards in a mocking, ironical smile. But

116

from under this mask there emerged a rounded girlish chin, poised on a slim white neck. The bust was imprisoned in a bright metal cuirass of shining brass scales. This breastplate stopped short of the hips, but descended to a point between the legs. The costume was completed by a pair of yellow trousers, made of gauze. They were puffed out below the waist, but caught in with ribbons just below the knee, and again at the ankle. The arms and shoulders were bare, and the limbs were bare under the gauze trousers.

The most striking thing about the apparition was the head dress. From the forehead of the violet face there arose a gleaming aureole of gold, like flames that thrust back the surrounding shadows. A movement of the head sent a ripple along these flames, and then I realized that they were feathers; feathers so long that they curved back and fell almost to the feet; feathers of gold, with shadows of dark green. Donald Parramoor was right. Never had a finer ornament been created to clasp round the brow of a king. No monarch ever had a crown like the crown of Montezuma.

Kuniang's voice, somewhat muffled, asked me what I thought of it. She came forward into the room, taking off her mask with a gesture of relief. The crown of feathers came away at the same time, revealing Kuniang's hair and the birthmark on her forehead shaped like a crescent moon.

She drew near to the fire and held out one bare foot to the flames.

'The Heavenly Trousers,' she said, 'are not warm.'

'Kuniang!' I exclaimed. 'You don't mean to say you came out like that, without a coat?'

'Only through the courtyards, from my room to yours. But there is a north wind. Feel my hands.'

And she laid her icy fingers on my wrist.

I quoted from the *Princess in Tartary*:

'Hab lib in colo lan'.
    Hab stop where ice belong,
What tim much solly in-i-sy
    She makee this sing-song.'

Exalted Virtue always puts a kettle on the hob for me on cold nights. I picked it up, and, taking a little brandy from a tantalus, I made Kuniang a tumbler of grog. She stood by the fire and sipped it. The firelight flickered on the metal scales of her cuirass and showed her slim figure through the gauze. When she had warmed herself, I went to the other end of the room and opened one of the camphor-wood boxes, where I keep my silks. I took from it the rose-coloured padded silk that Donald had admired.

When I got back to her, Kuniang was still standing beside the fire. She looked at me inquiringly, wondering, I suppose, what I was going to do. I spread the silk out on the sofa, and told Kuniang to lie down on it. She did so, still looking puzzled. Then I wrapped the silk round her, covering even her head and feet, and carried her to her room. Thus, through the courtyards of the palace, they used to carry to the Emperor the concubine of his choice. But there it was a eunuch who held her in his arms. Kuniang was so light I could have carried her for miles. Yet when I pushed open the door of her room with my foot my heart was beating fast. I laid her down on the bed, and as I did so the rose-coloured silk fell aside. Kuniang's face was close to mine; her soft hair brushed my cheek. I felt that I could never let her go. My own face was cold with the outside air, but hers was warm and sweet and fragrant as if all the flowers of summer were on her lips.

Elisalex had prophesied truly.

12 The Mettray Succession

Noise is not in the market-place, nor quiet in the hills . . .

I cannot remember where I came upon this Chinese
proverb, but I think it must have been in a missionary
pamphlet, published in Hong Kong. As is so often the
case in Eastern literature, the idea is only half
expressed. The reader must guess the conclusion:

> *. . . but in the ever-changing hearts of men.*

The Home of the Five Virtues had been for me a pleasant, tranquil place where I could meditate and write and
study the Eastern world. But its quietude was not in the
sheltered courtyards. It was in my heart. And after I
realized that I loved Kuniang my heart was quiet no
longer.

Kuniang and I had often considered the advantages of
imaginary suitors.

'Tinker, tailor, soldier, sailor . . .' It had become a sort
of family joke between us. I would suggest an officer in
one of the Legation Guards (a Highlander in a kilt, or a
naval officer in summer uniform), a student-interpreter,
a rich *tai-pan* from Shanghai, or even a Chinese War
Lord, with half a dozen wives already.

But now the humour of such speculations appealed to
me no longer. I wanted Kuniang for myself. The feeling
had been there for some time. It came over me, with all
the force of a sudden surge of passion, when I carried
her back to her room, wrapped, like an imperial concubine, in the rose-coloured silk.

But, in her position, was it fair to make love to her?

Might she not give herself to me out of gratitude, or a mistaken sense of duty?

And so I hesitated, and there was no more peace for me in the old Shuang Liè Ssè.

Meanwhile some one else came into the story.

That is why I must begin my tale anew, bringing in people and events which have nothing to do with the Home of the Five Virtues. I must tell of the opening of the Mettray succession, in Tientsin, in the second year of the war.

In those days, whenever I wanted advice on business matters, I used to go to Tientsin, to consult my old friend Jeremiah Mettray.

Jeremiah had come to China as a boy, in 1861, and had settled in Tientsin when they first opened the British Consulate there. He had made a fortune which, at the time of his death, was estimated at fifteen million dollars Mex. This calculation was made a few months before Jeremiah ceased absorbing his evening cocktail at the bar of the Country Club and was entombed in the large grey sepulchre which he had erected for himself at the time when he built a row of warehouses along the banks of the Hai Ho. Both the tomb and the warehouses were constructed of reinforced concrete, and had been contracted for with the same firm at the same time. Jeremiah used to boast that, in this way, the tomb cost him practically nothing.

Some months before his death Jeremiah Mettray gave the world another proof of that farseeing business acumen which had contributed so much to the success of his commercial ventures. He wrote to his brother, a retired clergyman, living in Plymouth, asking him to select one of his own grandsons (preferably the most serious minded) and to send him out to China in order to prepare the transfer of Jeremiah's estate, which before long would be at the disposal of his heirs.

Jeremiah was a bachelor, and, so far, had never taken much interest in his elder brother's progeny, though he might well have adopted one or other of the members of the younger generation, in order to continue the family

120

traditions in his firm. He preferred, however, to float a company and to leave shares, or certain sums of money, to his nearer relatives, with whom he had remained on cordial, if not on very intimate, terms. It was only when he felt his own end approaching that he manifested a desire to have some one of his own kin near him at a time when, as he expressed it, his last bond should fall due.

But it so happened that, at the time when Jeremiah wrote to his brother in Plymouth, all the young men of the Mettray family who were of a suitable age were either at the front or in service connected with the war. Even those who were not in the army had offices which they might not abandon for private reasons. The only member of the family who could come to China was a grandson of the old clergyman (a son of his daughter), whose delicate health prevented him from serving his country.

The young man's name was Paul Dysart. He was quite unknown to Jeremiah, who remembered only having heard that his niece, the clergyman's daughter, had married into a social sphere considerably above that of the Mettray family. The idea of having to deal with an aristocratic and sickly young man did not please the old Tientsin merchant. But it was too late to stop Paul Dysart's departure for China; he had already started, via New York, San Francisco, and Yokohama.

Jeremiah was often in Peking, and it was from him that I learnt of his great-nephew's arrival, in March 1917. Two months later, about the middle of May, he brought the young man to see me.

They arrived at my door at four in the afternoon, and for some unknown reason there was no one in the *k'ai-men-ti's* lodge to receive them, or to announce their visit. But Jeremiah, who was well used to the vagaries of Chinese servants and knew my house well, walked in and made his way through the courtyards to the door of my study.

I was at work on a translation of *The Dream of the Red Chamber* when I heard their voices outside. Jeremiah was saying:

'If he is at home, he will be here.'

Then came an exclamation from Paul Dysart, who had perceived Ah-ting-fu's sign of the Heavenly Trousers:

'Good Lord! Why has he got that thing over the door?'

'Better ask him yourself. I have long given up being surprised at anything people do in the East, especially if they have been here a long time. Old China hands are all a bit cracked. It comes from learning the Chinese language.'

At this moment there came a knock at my door, and as I said 'Come in' Jeremiah entered, followed by his nephew, who asked no further questions about the Heavenly Trousers.

I had heard much about Paul Dysart and I looked at him with interest. He did not appear at all sickly. He was pale, but not paler than many people who, like him, have dark hair and eyes. And he was tall and held himself very straight. His clothes were newer and smarter than usual among the foreign inhabitants of Peking. I noticed that he spoke little, and hardly ever smiled.

Jeremiah's visit to me was not a mere formal call. We had much to talk about, and for a part of the time we conversed in my study, while Paul Dysart strolled about in the garden. Kuniang was out riding and he did not meet her. I seem to remember that my tête-à-tête with Jeremiah was made possible by some fairly obvious hint, on his part, that he wanted to speak with me alone.

'Our young friend does not seem to be as ill as was reported,' I remarked, when Paul had left the room.

Jeremiah shook his head despondently.

'You are quite wrong,' he said. 'Paul is a very sick man. In fact I want to talk to you about him. I have reason to believe that he is dying.'

'What!'

'Yes. I don't mean to say that he is in any immediate danger. But he is suffering from some incurable affection of the spleen. The doctors say that he may last another year, but not more.'

'In that case why did he come out here?'

'I don't think he knew how ill he was when he left England. But he visited a specialist in San Francisco, what they call a "diagnostician", and that was the verdict.'

'But, then, all his journey has been for nothing?'

'No, indeed. He has been working with me very efficiently. I think he is pleased to have some useful work to do. He is a clever boy, and some of his suggestions have been most useful. It is by no means certain that he won't have the opportunity of winding up my estate. I don't suppose I shall last much longer.'

'You look good for another five years at least, and I hear that you still frequent the swimming-pool at the Country Club. You cannot be really ill if you do that at your age.'

'I ought not to do it. My doctor has told me I must give it up. But I hate leading the life of an invalid when I do not feel ill. My heart is weak, and I suffer from attacks of asthma. I have been on the point of handing in my checks several times, and have just managed to pull through. I dare say I might last much longer if I were more careful, but that is just what I do not want to be.'

'I believe you would like to pass out first, just to give your nephew a chance to go on with his job as executor. But what an extraordinary situation: both of you going about in apparently the best of health, and both of you believing that you have not long to live! Are you sure that it is not all some stupid mistake of the doctors?'

'It may be. In Paul's case, I sincerely hope it is. Anyhow, I have put him down in my will as if he had a lifetime before him. If he hasn't, it may please him to make a will of his own. Should he survive me, I want you to do your best for the boy, as long as he stays out here.'

'You may count on me for that.'

'Thank you. That is why I wanted to see you alone. It is odd how fond I have become of Paul in the few weeks he has been with me.'

The old man's voice had in it a touch of pathos, very unusual with him.

Such a conversation would sound very improbable in Europe. But it appeared natural enough in Peking. People take the prospect of sudden death more naturally in China than in the West. Long illnesses are rare. We pass out quickly. I can well imagine someone who had not seen me for some days calling at the Home of the Five Virtues

123

and asking if I were in. And Exalted Virtue answering politely: 'Solly. No can do. Master makee die.'

When Paul Dysart re-entered my study he told me that he intended remaining in Peking for a week or ten days, whereas his uncle was leaving for Tientsin that same evening. So I suggested that Paul should occupy my guest-room during his stay in the capital. He accepted with evident pleasure. I think that, in his state of health, he rather feared the racket of a big hotel.

I have always been somewhat casual and absent-minded. When I asked Paul Dysart to stay with me, I never spoke to him about Kuniang, which perhaps I might have done. And I never said anything to Kuniang about his being asked to stay. She heard, of course, from the Five Virtues, that a friend of mine from Tientsin was occupying the guest-room and would be there for dinner. I noticed, when she came into my study at about a quarter to eight that she had put on her best evening frock. But I think she had understood that the guest was old Jeremiah Mettray. So it happened that, when Kuniang and Paul Dysart met for the first time, the meeting was unexpected on both sides. And that touch of the unexpected added to the immediate interest they took in one another.

Kuniang was standing near the fireplace when Paul came into the room, and the light from a tall standing lamp fell on her head and shoulders. The colour of her dress was the faintest green with silver shoes (Donald Parramoor had taught Kuniang to dress well). Her big grey eyes were like pools of water, and the jade bracelets on her arms had the lights and shadows of a running stream. She reminded me of a Rhine maiden, with the Rhinegold in her hair.

Paul remained for a moment near the door, staring in amazement at the lovely girl, and she gazed back at him, wondering, I suppose, who this could be, who had taken old Jeremiah's place. She stood in the full light, herself a creature of light and youth and beauty. He remained like a shadow among the shadows in the darker part of the room.

I got up and introduced them, and even as I did so it

came over me that these young people would love each other. It was as if I saw two flames drawing close together so that in a moment they must become one under my eyes.

Kuniang was then nineteen, with a heart all ready for love. Paul Dysart was a young man, still in the full possession of his strength, but with the threat of an immature death hanging over him. Doubtless Kuniang appeared to him as the embodiment of all that was most lovable in the world that he must leave. Love is often more sudden and more poignant when it is born within the shadow of death.

And there was something about him which Kuniang had not known before. He was a man whose good breeding, whose gentleness towards women, was manifest in every word and in every gesture, without ceasing to be as natural to him as the colour of his hair and of his eyes. He spoke to men with an assured authority; to women with an unconscious deference.

Donald Parramoor had been all bustle and fuss and pleasurable excitement. Every hour with him and his silks and his feathers was full of thrills. For all I know, he may have treated Kuniang as he did his manikin sisters.

But Paul Dysart was the type of man whose love encircles a woman with protecting arms. His glance, bent down towards Kuniang, was in itself a caress. He did not fascinate her by his talk as Donald had done, but he made her talk, and talk about herself. Donald had stood her before a mirror. Paul Dysart held up a mirror to her soul. Yet he could flatter her (a necessary accomplishment, if you want to make a pretty woman love you). I remember how, on the first evening, his words seemed to imply he had known her, by sight at least, for years.

'But you have only seen me to-night for the first time!' exclaimed Kuniang.

'I have seen those eyes of yours so often, in pictures by old masters! If I were Raphael, I would give your face to my Madonnas.'

My heart was sore within me. I had known that Kuniang might some day fall in love with another man, and that I might suffer all the pangs of jealousy should I lose her. But

125

I was not prepared for a tragedy such as I then foresaw. And how could I be jealous of a dying man?

Meanwhile Kuniang was radiant, with the short-lived radiance of a falling star.

13   *Buddha's Hands*

I

If Paul Dysart had been living by himself in an hotel in
Peking I doubt if he would have troubled to go sightseeing. But during the first days of his stay with us he
made no mention of his tragic state of health, and
Kuniang did what she thought would give him pleasure:
she took him to see the Temple of Heaven, the Lake
Palaces, as much as was then visible of the Forbidden
City (the little Emperor was still occupying a portion of
it), and one day they went and picnicked at the Summer
Palace. Paul's interest in Kuniang lent an interest to the
surroundings, and it was evident that he enjoyed these
excursions as well as the expeditions into the Chinese
City, to explore the curio-shops round the Liu-li-chang.

I did not accompany them, save on one occasion, when
they went to visit the Lama Temple.

People who have been in Peking longer than I have tell
me that the Lama Temple used to be a centre of anti-
foreign activity, and that at one time it was even dangerous, if not impossible, for a foreigner to visit it. But all
this has changed since 1900, and nowadays the Lama
Temple is one of the sights of Peking, though the habit of
the guides who show you round, to ask for money, and
more money, at almost every door as you pass in, and
again as you pass out, takes away from the enjoyment. It
was partly to make things easier for them that, on the
afternoon when Paul and Kuniang decided to visit the
headquarters of the 'yellow religion' in Peking, I decided
to go with them. For I had friends in the Lama Temple. I
had once been in the habit of going there regularly, to

visit two old priests, or lamas, whom I had met years before and with whom I had become almost intimate, at a time when I was making a not very successful attempt to learn the Mongol language.

It is a very long way from the Shuang Liè Ssè to the Lama Temple, and by the time we got there we were all feeling almost as tired as our rickshaw coolies. The prospect of a rest and a cup of tea in one of the minor pavilions was not unpleasant to any of us. So, after a tour round the temple buildings and a very casual inspection of the colossal Buddha and other items of interest, I asked to see my old friends, and we were taken to them through a maze of small courtyards and passages, to the east of the central pavilions.

The two lamas were in the company of a much younger man, to whom they gave the Mongol title of Kagan (prince), and also that of Chubil Khan, which I think can best be translated as 'abbot'. We found them all out of doors, in a courtyard, examining some small hairy objects, which on closer inspection turned out to be the severed paws of a bear. These represented, so we were told, a great delicacy on Chinese and Manchurian banqueting tables. They had been sent to the abbot from the north, and he was telling his hosts how they should be cooked.

We were invited into a big hall, that might have been a refectory, except that Eastern friars and prelates do not take their meals in company. But a young *chela* brought us cups of tea and we sat there for some time. Paul admired the dark red and orange robes of the priests, and their curved and plumed head-dresses, which they wore in anticipation of some ceremony that was about to take place in the principal hall of the Temple.

But the interest of our visit lay in the fact that we made the acquaintance of the Mongol abbot. I sometimes wonder if it would not have been better for all of us if we had never met him.

It is always difficult to guess the age of an Oriental, especially of one whose head and face are shaved. Our new friend might have been anything from twenty-five to forty-five. He was very tall and had a straight, elegant figure that even the padded Mongol coat could not hide. The slimness of his waist was accentuated by a silk sash, with two beautiful jade buckles. In a corner of the room was a pile of luggage, which must have been his: a saddle and saddle-bags, a fur cap and felt riding boots, also a pair of Mauser pistols.

Judging by these accoutrements, the abbot might have been one of those militant bishops of the Middle Ages who wore armour under their vestments and were not averse to wielding a battle-axe in a good cause. His features were not of the pure Asiatic type, but the shape of the eyes was that which is so characteristic of the Mongols. His clothes, though worn and travel-stained, were clean. Most lamas, in North China and in Tibet, have the obnoxious habit of never taking off their clothes, and one can smell them a mile off.

One of my lama friends told me that the abbot had arrived, some time before, from the famous lamasery at Kum Bùn, but that his home was much farther north. His own lamaseries were situated in the basin of the Amur and Sungari rivers, and they had been looted and destroyed by bands of *tung hudze*. Many of the monks had been killed and the survivors scattered. This was, apparently, the reason for the abbot's coming to Peking. He was anxious to win back the possessions of his order, and to collect a new band of followers. But to do this he had need of money, and this was difficult to come by. Business men in Peking had not been encouraging. The days of richly endowed Church foundations had passed away in China as elsewhere.

For some time we sat together on either side of a narrow table, made of one long polished beam of teak, resting on trestles. I conversed with the two elder priests, while Paul and the abbot gazed at one another with a certain mutual interest that found no expression in words. Kuniang sat a little way off, at the end of the table, with her eyes on Paul. I don't think she paid much attention to the others or to what was said.

At first there appeared to be no possible means by which we could communicate with the abbot. The two priests told us that he could speak no Chinese, only

Mongol and Russian. But when our hosts and I had almost exhausted all the usual exchange of compliments that accompany a Chinese visit, the abbot caught my eye and very diffidently pronounced a phrase that at first I did not recognize only because I did not expect it. He said:

'*Nous pourrions peut-être parler francais.*'

Thus we discovered that he could understand French quite well and speak it fairly correctly, but with an exasperating slowness. As Kuniang said afterwards: 'You felt that he must be eating a grape between each word.'

This slowness of speech lent a peculiar interest to all the abbot said. We hung on his words, waiting breathlessly for the end of his sentences. Luckily he did not speak much. From what he told us himself, supplemented by explanatory comments from the two lamas, we gathered that he had first learnt French from some missionaries in Mongolia, and that later he had perfected it in St. Petersburg, where he had stayed for some time. As a semi-independent Mongol prince he had been treated with much honour by the Tsar, and even entrusted with a military command, though this had probably been more honorary than effective.

A certain mutual sympathy became immediately apparent between Paul Dysart and the abbot. Paul was obviously much impressed by the first outstanding personality that he had met in the Orient.

The conversation took an unexpected turn when the abbot asked Paul (letting his words fall like drops out of an eye-dropper) if he were glad to have come to China. The answer was:

'Yes, I have always longed to see China, though I knew nothing about the country. Indeed, I had an entirely false idea of Peking, taken from a description made up in a dream.'

I asked Paul what he meant.

'I was alluding,' he explained, 'to the much-quoted poem *Kubla Khan*. It was conceived by Coleridge while he was asleep. When he awoke he wrote down the first fifty-four verses, and he might have written more, for in his dream the poem was longer. But he was interrupted, and when he sat down again he had forgotten how it went on.'

For the benefit of the abbot, we did our best to render, in French, the well-known lines:

In Xanadu did Kubla Khan
  A stately pleasure-dome decree,
Where Alph, the sacred river, ran
  Through caverns measureless to man
Down to a sunless sea.

After which we talked about dreams.

I recalled the case of Condorcet, who discovered in a dream the solution to a mathematical problem which he had not been able to solve in his waking hours. The abbot listened attentively and appeared to have no difficulty in understanding what we said. He remarked that, in certain circumstances, it was possible to exert an influence on the mind of a sleeping man, and to give him, by means of a dream, such experiences as he might desire.

It was better, I found, when the abbot was speaking, not to look at him direct. His slowness of speech was less exasperating, and he even seemed to speak quicker if one did not meet his eye. So it happened that when he mentioned the possibility of a suggested dream I was looking, not at the speaker, but at Paul Dysart. And I was surprised to observe a sudden flash of interest, which lighted up his expression, as if the idea opened out to him a new field of thought.

But the idea was not clear to us, and though the abbot appeared willing to explain, it was difficult to understand what he meant.

'It is done,' he said, 'by changing the thought-soul for another, while the person is asleep.'

'And the result is a dream?'

'Yes.'

'It reminds me,' said Paul, 'of Du Maurier's *Peter Ibbetson*. There is a young man in prison who comes out every night, in his dreams, to meet the woman he loves, and they go over their past life together.'

Kuniang began to say: 'And there is the dream in . . .' But she left her sentence incompleted. I suppressed a smile. Evidently she did not want Paul to know that she had read *Aphrodite.*

The matter might have ended there, but Paul was not inclined to let the subject drop. The abbot, realizing that his own laboured French was not sufficient to define a technical process in the realms of experimental psychology, suggested at last that he should give us a practical illustration of what he had attempted to describe. And Paul agreed.

At that moment the two old lamas were called away to take part in the ceremony that was just about to begin. We all stood up while they took their leave. Kuniang came close to me and whispered anxiously:

'Do you think it safe to let that man try experiments on Paul? You know these priests are not to be trusted.'

I looked at her and then at Paul, who was now talking to the abbot, a little distance off. Paul's interest, and his apparent willingness to do anything that the abbot suggested, were rather surprising, unless one knew, as I knew, that the young man was living under the shadow of death. I understood that he might be only too happy to be taken out of himself. In the circumstances it did not seem to me that the abbot could do him any harm. Nor could I think of any way to interfere. I did my best to reassure Kuniang, telling her that it would be all right as long as we were there. Then we followed Paul and the abbot into an adjoining room, which had a *kang* in it, or Chinese bed. But Chinese beds are hard. They are not adapted for an afternoon snooze, so the abbot went and collected some padded Mongol coats, smelling slightly of camphor, and spread them over the *kang*.

Then he asked Paul if he thought that, lying down on that couch and being left alone, he could possibly fall asleep. Paul answered that he might try, but that it would be difficult, at that hour. So the abbot said that, if Paul would do his best, it might be possible to assist him.

'Do you mean that you would help me to go to sleep?'

'Yes.'

'But then it is pure hypnotism that you wish to try on me?'

The abbot shook his head, but did not attempt to

132

explain. He made a sign that we should wait, and left the room.

'He has gone to fetch opium, I am sure,' said Kuniang. 'I should not let him play tricks on you, if I were you.'

'Surely,' said Paul, 'they do not keep an opium den in the Lama Temple?'

'No. But every Chinese who can afford it has opium in the house.'

The abbot returned, carrying a small lighted brazier, and we noticed the drowsy smell of poppies. Kuniang had been right. But Paul did not seem inclined to take heed of her warning. Although protesting half-heartedly that he felt an utter fool, he took off his shoes and his jacket, and lay down on the *kang*. Then the abbot made a sign to me and to Kuniang to follow him. We passed out together into a small courtyard.

II

My idea of visiting the Lama Temple had not comprised experiments in new forms of hypnotic suggestion. I took no interest in the possibility of substituting the 'thought-soul' with another (though I recognized the Eastern conception of a soul divided into component parts). Therefore I was naturally impatient at having to wait about while Paul Dysart tried to sleep on a Chinese *kang* under the influence of opium.

But Kuniang appeared quite content. She sat down on the edge of a marble platform, to the side of the steps that led up to the door from which we had just come out. Taking off her straw hat, she laid it down beside her. The abbot was standing close by. I think he also felt uncertain what to do, while we waited for Paul to fall asleep. But, unlike myself, he showed no impatience. As Kuniang took off her hat, his eyes fixed themselves on her forehead, on the mark of the half-moon. He came nearer, and with one hand gently lifted her hair in order to see better. They made a pretty picture, against the background of the temple courtyard: the young girl, looking up, and the tall Oriental, bending over her. The beauty of her hair was equalled by the beauty of his hands.

I have always admired Chinese hands. How often have I seen plutocratic European and American men come out of the Hôtel des Wagons-lits, beautifully shaved and groomed and manicured, holding fat cigars in their ringed fingers, while the rickshaw-coolies raced to the doorstep and fought for the fare. The 'foreign devil' would make his choice, and they would start off, with a great show of initial speed, to the curio-shops, or the Winter Palace, or to some foreign Legation. Between the Lord of Creation, inside the conveyance, and the beast of burden, running between the shafts, it was the latter who had the better hands.

The abbot's hands were strong, though the sinews were hidden under the smooth skin. they were powerful, though their power was more spiritual than physical: the hands of a thinker, of a creator. And they were quiet – so very quiet. An Italian, or a Frenchman, speaks with his hands. But the abbot came of a race in which, for many generations, men had kept their hands hidden under long sleeves. They were silent hands, aloof and mysterious. Sometimes I think that the Buddha must have had hands like those.

When he had looked at the mark on Kuniang's forehead, the abbot smiled at her and said, in his hesitating French: 'If your friend can sleep, we will make him dream of you.'

He strolled off to the middle of the courtyard, where some lilac bushes were just coming into bloom. Two white butterflies were fluttering over the lilac. The abbot was evidently a nature-lover, for he examined with interest the panicles of still-unopened flowers. When he noticed the butterflies, he turned his attention to them. And then he did a very remarkable thing. He stretched out his arms in the gesture of one who blesses. And immediately, on to the tip of the middle finger of each hand, there came a butterfly, and posed itself with closed wings. There the abbot stood, with a white butterfly on each hand. He turned his face towards Kuniang and smiled, as if to draw her attention to what he had done.

'Surely,' said Kuniang to me, 'they have gone to him by

chance. He could not have called them?'

'I don't think it was mere chance,' I answered, 'though I have never seen it done before. It reminds me of Kipling's story of the Butterfly that stamped:

> 'There never was a king like Solomon,
>   Not since the world began;
> But Solomon talked to a butterfly
>   As a man would talk to a man.'

Kuniang got up and walked very quietly to where the abbot stood. He let her come quite close, so that she might see the butterflies resting on his fingers. Then he gently waved them off. Kuniang gazed at him with wonder in her eyes.

'Can you do it again?' she asked.

The abbot raised his hands above his head, for the butterflies had flown to a higher level. For a few moments it would seem that they did not see his hands. But he waited patiently and, sure enough, back they came, first one and then the other, and rested on his finger-tips.

A few minutes later the abbot went and looked in at the door of the room where we had left Paul. Then he made a sign to us not to make a noise, and disappeared within. With the help of the opium fumes from the brazier, Paul had succeeded in falling asleep. Kuniang and I tiptoed to the open door, and I looked in over her shoulder. The abbot was seated on the *kang*, with his fingers resting lightly on Paul's wrist (I wondered what other miracle those fingers were about to accomplish). The room was dark and cool.

As nothing happened that I could perceive, I soon got tired of watching, so I strolled out again into the courtyard. Kuniang remained standing near the door.

The butterflies were still circling over the lilac bushes. I held out my hands to them, as the abbot had done, to see if they would come to me, but they fluttered off and disappeared over a low wall which separated the courtyard from the central part of the temple. As I turned away I noticed some small objects lying on the

135

soft earth under the bushes: a small envelope, open, with a letter inside, and two walnuts, with their shells highly polished. The Chinese use such walnuts (or little metal or ivory balls) to hold in their fingers, moving them round and round to keep the hands supple. The abbot had probably dropped them out of his wide sleeves when he lifted his hands to call the butterflies. I picked them up, together with the letter, and laid them on the marble flags to the side of the steps that led up to the door of the room where Paul was sleeping. I put the letter under the walnuts, so that it should not blow away. The abbot could not fail to see his belongings when he came out.

As I turned the letter over, wondering that it should be written on heavy foreign paper and not on the light rice paper used by the Chinese, I noticed the address, written in a bold feminine hand:

Le Prince Dorbon Oirad
Pékin

There was no stamp on the envelope, and the notepaper was scented, with a scent that seemed strangely familiar.

I do not know how long Paul might have slept, had not a tremendous noise of drums and gongs broken out in one of the principal courtyards, not far from where he was. The ceremony had begun that my two old friends had gone away to attend. Ceremonies in the Lama Temple are generally accompanied by a lot of noise. The *chelas* are given gigantic rattles, which they agitate at intervals with great religious fervour. The sound produced is like the rolling of thunder and is sufficient to wake the dead. For all I know, that may be the object in view.

I went in again and looked at Paul. He was sitting up on the edge of the *kang*, very much dazed. Kuniang asked him something about what he had dreamt, but he shook his head without answering. Possibly he was half stupefied with opium. I suggested that we should go home. After the usual ceremonious farewells, in which Paul took no part, we reached the outer door of the temple, and got into our rickshaws.

*   *   *

It was about six o'clock when we reached the Home of the Five Virtues and separated to go to our respective rooms. Only when we met again in my study, an hour before dinner, did Paul appear to have shaken off the effects of his afternoon's experience. The opium fumes had given him a slight headache, but his brain was clear, and he could tell us about his dream.

'It was the most astonishing thing,' he said. 'I might have expected something Mongol or Chinese. But there was nothing Oriental in the dream at all. I was with you' – he looked at Kuniang – 'in a lady's dressing-room, your own dressing-room, in a house in Europe.'

'The abbot told us he would make you dream of me' said Kuniang. 'But how do you know it was Europe?'

'Because I can tell you what town it was: St. Petersburg. I know that, although I have never been in St. Petersburg.'

'And what happened?'

'Nothing happened. I was in a chair, by the side of a large toilet-table, with a Venetian mirror on it, in a glass frame. You were standing in front of the mirror. You had on a white ball-dress, and two maids were helping you to put on your jewels.'

'That doesn't sound like me! Jewels, and two maids to put them on. What jewels were they?'

'Diamonds. Nothing but diamonds. There was a diamond star, in a leather case stamped with the imperial arms. At least, I suppose they were the imperial arms: a double-headed eagle under a crown. We were discussing whether you should put it on or not. You called it the Cross of Alexander.'

'Why call it a cross if it was a star?' Kuniang did not seem willing to allow for any discrepancies.

'It was both. There was a star of diamonds. And, on top of the star, a cross of enormous brilliants. They were dazzling to look at. But you were wearing quite enough jewels without that: great diamond drops, as ear-rings, and a Russian head-dress, like a tiara, all of diamonds, to which was attached a lace veil that fell down behind. I persuaded you to leave the Cross of Alexander at home.'

'What language did we talk in?'

'I seem to think it was Russian.'

'I don't speak Russian, or very little, just a few words I have picked up at Matushka's.'

'Neither do I, in real life. But I was not the same as I am now. I felt a bigger man, in many ways, and quite important. We were going together to some reception, or to a ball. I was dressed all in black: a long skirted coat, and a belt, and silver cartridge cases. An astrakhan cap lay on the floor at my feet. Yet there were two things about the dream that make it seem real, even now. I kept telling you that if you did not hurry up we would be late. You never are ready for anything, you know.'

'And what was the other thing?'

'That I was in love with you.'

Kuniang's eyes sparkled, like the diamonds in Paul's story.

'I'm not surprised,' she said mischievously. 'I must have been quite an heiress, with all those jewels!'

14 'Love Pidgin'

I

A few days after our expedition to the Lama Temple,
Kuniang had a headache and did not come to lunch. In
the evening she appeared as usual, in my study, about
an hour before dinner, but she was pale and nervous. I
realized that something must have happened, and from
the few words that she said, in answer to my questions, I
understood she had learnt of Paul's illness and the fact
that he had not long to live. Poor girl! Whatever her
dreams may have been, the awakening had not been
long delayed.

Our dinner, that night, was a melancholy meal. After
we had left the table, Kuniang went away to her room.
Paul sat with me for a short time, smoking and saying
nothing. Then he also retired for the night.

I sat in my study for an hour, or more, trying to read.
But I could not keep my attention on the book. So, about
eleven, I went to my room and to bed. But I could not
sleep. The windows were wide open and I could smell
the lilac and the yellow briar. Scents always make me
restless. I felt like the animals in the jungle-book, at the
time of the 'spring running'.

After tossing about for a couple of hours I got up, put
on a dressing-gown and a pair of slippers, and strolled
out into the silvery light of a waning moon. It was very
warm and still.

I took a turn in the garden, disturbing some cats who
had come in over the wall. Then I walked through the
courtyards. They never look so fascinating as on a moon-
lit night.

Kuniang's room and the guest-room, now occupied by Paul, faced each other across the courtyard. The windows of both were dark. But the sound of my footsteps provoked a sharp bark from inside Kuniang's pavilion. I had woken up Uncle Podger. A moment later a light was lit inside and faintly illuminated the window. It showed Kuniang's shadow as she came to the door and looked out. I could just make out her presence, but it was too dark to see clearly.

'Is that you?' she asked.

She had not specified who. But I stood in the full light of the moon.

'Yes,' I answered. 'I could not sleep, so I am prowling about. Uncle Podger took me for a burglar.'

'Wait a moment,' said Kuniang. 'I will come out too, I cannot sleep either.'

She closed the door and did not reappear for almost five minutes. Then she came out and down the steps into the courtyard, with Uncle Podger trotting after her. I wondered if he too felt the 'spring running' in his blood. If so, he was too dignified to show it.

'Sorry to have been so long,' said Kuniang. 'I could not find my new pyjamas.'

I noticed that her blue silk pyjamas looked very fresh and that all their creases were still there. Evidently she had just put them on.

'Weren't you in bed?' I asked.

'Yes. But I got so used to wearing nothing in bed that, although I have all those lovely pyjamas that you gave me, I do not often remember to put them on. I am sorry if I seem ungrateful.'

Kuniang spoke calmly and even languidly, as was natural in a person who had left her bed to come and stroll in the moonlight. She glanced across at Paul's darkened windows, and added:

'He must be asleep. He tells me that he takes veronal when he cannot sleep.'

We came out into the middle of the courtyard, and I saw her more clearly in the moonlight. I was surprised, for her face was quite calm and serene. Her expression was a little weary, but there were no signs of the

140

nervous tension that I expected her to be suffering from since she had found out about Paul's state of health. She gave one more look at his windows and then turned away with me, putting her arm in mine.

'Let us go and lie on the grass,' she said. 'I feel I want to talk to you. Do you mind?'

'There is nothing I would like better.'

We went to the grass plot opposite my study door. I got a rug and some cushions and said to Kuniang that we had better sit on them and not on the grass. She did as I suggested and thanked me absent-mindedly. Her thoughts were evidently elsewhere. But when I had lain down on the rug, she came and sat down close to me, with what seemed a little sigh of content.

'I am glad Uncle Podger told me that you were outside,' she said. 'It is a great relief to have you to talk to.'

'I thought you would be in trouble,' I said. 'It is about Paul, is it not?'

'Yes. I am very much worried about Paul. I do not know what to do about him. That is why I could not sleep.'

'I do not see what you *can* do about him,' I answered. 'Nobody can help, I am afraid.'

'It is true the doctors cannot cure him. But that is just why I ought to do what I can to make him happy. He is madly in love with me.'

'Yes, I guessed that. And you?'

'At first I was quite sure that I loved him and no one in the world but him. But now I just feel dreadfully sorry for him, and I do not really love him any more. It is like a candle that has been lit and then blown out almost at once. I do not understand it, but I feel so hateful, so mean!'

This was not what I had expected. But, then, I rarely came upon what I expected when talking to Kuniang. After a moment she went on:

'Those first days, when I began to realize what was happening, were the happiest I have ever known. I was in heaven. Paul had not said that he loved me, but he made no attempt to hide it. Then came the moment when I learnt about his health. It seems years ago. Really, it was last night. Paul was with me in my Japanese room and we were talking about the dream. He said that he meant to ask the abbot to make him dream again about me: he would go to the Lama Temple every day and sleep. The abbot should give him a new life to be passed in a dream: a new life with me.'

'I thought it was a pretty idea. But Paul was so solemn about it that he made me laugh, and I asked him: "What am I to do, while you are dreaming about me? Am I to go to sleep too, and dream of you? It seems very complicated!" But soon I realized that it was not a joke, and that there was something that must keep us apart. In the end he told me that there could never be a real life together for us two, for he had not much longer to live. Any day his illness might lay him low, and then in a few months he would die.

'I felt like a flower that shrivels up in a cold wind. I cried, and dried my eyes, and cried again. Paul kissed me and tried to console me, and blamed himself for having spoken.

'He left me about midnight. And I undressed, and put on my little Japanese kimono, while I sat in front of the looking-glass and brushed my hair. But all the time I seemed to see Paul alone in his room, thinking that he loved me, and I him, and that soon he must die. I have heard of girls in Europe who gave themselves to men, just before they started for the front. Yet none of those soldiers was so sure of death as Paul. I felt that, as he loved me so, I ought to give myself to him. That night, and perhaps for many nights to come, we could be together. And the end of his life would be happier because of me.'

'You could marry him, Kuniang, even now,' I said, 'if you both feel like that about it.'

'Yes, I had thought of that. But what mattered was that I should offer myself, without his asking, because he might not dare to ask. And I should do it at once, for there was no time to lose. I should cross the courtyard, just as I was, and go to him in his room. I pictured him sitting in his arm-chair, as you were, when I came to you that evening wearing the crown of Montezuma. He would turn and look at me, as you did.'

'Well, Kuniang,' I asked, 'and did you go?'

'No. I didn't. And that is why I cannot sleep.'

There were a good many things that I might have said, but I feared to stem the rush of her confidences. Obviously she felt the need of unburdening herself. Better not to interrupt. Soon she continued:

'I know that no one can blame me if I keep my honour and my purity. But if I had really loved I would not have thought of that. Like the girls in Europe, I would have refused nothing to a man who faced pain and death. To give myself would be almost a duty, especially for a girl like me.'

'Why for a girl like you?'

'Because I am practically alone in the world. What does it matter what I do?'

I expostulated: 'There is your father, Kuniang.'

'Yes, poor father. But since I was a child I have never lived with him. He comes to see me in Peking, and then says good-bye and goes away again. And at every good-bye he feels, and I feel, that it may be for the last time. He tells me that he expects to be killed, some day, on the line. I am hungry for love and affection. But all around me there is only death, and the danger of death.'

Kuniang moved closer to me, as if for protection.

'And that is the real reason,' she said, 'why I cannot give myself to Paul. It is hateful of me to throw him over, like this, just because he is ill. If he were a soldier, leaving for the front, I would count the minutes in which I could be with him. But I feel a horror of disease. Ever since I thought of going to him, it is as if a skeleton were waiting for me in the arm-chair in his room. If I went in, I feel that not Paul's face would look up at me, but the face of a skull, with empty eye-sockets and dreadful grinning teeth. It would not be Paul who would rise up to greet me, but a figure such as might rise up from a tomb. Hideous arms, with bones not yet uncovered, would stretch out to clasp me, and cold, rigid fingers would caress my skin.'

Kuniang covered her face with her hands and pressed close up to me, her whole body trembling.

'And yet Paul loves me,' she said. 'And for a few short

143

days I loved him. How can I be so unkind? What am I to do?'

I knew now what was wrong. Kuniang's nascent love had never had time to take root, and it had been thrown back upon itself, nipped in the bud, by the revelation that Paul was not what he had first appeared to be, a healthy, normal young man. So sudden a blow had destroyed the natural response of a loving nature to the passion which it inspired. The shock might have been less brutal, had all the horror of mating with a diseased man not been brought home to Kuniang by her own willingness to sacrifice herself. This readiness to ignore all moral restraint, in order to be kind to the man who loved her, came from a generous nature, but was also the after-effect of too much loneliness in her first youth. From force of habit she still considered herself as alone in the world, without protection and without responsibilities. She might give her body, because it was all she had to give, and she felt less ashamed of a lack of chastity than of a lack of kindness. What was significant was that she should confide in me. And my love for her gave me understanding.

'There is only one thing that you can do, Kuniang,' I said. 'You must encourage Paul to carry out his own idea. Let him ask the abbot to make him dream of you, of a lifetime with you. Time is not measured in dreams, and one could perhaps dream of a whole life in one night. But there is no need for that. Paul has still many months to live. Let him pass them dreaming of you. Who knows that, for a sick man, a dream woman may not be better than the real.'

'As in *Aphrodite*?'

'Yes. As in *Aphrodite*.'

'I believe you are right,' said Kuniang. 'If he could dream of me, he would not feel so much alone. And, at the end, I could nurse him.'

She was silent for a few moments, and then added: 'You must not think that my sorrow is all for Paul. It was nice to be really loved.'

I looked at her without answering. Then I got up and went in to my study, turning on the light as I entered.

144

From a drawer of my desk I took a little brass box, with some Chinese characters engraved on the lid. It contained my half of the crystal seal.

Then I went back to Kuniang. She was sitting where I had left her, gazing towards the bushes whence came a sound of scuffling. Uncle Podger had found something to interest him.

I sat down once more on the rug, and as Kuniang turned towards me I handed her the box. She opened it, and the crystal glimmered in the moonlight.

'What is it?' she asked, and it seemed to me that her voice trembled.

'You know what it is, and what it means.'

'That you need help?'

'I need you.'

'Me?'

'Yes. I need you more than Paul does, for I am not a dying man. I am not even an old one, though perhaps I may seem so to you.'

'How old are you?'

It was an odd question to put, at that moment. But Kuniang was a little stunned. I answered in Chinese:

'Great lady, I have wasted thirty-four years.'

'And do you really want me?'

'I cannot do without you.'

'Why did you never say so before?'

'Because I thought it was unfair to ask you. You are so young, and you might have thought you were in some way in my debt. But now I do not care how young you are, or what you may think. I need you. I am giving you the token. Will you come to my help?'

Our night had begun in the shadow of a tragedy, and had continued in a vein of pure romance. It was destined to end in farce. For the most appalling row broke out suddenly in the yellow-briar bushes, near the wall that encloses the garden to the north. Apparently Uncle Podger had got mixed up with two cats, who were pursuing the course of true love in the darkness. For suddenly he emerged into the moonlight, emitting fearful howls, and disappeared again precipitately, in the direction of the courtyards.

Kuniang and I stared after his retreating form, and then at each other. And we began to laugh.

What Kuniang's answer to me would have been if we had not been interrupted, I cannot say. But, when she had finished laughing, she lifted her face to mine, and repeated the time-worn formula with which the Five Virtues answer me when I ask for something:

'Yes, master. Can do.'

15 Interlude

Noise is not in the market-place, nor quiet in the hills . . .

Quiet had come back to me, in the Home of the Five Virtues, when I knew that I would not lose Kuniang any more. But we both felt a little conscience-stricken about Paul, though neither of us had done him, or wished him, any harm. Had he enjoyed normal health Kuniang might well have preferred him to me. On the other hand, if he had enjoyed normal health he would never have come to China at all. His illness was the obstacle, not only to his marrying, but even to Kuniang's loving him. She had begun to do so, and then, at the very outset, a reaction had set in. And her short-lived love-affair with Paul had thrown her into my arms. But we felt ashamed of ourselves. Our future happiness would be based on another's sorrow. In my case, at least, it was *Mors tua, vita mea.*

When Paul left for Tientsin, Kuniang and I went to see him off at the station. We watched him settle in his railway carriage, and we talked with him through the wire netting with which the windows of the Peking-Mukden express are furnished to keep out the flies. We sent the usual messages to Jeremiah and to mutual friends in Tientsin. But they all rang false, somehow. Though we knew that we would see him again, in a sense Paul was passing out of our lives. And we said good-bye not only to him but to what might have been.

For some time after the train had steamed out of the station and, gathering speed, had passed under the archways that pierce the lunette outside the Hata Mên,

147

Kuniang and I did not speak to each other. Our silence had in it something of the respect for the dead.

Twenty minutes later we arrived home together and passed over the threshold, turning to the left, to avoid the brick screen that, as in all Chinese houses, is supposed to impede the entrance of evil spirits. I stopped for a moment to look at the two characters which offer welcome, like the Roman *Salve*. They read, *Han Hsian* (Ocean of Felicity). I felt just like that: life to me shone like a smiling blue ocean under a summer sky.

But I was not to settle down at once to enjoy my new-found happiness.

A week later I myself left Peking for Shanghai. In former years Jeremiah Mettray had advised me to make some investments in landed property in the French Concession. He now wrote to me that it might be advisable to sell. Landed property was not likely to depreciate in Shanghai, but the currency value of the silver dollar was then abnormally high. Might it not be advantageous to realize, and to re-invest elsewhere? Jeremiah could not give me any definite advice in the matter. But he suggested that I should look into it myself. A trip to Shanghai might be justified, in order to talk the matter over with people on the spot.

I was touched by the old man's continued interest in my affairs at a time when he might well have been thinking of other things. And, after some hesitation, I decided to do as he suggested. But it was painful to leave Kuniang.

Had she been old and ugly I might have taken her with me, in her capacity of secretary-typist. But she was not old or ugly. Youth and beauty and love make life worth living. They also make it very complicated.

Kuniang had been asked by the Russian family to go with them to Shan-hai-kwan, where they had taken a bungalow for the summer months. This meant sea-air and sea-bathing. I asked Kuniang if she thought she could face several weeks, if not months, in the Russian *ménage*, and she said that she could. Things had changed since the days when Matushka had chastised her for upsetting a row of bottled spiders.

'Even Fédor and Natasha don't get birched since they had a revolution in Russia.'

'What has the revolution got to do with it?'

'Only that now Fédor and Natasha think themselves as good as their parents, if not better.'

'And do you think you can keep Fédor in order?'

'Oh, yes, easily. I don't mind him now that I know that you are in love with me.'

I could not quite follow this piece of reasoning, but as long as Kuniang wished to accept Matushka's invitation I supposed it was all right.

The sale of my property in Shanghai detained me for much longer than I expected. Indeed, I was there for most of the summer. And it was during those months that old Jeremiah died suddenly, of heart failure, at Pei-ta-ho.

In spite of his age and growing infirmities, he had insisted on taking his daily swim. One morning he had been caught by the outgoing tide and had only succeeded in reaching land again with great difficulty. When he emerged from the water and made his way across the sands to where he had left his clothes, the people that were sitting about on the beach saw him stagger and grope with his hands like a blind man. They ran to his help, but even as they did so he collapsed. His last words, spoken between gasps for breath, were:

'Tell Paul Dysart that now it is up to him!'

I wrote my condolences to Paul and reminded him that I was an old friend of his great-uncle's, and in this capacity I would be glad to do anything I could for Paul himself, if ever he should need assistance or advice, during his stay in China.

After ten days I received an answer from Paul, thanking me and adding that his uncle had left him a million dollars Mex: 'I am very grateful to the old man for his kind thought of me. But I am afraid that I will have very little use for all that money, unless I give some of it to the Mongol abbot, in exchange for dreams.'

When I had finished all my business in Shanghai and was on the point of leaving once more for Peking I did a stupid thing. I fell ill. Not very ill, but enough to delay my return to the north for another three weeks. And it was all my fault; for I partook unwisely of a dish of land-crabs, at a Chinese dinner. One sees these crabs being hawked about, still alive, at Chinese railway stations, wherever there are swamps in the vicinity. I had always wondered how the poor brutes could be so active, when suspended, one underneath the other, on a string. But I discovered that they could display an even greater activity when dead, and in the process of digestion, in my inside.

On my arrival at Shanghai, the director of the hotel, who was an old friend, had insisted on giving me what he considered the best room in the building. It was a room on the ground floor, and it had been furnished and decorated by a Chinese millionaire to suit his own tastes.

The room was a large one, but dark, and there were no windows from which one could see out into the street. Two glass doors opened on to a glass-covered veranda, and this looked out on to a small and dingy courtyard, or well. The glass of the doors was profusely decorated with a massive and flamboyant floral design in oxidized metals, mostly brass. This excluded even the small amount of daylight that might have come from the courtyard. The Chinese millionaire's idea was that the electric lights in his room should be turned on all day. The same floral design that beautified the doors reappeared in a metal dado round the room and in the ornamentation of the fireplace, where burned (if turned on) an electric fire, simulating flames which glowed without a flicker above a pile of artificial logs.

This apartment had its advantages in the summer months. For some unexplained reason it was deliciously cool. But it was a depressing place to be ill in. The absence of daylight gave the impression of being buried in a crypt.

My only consolation, during the first ten days of my illness, were some books that were lent me by kind friends, and such letters as were delivered to me by the morning post. As these were few and far between, I was reduced to reading again and again the correspondence of the previous months.

The gem of the collection was a letter from Donald Parramoor. It had been forwarded from Peking, where it had been addressed to:

The Maker of Heavenly Trousers
    Shuang Liè Ssè
      Tartar City, S.W.

Some one had added my name before forwarding. The postmark was that of Paris, but the letter began without any date or greeting:

'Say, old man! How are the celestial pants getting on? Fine? So glad!

'I thought you would like some news of your Uncle Donald. Please exchange with all information available as to the Home of the Five Virtues and inmates thereof.

'When Norah and Elsie and I arrived in Europe we found there was a war on. We had heard something about it already, but had not paid much attention. They will tell you anything in China! However, it was true. And the Americans were in it, making as much noise as anybody. Now, when there is a war on, or any little thing like that, your Uncle Donald is all over it in no time. So I went to offer my services. The first person I ran across was Ikey Rosenstein, whom I hadn't seen since his second wife divorced him in Old Chester. When I asked him to get me a job in one of the Allied armies he started singing:

"Would you rather be a Colonel, with an eagle on
    your shoulder,
Or a private, with a chicken on your knee?"

'Then he asked me what I could *do*? I told him that I could dress him up so that his own mother would not recognize him, in spite of his nose. "That's fine!" he said. "We've been looking for months for somebody that knew something about camouflage." And he took me to Head Quarters, where they told me to go and paint huts so that nobody would know that they were huts. Ikey was acting as liaison officer between the Scotch and the Americans, who could not understand

151

each other's language (Ikey talks like Hans Breitman, himself!). So he suggested that I should begin with the Highland regiment to which he was attached. I half suspected that he was trying on the old joke about the Jordan Highlanders (no advance without security). But no. They were the real thing. The Colonel came from Carnoustie. I taught him how to mix cocktails in a teapot, and I painted his hut so that when the poor man came out after a meal he thought he had *delirium tremens*.

'After that I took on the hut that Ikey shared with the chaplain. I painted it all round and on top with a series of Chinese gods, like the ones they have in the Lama Temple in Peking (only they keep them covered up, so as not to shock respectable spinsters from Boston, Mass.). You know what I mean. The gods all look very fierce, and each one has a young lady on his knee, wearing a crown and several necklaces, but nothing else. Very hot stuff! Ikey was real mad, but I told him that he had brought it on himself by singing me ribald songs about "a private with a chicken on his knee"! The chaplain moved into another hut.

'When I first saw those pleasing groups in Peking I thought of making up a musical comedy about them. The story would tell of a young lady who loved an Eastern god, and found that she had bitten off a larger bit than she could chew. The costumes might be very suggestive, but I doubt if they would produce it any-where out of China. We are not yet educated up to that sort of thing in the West. After I had finished with Ikey's hut, they would hardly let me do any camou-flage any more. I offered to decorate the Officers' Mess, but they said they would rather be shot at by German aviators any day. You can't expect military men to have an artist's soul.

'Elsie and Norah went into the Hot Cross Nurse business at Etampes. Elsie has got a beau: a French officer with a broken leg. He cooled off after Elsie had been nursing him for a week. I guess she must have sat down on his bed and broken the leg again. But they may patch it up again, leg and all.

'Do you know, I got mixed up in a battle, a real battle? I didn't want to. It was all a mistake. I was trying to organize some private theatricals in the trenches. We thought of giving "Midsummer Night's Dream", with gas-masks and a ballet, when the Germans made a surprise raid (at least, it was a surprise to me!). The next thing that happened was that your Uncle Donald had thrown a hand-grenade into the thick of them. Nobody else dared throw anything, because the Germans and our people were so mixed up that you couldn't tell which was which. But I was afraid that the beastly thing would explode in my hand, so I threw it away without thinking. As it happened, I killed more Germans than Allies, so we won! And now your Uncle Donald is a great man, and they are going to make a statue of him with a Mills bomb in one hand and a paint-brush in the other.

'I am now collaborating in a new French-American revue: something too cute for words. It will make the world feel sweet and sentimental again after the war. It's to be called *Golden Slippers*, after the old coon song:

Golden slippers on a golden stair,
    Golden slippers on my tirèd feet.
Golden slippers that we all must wear.
    Because dey am so sweet!

'Tell Miss Kuniang that, if the revue is a success, as it must be, I will send her a pair of slippers, pure gold, to match the light in her hair!

'If you come to Paris, look us up. You will find me at the bar of the Ritz, from 6 p.m. till dinner. And Norah and Elsie are generally at Rumpelmeyers about tea-time.

                        'Ever yours
                        'Donald Parramoor.'

'PS. – The girls at the Folies Marigny don't put enough rouge on their knees. I shall have to teach Paris how to dress! – D.P.'

16   Kingdom Come

I

Kuniang wrote to me often: quite long letters. Her literary style showed signs of my own influence, which was natural, as she had copied out so many articles of mine. Soon after my departure for Shanghai she had started with the Russian family for Shan-hai-kwan. She wrote from there and, much to my surprise, her letters contained quite a lot of news of a semi-political nature. Her first was dated 20th of June 1917. It ran as follows:

'Uncle Podger and I have been here now almost a week, and it is perfectly lovely. Lovely sands, beautiful woods, and mountains in the background, with the Great Wall rising from the sea, crossing the plain, and then climbing up into the hills. This side of the Wall is China, the other side (the north) is Manchuria. Uncle Podger has a lady friend in Manchuria. She is black and white and belongs to some Japanese who have a bungalow just outside the Wall.

'Everybody has bungalows here. They call them that, but some of them are quite fine houses. The one Patushka has taken is in the "second row". That means that it is not quite on the beach, but it is very nice all the same. Plenty of bedrooms. But we all sleep on the veranda. (Don't be alarmed! I wear my pyjamas every night.)

'It is early in the season, and there is trouble along the line, as there always is in China. So most of the bungalows are empty. But the place is full of Italians, camping in the woods, round the Italian fort. Think of finding my own compatriots at Shan-hai-kwan! There must be about 500, or more: what they call *irredenti*. They come from Trent and Trieste and Zara. I could not make out who they were at first and how they came to be here at all. But they have explained to me that they are Austrian subjects of Italian nationality. When the war broke out they were called up for military service in the Austrian Army and sent to the Russian front. But they would not fight against an Ally, so they let themselves be taken prisoners by Brussilow. The idea was to send them to Italy by sea from Archangel. But things are going badly in Russia, and for some reason which I do not understand they were sent to the Far East, via Siberia. They are not all here. There are others at Vladivostok and in Tientsin, and even in Peking. They are now waiting for a ship to take them to Italy.

'All the Russian family are wildly excited about them, because they bring news from home. And the odd thing is that all the Italians are perfectly wild about Russia. They say it was the most heavenly place. Though there was a war on, everybody was anxious to have a good time, and everybody seemed perfectly mad. It sounds rather like the Russian family on a big scale.

'The *irredenti* don't seem to be able to answer all the questions that Patushka and Matushka and Fédor want to ask them. But possibly that is because I have to interpret, and the Italians would rather tell me about themselves. They have a lot to say, and all seem to have had lots of love-affairs in Russia. One young man told me that he had done the journey three times from Vologda to Moscow, to see a girl. He had no railway ticket and no money. But he told everybody that he belonged to an Italian Mission, and showed them an illustrated postcard of a place called Fermo, in the Marche, where he comes from. Some one had put a large official stamp on the postcard, and this impressed people so much that my friend travelled for nothing and got all the food he wanted. I am not surprised that he thinks Russia was great fun!

'They all say that the revolution of last February

was only a beginning. There will be another one quite soon, and then there will be the devil to pay! Fédor is wildly excited about this. He wants to start for Russia at once. He says that one of the first things they will do will be to nationalize everything, factories and shops and food and even women! But from what the *irredenti* say there seems to be confusion enough with the women as it is.

'I have had letters from Paul. He is in Tientsin. The abbot has been there and they have seen each other and arranged about the dreams. If they go off well Paul will give the abbot money to help rebuild his monastery in Mongolia. It will be the price of a dream about me! This seems too fantastic to be true. I could never believe it had I not been there when the abbot made Paul dream. I am still very sorry about Paul, but I am no longer worried about what I should do. If he can dream of me, and it makes him happy to do so, that is all that matters now.

'Elisalex is in Peking. She says she will not come down here. I cannot make out why. What can she have to do in Peking? There are no servants left in Patushka's house, so she has gone to an hotel, the Telegraph Hotel, on the Austrian glacis (the glacis is Japanese now, but they still call it Austrian). It is a very cheap hotel. I thought that perhaps Elisalex might be hard up, but Fédor and Natasha say that she has plenty of money. She writes me letters, quite short and full of affection. But she does not tell me what she is doing.

'I hope you will come north again soon. It is very nice here, but I would like to be with you again in the Home of the Five Virtues.

'Yours very affectionately
'KUNIANG'

Another letter, also from Kuniang, was dated 17th of July. I noticed how easily she wrote about Paul. I felt rather sorry for Paul. The letter began, as before, with news of Shan-hai-kwan:

'Do you know there are a lot of musicians among the

irredenti? Practically all the chorus from the opera at Trieste is here. Yesterday they got hold of some barges, which were at anchor at the mouth of the river, and they rowed up and down, not very far from the beach. Then, as the sun went down, they rested on their oars and began to sing the fishermen's songs of the Adriatic. It is odd to hear Italian voices off the coast of China and Manchuria. To please Matushka they also sang an evening prayer that they had learnt in Russia. It was perfectly lovely! They told me afterwards that the Russian soldiers sing it, or used to sing it, at sunset, sometimes to the accompaniment of distant guns. We have all learnt that prayer now, and sing it every evening.

'Patushka and Matushka are much more civilized than they were in Peking. I think that they feel they must be on their good behaviour. They all wear quite respectable bathing-suits. Patushka throws no more plates, and nobody gets whipped any more. It is really quite dull! But every now and then one of them gets absent-minded and strolls out on to the veranda without any clothes on.

'Uncle Podger is getting tired of Shan-hai-kwan. He does not care much for country life, and he misses the nice smell of Chinese cooking that comes over the Tartar Wall when the wind is from the south.

'You have heard, I suppose, of poor old Mr. Mettray's death at Pei-ta-ho. It is extraordinary that such an old man should have gone out swimming. I am not surprised that his heart failed, after fighting the tide. There is a sandbank here, about a hundred yards from the beach. We swim out to it sometimes, and when the tide is going out it is quite a struggle to get back to shore.

'Paul writes that now his uncle is dead he will not stay much longer in Tientsin. He has rented a house in Peking, miles away, near the Lama Temple. It was once the Palace of the Duke Lan, the Boxer Duke. Paul says that he will live there, so that the abbot can come and see him and make him dream. He has had several more dreams already, but they were all of Mongolia and the highlands of Asia. In these dreams Paul was quite a little boy, and I had not come into them yet. The abbot says that he will bring me in later. How can the abbot make up the story of a whole lifetime? It seems impossible. Perhaps he just makes Paul dream of things that he, himself, remembers, or has heard about. I will be glad to see Paul again, when we all get back to Peking. I hear that he is beginning to suffer very much from his illness. If he needs a nurse I should like to go to him. It is the only thing which I could do to help.

'Fédor is quite determined to go to Russia. Everything that the *irredenti* have told him makes him sure that there is a much bigger revolution coming on, and he wants to be in it. His parents are much worried about him; they do not seem to be able to control him in any way. Patushka said quite a clever thing the other day. He said that revolutions always bring about a break between successive generations, between parents and children. So it will happen some day that he and Matushka will go to Russia, and will find that Fédor is in the Government. But he won't be kind to his aged parents. He will have them up before a firing squad and shot, because they are reactionaries.

'The only person here who does not take any interest in politics is Natasha. She is in love with one of the *irredenti*. He comes from Sussak and seems to be more of a Slav than an Italian. He can talk Serbian, and somehow he and Natasha understand one another. Anyway, they go for walks together on the sand-dunes, or along the river, and he puts his arm round her waist.

'I *do* so want to see you again. I am lonely without you, and you always said it was bad for me to be lonely. When are you coming north again?

'Your loving
'KUNIANG'

Kuniang's last letter from Shan-hai-kwan was dated 28th of August:

'Elisalex is here. She came down on purpose to see the *irredenti*. She makes me interpret for her, when she talks to them, and she asks them the oddest questions: "Do they like Russia? What did they think of Siberia? Would they like to go back there? Do they want a job?"

'I think she would prefer to talk to them direct, without my help. She has found a few who are Slavs and who can understand her. She has long conversations with them. They are much struck with her. I don't wonder.

'Yesterday evening, after we had been talking to the *irredenti*, Elisalex and I went for a walk along the Great Wall. There is a broad path on the top, and it is very pleasant up there. When you walk towards the west, you have the mountains before you, and behind you is the sea. It was a sultry evening, with thunder among the hills, and the swallows were flying low. They darted backwards and forwards close to our feet, to get the flies that rose up as we passed. I asked Elisalex why she was so interested in the *irredenti*. She answered with a long speech all about politics. She says that Russia is crumbling to pieces, and not only Russia. All civilization is in danger. We have progressed in science and in mechanics, but we have forgotten how to live. This is true not only of the West, but of the East, since China and Japan have entered into the *Weltpolitik* (whatever that may be) and lost their old aloofness.

'There are a few oases left here and there, but these also are in danger of disappearing. One of them is in the highlands of Central Asia, which were the cradle of the human race.

'Elisalex says that a resolute man, with a band of faithful followers, might carve out a kingdom for himself on the northern Asiatic plateaux, in Siberia, or in Mongolia, and hold it as a last stronghold of the ancient wisdom that the world has lost. She adds that she knows such a man and could help him to realize his ideal. That is why she wished to talk with the *irredenti*. Some of them might be ready, even eager, for adventure. And she wants to enlist them as soldiers of a kingdom yet to be born: the kingdom over which, some day, she hopes to reign.

'When Elisalex talks to me like this I cannot make out if she is serious, or if it is all a joke.

'Last night we had our beds out on the veranda, she and I, but all the others slept indoors. At this season they are afraid of the thunderstorms. I woke an hour before dawn, when the sky was just beginning to lighten. Elisalex was sitting up in bed, with her chin in her hands, looking out towards the mountains. For some time I watched her, very sleepily, and then I asked what she was thinking about.

' "I was thinking of my kingdom," she said, "and wondering if, when I reach it, I will find it is all a mirage, such as you see when travelling on the steppes: a vision of forests and lakes and palaces, which melt away as you approach."

'I tried to see her face, for I could not make out if she were smiling. But there was not enough light.

' "What is it going to be called?" I asked.

' "I have no idea," she said. "Can you suggest a name?"

'So I suggested *Kingdom Come*, and I told her that we would all go and live there, and be happy ever after: you and I and the Russian family, and the Five Virtues and Uncle Podger. Wouldn't it be fun?

'Do you know, I believe it is not all a mirage, nor an earthly paradise like the Fortunate Islands, such as the Chinese have (or say they have) at Pu-to? I am sure that somewhere, outside the Great Wall and beyond the desert, there is really a country which Elisalex hopes to reign over, some day soon. But if she is Queen there, who will be her King?

'I have so much more to tell you that I cannot write.

'Meanwhile a thousand kisses,

'KUNIANG'

'PS. – Just think how fine Uncle Podger would look on the footsteps of a throne! But there ought to be two of them, one on each side. Only it would be better if they were not both gentlemen, like the marble lions outside the Shuang Liè Ssè. Before we leave for Kingdom Come we must get another Pekingese out of the *k'ai-men-ti*. We might call her Lady Podger! – K.'

17   The Ivory Cage

I

As soon as I was well enough I travelled up north by sea, on the *Ting San* of the 'China Merchants Steamship Co.' The *Ting San* is a comfortable old boat which has been sailing up and down the China coasts for so long that even the typhoons know her by sight and regard her with a friendly feeling; and she never seems to mind them. The captain was a Scotsman, who had taught his Chinese cook to make porridge and Scotch broth, such as in Europe can only be found north of the Tweed. These advantages, coupled with a mild breeze off the land, made for a very pleasant journey. The other passengers were some Chinese business men, an Italian naval officer, a pretty young woman with bobbed hair and an exiguous skirt (I discovered that she was a Rumanian going to Tientsin to meet her husband), and finally two austere-looking ladies from Boston, who seemed to be under the impression that some responsibility rested on them for putting the world to rights when the war should be over. They told me that they were travelling around to acquire knowledge, in order to 'start a movement' when they got home. I was not sufficiently interested to inquire what the movement might be.

We had the usual interminable wait for the high tide outside the Taku Bar, and the last part of the journey (from Tang-ku) was accomplished in a goods train, which brought us wheezily into Tientsin about six p.m.

The manager of the Astor House Hotel is a Swiss, and, like all good hotelkeepers, he knows all there is to know about his regular clients, and a bit more. When he saw me getting my room-key at the reception office, he volunteered the information that Mr. Paul Dysart was staying in the hotel. I was surprised, for I had understood from Kuniang's letters that Paul was already established in Peking, in Duke Lan's palace. After I had taken possession of my room and had a bath, I rang up Paul on the telephone and suggested that we should dine together.

His answer (down the telephone) was unexpected. He said that he was not well enough to take dinner: his evening meal consisted of a cup of warm milk; but later in the evening he meant to go to a fête in the Italian Concession in aid of the Red Cross. Apparently he considered it his duty to patronize these forms of patriotic entertainment, and to spend as much money as the occasion warranted. He proposed that I should accompany him, and we arranged to meet, at half-past nine, in the hotel lounge.

I had been wanting to see Paul again, ever since Kuniang had written to me that he had come to some arrangement with the abbot, and had actually begun to carry out that strange proposal of a life to be passed in a dream. If Kuniang's information was correct, Paul had already started on a series of dreams similar to that which the abbot had given him in the Lama Temple.

That such an experiment should be tried in the old world atmosphere of a Manchu palace was not unnatural. Nowhere is the 'glamour of the East' so manifest as in Peking (at least outside the Legation Quarter). But in the industrial atmosphere of Tientsin the poetry is that of commerce, and the only glamour is that which illumines trade with distant lands. Ships and wharfs and bales of merchandise, imports and exports, fluctuations in currency, the silting up of Chinese rivers, the dangers of civil war: these are the things on which men's interests are centred. There is no place for esoteric mysticism and unexplored by-paths in knowledge of the soul.

So it was that when I met Paul that evening, to go with him to a bazaar in aid of the Red Cross, I decided to postpone any mention of the abbot and his dreams. Such a subject of conversation appeared incongruous in the busy up-to-date atmosphere of a Treaty Port.

* * *

We started off from the hotel in rickshaws, and reached our destination, which was on the other side of the river, in about ten minutes. But once inside the grounds, where the bazaar was being held, we each had friends and acquaintances to greet, and soon lost sight of each other. I found Paul later in the evening, sitting in the open near a bandstand.

When we had first met in the hotel lounge, I had hardly noticed any change in his appearance; but now, in the glare of the arc-lamps, his face showed wan and tired, and for the first time I realized how ill he was looking. His malady was beginning to show in sunken eyes, in deep lines round his mouth, and in a weary, listless expression, as if life had no more interest for him. I felt a sudden wave of pity, and decided not to leave him again that evening until it was time to go home.

The very gaiety of the scene accentuated Paul's air of lassitude. Around us were the uniforms of many nations: English, French, Italian, American, and Japanese. I was told that, among those wearing the Italian *grigioverde*, were many ex-soldiers of the Austrian Army: the *irredenti*, whom Kuniang had seen at Shan-hai-kwan. An open-air cinema showed scenes from the Italian front, with a backing of snow mountains. A group of children, who ought to have been in bed, were playing round a newly erected fountain (a great novelty in Tientsin) with jets of water spurting up and falling into four different bowls. As in all open-air meetings in China one heard on all sides a medley of languages that would have shamed the Tower of Babel.

Paul was unwilling to sit still. Sick as he was, he had come to the fête with the laudable desire to spend money for the Red Cross, but so far he had only succeeded in getting rid of some thirty dollars. Having rested, he started off again, to spend some more.

Among the stalls was one showing a collection of gifts which were to be sold by auction later on in the evening. They were mostly war relics and mementoes, but among them were also a few Chinese *objets d'art*. Above the table where the gifts were laid out, and hanging by a string from the roof of the stall, was an ivory cage.

164

Paul glanced at it and asked if it were for sale. He was told that it would be put up for auction in about an hour's time, that is to say, after midnight. With a sigh of weariness he moved away. Then apparently an idea struck him, and he turned to me.

'Will you do me a favour? I am so tired that I must go home. If you are staying on, will you buy that cage for me?'

He handed me a packet of bank-notes.

'How much are you willing to spend?' I asked.

'I do not know. How much do you suppose the cage will fetch? I have a little more than a thousand dollars here.'

'The cage may be worth about three hundred dollars. But in an auction for a patriotic purpose there is no saying what may be offered.'

'Well, it does not matter much. Do what you think best.'

He gave me the notes and moved away along the brightly lit avenue, among groups of officers and ladies. He walked with difficulty and his face was drawn and haggard.

Next morning I was surprised to find Paul breakfasting on the hotel terrace which overlooked the Victoria Road. He looked well and said that he was without pain: his illness often gave him periods of respite.

On a fine day the terrace of the Astor House is an amusing place to have breakfast. One can watch the consular and business community of Tientsin going to the office on foot, in rickshaws, and in motor-cars (it is the more important class of workers that goes on foot). On the opposite side of the road the public garden begins to fill up with children and attendant *amahs*, pottering about on diminutive feet.

I ordered coffee and eggs at Paul's table, and then went up again to my room to fetch the ivory cage which I had bought for him the night before. Of the thousand dollars he had given me I had spent six hundred.

Paul examined his purchase with interest. It was a fine cage of beautiful old ivory. The seed-box and water-trough were quite plain, but the door of the cage was made in the form of two sliding gates, which met in the middle of an opening in the bars. They were ornamented with those minute carvings which are so popular among Far Eastern peoples.

'These double gates,' said Paul, as he moved them up and down with his forefinger, 'are like the *geminae somni portae* of the Aeneid: the Gates of Sleep, which are made of horn and ivory.'

'You remind me that I too once had a classical education. *Et ego in Arcadia vixi.* If I remember rightly, the dreams that issue from the gates of horn come true, but those that pass through the gates of ivory are deceptive. Is there not something about them also in the *Odyssey*?'

'Yes. But there the twin gates are called the Gates of Dreams.'

For some moments he remained silent and absorbed, till at length I asked him what he was thinking about. He started, as if indeed awakened from a day-dream, though the veranda of the Astor House is not exactly the place for a reverie.

'I was thinking,' he said, 'that it has become almost a platitude to say that every man has more than one personality. We all try to escape from the consciously thinking self of our everyday life. Even you are not one and indivisible. Besides being yourself, you are a Maker of Heavenly Trousers.'

Falling into his mood, I answered: 'Quite right. And I put them on when I go into my study to meet the people whom I tell about in my stories. So it was with Machiavelli. When he wrote his histories he lit the candles and put on his best velvet robe to meet the great ones of the past.'

Paul smiled and added:

'We all have something to take us out of ourselves. I now have an ivory cage.'

'Which means?'

'It means that I have the dreams that the abbot gives me, and, thanks to them, a second existence. As Baudelaire would say: an artificial paradise.'

'Why call it an ivory cage?'

'Because in my other life I am suspended above the

realities. And through the ivory gates of my cage pass dreams that will never come true.'

'When do you dream? Is the abbot here?'

'No. He is in Peking. But I go back there in a few days. I have rented the Duke Lan's palace, and there we have our séances. I know very little about Eastern people, and I never imagined anybody could be like the abbot. In some ways I feel that he is hardly human. Are there many like him in China?'

'The only person I ever met who was in the least like the abbot was an actor belonging to the troupe kept at the Summer Palace for the old Empress Tzu-hsi. He used to gild his face and take the part of the Buddha in a play called the *Tien Nu San Huà*, meaning the Celestial Lady Distributing Flowers. Like the abbot, he was slim and extraordinarily handsome. And, strange to say, he too came from the far north, beyond the Amur.'

'You would hardly call that China.'

'Not now, though it once formed part of the empire. When people speak of the East, they seldom realize that there are Eastern people who live within the Arctic Circle, and see the northern lights, and use the reindeer as a means of transport. The abbot is no pure Mongol. Strange to say, I should have thought him more like the *tung-budze*, who apparently have made war on his monasteries.'

'But surely these northern people don't know anything about hypnotism?'

'They know much more about it than we do, though they call it exorcising spirits. Shamanism, which is their religion, is based on hypnotism. Their priests are very clever in inducing autohypnotic phenomena. I remember a German doctor once telling me that the Tungus priests, if they could speak our language, might make fortunes in Europe, curing people of nervous diseases.'

'One might suggest that to the abbot. He speaks French.'

'His magnetic powers must be quite exceptional. Did Kuniang tell you about his calling the butterflies?'

'Yes. And I believe he can call the birds too. But what surprises me about him is the kind of life he has chosen to make me dream about. You might think that he would do his best to make it as pleasant for me as possible. But not at all. There is a most unexpected realism in the life he is making up for me, and I have to take the rough with the smooth. So far, in my dream, I am only a boy of sixteen, and not what, in my waking hours, I would call a very nice boy. I have already begotten two children. I live with my parents on the edge of the desert. There are flocks of sheep and a few small horses and countless camels. The camels are used to carry wool and furs into China, or tea into Russia. I have taken many journeys with them and suffered hunger and thirst. Once I was ill for months because of a bite that a camel gave me. I never knew that camels *did* bite. Perhaps they don't, in real life.'

'Yes they do. But very rarely, and their bite can be very bad. They move their teeth sideways and make horrible wounds.'

'So I have discovered – or, rather, the abbot has taught me. But what a strange thing to make a person dream of! If his handiwork reflects the soul of an artist, then the abbot has a very remarkable soul.'

'I had never thought of a dream as a work of art.'

'Neither had I. But what else would you call it? It is not a real life that the abbot gives me. Only the Creator can do that. But will not even our real life seem to us an illusion when we look back on it from whatever lies beyond?'

I did not know what to answer, and for a few moments I attended to my bacon and eggs. At length I said:

'There does not seem to be much fascination about your dream: nothing like the garden of Klingsor. Is it all stark realism? Is there no beauty in it?'

'There is an extraordinary fascination in the isolated life of the steppes. To people living such a life contact with other peoples appears a danger, like a poison that might make them ill. We Mongols (I speak of myself as a Mongol!) might be living in another planet. We are cut off from the world, and primitive beyond words. We are thieving and ignorant and superstitious. Our huts are always full of the acrid smoke from the fires of camel-dung. Our table manners would make you sick, especially when we eat clotted cream from a common bowl, with no spoon, only our dirty fingers. Our great delicacy is brick-tea with lumps of rancid butter floating in it. But you should see our cavalry ride out to meet the dawn, with the gold of their peaked caps catching the first light of day! Thus did our war-lords ride out to conquer Asia when the world was young! We have the feeling of being a privileged people: the chosen of God, like the Jews in the Old Testament. It dates from the time when all the north of this continent was ours from the Volga to the Yellow River. The air of the steppes on frosty mornings may have something to do with that feeling. It is what I imagine the air must be like in Paradise. In that pure air, men and beasts seem to be utterly tireless. We move about with our herds as the grass becomes scarce, and there are no boundaries and no frontiers. Only in the north-west have I seen a furrow in the sand, made by dragging a heavy tree-trunk along the ground. That furrow was supposed to represent the borders of Russia. There are no land-marks except a few cairns on the higher downs. And the signs of animal life are few and far between, in proportion to the vastness of that great prairie: little gophers scuttling about, like rabbits in a warren; moving herds of antelope, or passing strings of camels. Round our felt huts are fierce black dogs, and the cattle lie about and chew the cud. The wild ponies breed in liberty, but they never wander far from the wells.'

There was a note in Paul's voice, as he described the home of his dream, which reminded me of Signor Cante when he spoke of his life on the Yellow River. Here again was the lure of immensity, the magic of far horizons, something of the mystic love of Jauffroi Rudel for a *Princesse Lointaine*.

A sudden and violent altercation on the other side of the Victoria Road interrupted our conversation. A rickshaw coolie and a French petty officer were having an argument which threatened to arrest all traffic in the streets. It lasted about five minutes. Two turbaned Sikhs of the municipal police succeeded at last in restoring quiet. When it was all over, Paul pushed the ivory cage towards me, among the cups and saucers.

'I hope you will accept this little souvenir,' he said, 'of some one you have been kind to. You might hang it near the sign of the Heavenly Trousers.'

I objected that it was too valuable a present, but he answered that if I took it there and then it would save him the trouble of mentioning me in his will.

18   Home-Coming

I

I have done the journey between Tientsin and Peking so many times that I recognize even the stray dogs (known locally as *wonks*) that frequent the platforms in the hopes of picking up something thrown out from the carriage windows. As usual in September, the floods were out on either side of the Hai-ho, and the so-called motor-road that unites Tientsin and Peking was partly under water; one could see the unsubmerged tracts of it from the train, during the first part of the journey. But the rains were over and it was a clear sunny day, which brought out all the glory of autumn tints in the clumps of trees, and in the cobs of Indian corn, drying on the roofs of isolated farms, or of the smaller villages.

Never before have I been so impatient to arrive in Peking. And my impatience was shared by some one who was waiting, or, better still, who would not wait, for my train to arrive at the Chen Mên. For when we came in sight of the Western Hills, and the train stopped at the junction of Feng-tai (which is still half an hour's journey from the capital), a radiant young form in brown sweater and 'Jhodpur' riding-breeches came running down the platform and burst into my compartment, greeting me with a boisterous affection that much disturbed the elderly Chinese couple who occupied the corner seats near the corridor. The railway line takes a big curve before entering the city, and Kuniang had ridden out from the southern gate. She was brown and healthy-looking after her summer at the sea, and her eyes shone with happiness. She came home with me in the train,

171

leaving the *ma-fu* to take the horses back to Peking.

What a glorious thing is a home-coming when there is some one you love to greet you! I was met by the smiling faces of the Five Virtues (backed by the Old Lady, Little Lu, and his mother), and a rattle, like musketry fire, of the crackers they let off to chase away the evil spirits who might have accompanied me home. Even Uncle Podger kindly manifested his pleasure at seeing me again. None of these things were needed to make me happy, since Kuniang was there. But they added to my pleasure and gave me the sense that the old temple was indeed my home.

There is something very welcoming about a Chinese house, with its sunlit courtyards and red lacquer columns rising up to the sloping roofs. But for Kuniang also there had been a home-coming. She had flown to me like a bird to its nest: her home was within my encircling arms. It was sheer ecstasy to think that now she belonged to me: the real Kuniang, not a dream one, such as the abbot might give to Paul. I wondered how I could ever have hesitated to take her for myself. She was so happy in the security of my protecting love. That security, and the consciousness of her own charm, gave her a gentler and more feminine outlook than the old brave facing of a difficult world. I asked her, and she asked me, the foolish old questions that lovers never fail to put to one another: 'Do you love me? Do you really love me?' And we answered, as lovers do, without words. But when she spoke of all the happiness she owed to me I answered with the old French phrase: '*C'est moi qui te doit tout, puisque c'est moi qui t'aime!*'

That evening we sat together on the sofa and made plans, a whole lifetime of plans. They began with getting married quite soon and being happy ever after.

I sometimes wish I could end my story here, with Kuniang and me on the sofa and Uncle Podger at our feet: I mean, of course, on the arm-chair opposite! It makes so suitable a picture for a conclusion: Kuniang with the lamplight shining on her hair and on the mark of the half-moon; my arm around her, our lips meeting in a kiss. How many novelists have written the word FINIS under such a scene? And indeed love is always the beginning and the end, and there can be no finer climax than a young girl gathered into her lover's arm. But my story does not end here. Though at the time we knew it not, Kuniang and I were minor figures in a greater story. And this had not yet reached its climax or its end.

19   In Duke Lan's Palace

I

A week later Paul Dysart returned to Peking and took up his quarters again in the Duke Lan's palace. Kuniang went at once to see him, and came back after a few hours with a very grave face. She told me that Paul's illness had taken a sudden turn for the worse. And she added:

'He has got some Chinese servants. They are relations of the Five Virtues, and I should say awful thieves. But they seem to look after him well. At the same time I don't think he should be left there with nobody near him but Chinese Boys; it is not as if he were used to living in the East.'

'Could he not have a nurse from the hospital? There are some professional nurses in Peking.'

'No. He won't have anybody round who might interfere with his dream. The abbot comes to him daily and makes him dream. It is the only interest that Paul has left in life.'

'Does this mean that you want to go and nurse him?'

'I feel that I ought to.'

'It is not I who would prevent you going on an errand of mercy. But I am afraid it will be a long business, and a great strain for you.'

'I need not stay there all the time. But I could have a camp-bed put in one of the pavilions, so that I could pass the night there when required.'

And so it was arranged. For the next few weeks I saw Kuniang only when she came home for an hour or two, or when I went to see her and Paul in the Duke Lan's palace. I had never been there before, though I believe it is often shown to foreigners as a typical princely residence of former days. To me it seemed much like other Manchu palaces in the Tartar City, except that the garden was larger and better kept than most.

It was in the garden that I used to stroll about with Kuniang, before going to see Paul. It was very quiet there. The rooks would call to each other from the tops of giant acacias, and here and there a lizard made the most of the last warm days, sunning himself on a marble seat, backed by a sheltered rockery. With the self-ishness of lovers, Kuniang and I would linger together on the grass-grown paths before going to Paul.

The first time I saw him after his arrival in Peking he was lying on a Chinese couch, or *kang*, of teak and cloisonné, and he was half covered with furs, which he tossed off and drew on restlessly. Although he was without fever at that moment, he appeared much exhausted, and it occurred to me that the dreams given to him by the abbot must deprive him of his normal sleep. He lay back on the cushions and idly traced with his finger some little figures on the cloisonné sides of his couch.

'This bed was part of the original furniture of the palace,' he said languidly. 'You see, the figures are European, in eighteenth-century costume. Here are a couple of little men in three-cornered hats, carrying a big clock, Chinese fashion, on two sticks. I suppose the artist meant to represent them as bringing tribute to the Emperor of China.'

Paul had not greeted me when I came into the room, and he seemed to take my presence there, and Kuniang's, as a matter of course, almost as if he did not realize that we were there expressly for him. This struck me as showing how much his dream-life must be taking hold of him, and how he was becoming indifferent to what went on in the world he lived in. The little figures on the cloisonné were as important as anything else, which was not saying much. His own illness appeared to trouble him but little. To my questions as to how he felt he answered perfunctorily, as if he were speaking of some third person, or perhaps of that other Paul Dysart who had come to Peking months before with old Jeremiah Mettray, and had fallen in love with Kuniang, even inspiring, for a time, an answering love in her. All that might almost have been in another incarnation.

Since only his dream interested him, I spoke to him of that:

'Can you tell me something more,' I said, 'about the ivory cage?'

'I can tell you something, but not all. For the ivory cage is my life, and who can remember all the details of his life?'

'Has Kuniang come into your dreams?' I asked. 'You did not mention her when you spoke to me about your boyhood on the edge of the desert.'

'She did not come into the dream for many years after that. All my youth was spent in wandering about Asia, though I could not tell you exactly where I went. The names of the places, even when I remember them, do not seem to correspond to anything I have ever heard of or read of in my waking hours.'

'Mongol or Chinese names are different from those we use. They are often quite unrecognizable, like Tung-ching for Tokyo, "the capital of the East".'

'The names all have a meaning. The places themselves appear to me, when I am awake, like lantern-slides projected on a screen. I could describe a few of them, but I forget how much I have told you when we talked about it last.'

'You were speaking of life on the steppes, and the pure air of frosty mornings.'

'Yes. On the rare occasions when there is no wind to raise the dust the air is crystal clear. The smoke from the yurts goes up like a thin line straight to the sky, and the wild geese pass over at dawn, with the sunlight giving their white wings a tinge of pink.'

'But you travelled. What were the places like that you visited?'

'They were very different, for at times I was in the heart of the Himalayas, and at others in the far north. I remember a great valley, so deep that the sun never penetrated as far down as the river that runs through its

176

gorges – deserts where the sand moves over the ruins of long-dead cities – strings of camels, travelling in winter, with packs of ice which represent the provision of water for many weeks – golden pheasants, rocketing up in the sunshine, like flashes of light that dazzled the eyes – great rivers, flowing northwards, between fields of lily of the valley, and a few months later those same rivers frozen hard, so that an army could light its campfires on their surface. My tent is of white felt, lined with the skins of bears and leopards and with rugs from Turkestan. The carpet is of silk and silver thread. It is cut into triangles, like the slices of a cake, so that it can be divided up and pieced together again as we move about. My horses are the shaggy, half-tamed ponies whose ancestors carried the hordes of Attila into Europe.'

Paul spoke slowly, as if piecing together his memories. After a moment's pause he continued:

'When I was twenty-five I went to St. Petersburg, to render homage to the Tsar. My recollections of that time are less disconnected. I was popular in Russia. They seemed to like me, and they did their best to make me stay. They gave me a military command and a place at Court. It was there I met Kuniang. Once again I have been through the scene in the dressing-room when she put on her jewels. I have learnt about the Cross of Alexander. It was given to a great-grandmother of Kuniang's by Alexander the First. Apparently she was a lady-love of his, and he had the cross made out of the finest of the Court jewels and mounted it on a diamond star. Kuniang never liked it; she said it always felt to her like a piece of ice on her bare skin. There is a superstition about that jewel. It must never leave Russia. When it does the Empire of the Romanoffs will fall.'

'It has fallen, so I suppose the Cross of Alexander has gone abroad.'

Paul looked at me in a dazed way and then said:

'I never thought of that. It is extraordinary how I have forgotten everything. Is the war still going on?'

'Of course it is. You knew that when we were together at Tientsin.'

177

'That seems years ago to me. I suppose they are the years of my dream.'

It was quite obvious that in Paul's double personality it was the Mongol ego that now predominated, even though it consisted only of such stuff as dreams are made of. I asked him:

'Where are you now? Are you still in St. Petersburg?'

'No. I am Governor of an Eastern province, and I live in a place that they call the Fortress, though there is not much in the way of fortification. Only some stockades and watch-towers in the surrounding woods. I have a very fine house which might be the principal residence of a big estate, had it not a guard-room attached, and some barracks and a prison. The less said about that prison the better.'

'Where is all this? In Siberia?'

'I could not say, but it might well be a place of exile. There are quite a number of people there who may not go away: handsome men and beautiful women, whose clothes were made in Paris, though they are no longer in the fashion. These people live in very modest houses, but are not molested in any way, as long as they give no trouble. If they try to escape, and are caught, they go to prison, and they don't often come out of it alive.'

'And this is your dream-life! Are you satisfied with it?'

'Is any one ever satisfied with his life, whether real or a dream? I wish I were not separated from Kuniang, though the abbot tells me she will soon come back.'

Paul lay back among the fur rugs and shut his eyes. He had tired himelf out with talking.

I left him and strolled out of the room with Kuniang, following her till we reached a little courtyard that faced the pavilion she had taken for her own use. She pointed out to me some pots of chrysanthemum in bloom.

'These flowers,' she said, 'are appropriate enough in a house where some one is dying. I wonder if Paul will be here to see the lilac blossom in the spring.'

I did not go often to Duke Lan's palace, but Kuniang came to see me nearly every morning and went back again after lunch. She told me that Paul was growing weaker. The strain of the double life was telling on him. The hypnotic séances sapped his scanty reserves of strength. The dreams were less satisfactory than before, and they no longer soothed him. His sleep, even when under the influence of opium, was agitated, and in his waking hours Paul was always thinking of the other life. His real personality was disappearing, like that of Dr. Jekyll in the personality of Mr. Hyde.

Kuniang was looking pale and distressed. The task of nursing a hopeless case was one that might well be too heavy for her, and I began to feel anxious, though she assured me that Paul gave very little trouble.

'It is strange,' she said, 'that Paul's dream-life has ceased to be a happy one since I have come back into it. Something painful is happening, but Paul will not tell me what. It makes him suffer, even more than his illness. And yet he never wants the dream to stop. Yesterday, when he awoke, he begged the abbot to keep on, and they have been together all night. This morning they rested for a few hours, but they meant to begin again as soon as I came away. I wish the dream could end. I do not know how, but I feel that it hurts Paul horribly.'

I remembered what Paul had told me, in Tientsin, about the unexpected realism in the dream-life that the abbot was giving him. Evidently he was now in some trouble. What could it be? And how was it that, if his dream was so very painful, he did not wake up, as generally happens when one reaches the climax of a nightmare?

'It is bad for you, Kuniang,' I said, 'to be alone with a dying man and his hallucinations. To-day I have some work to finish, but to-morrow, after you have been here, I will go back with you to Duke Lan's palace. I will take a camp-bed with me, as you have done, so that, if necessary I need not come home at night.'

Kuniang brightened up at this suggestion, and when

she went back to Paul she was looking happier.

I worked hard that evening, both before and after dinner, finishing an article for the Shanghai papers. I wanted to be free on the morrow. It was almost midnight when I got up from my desk and went to the tantalus to mix myself a drink. At that moment Exalted Virtue came in and told me that somebody wanted to see me: the *tai-tai*, who was a friend of the Russian family. It was Elisalex.

I am not accustomed to receiving visits from beautiful ladies late at night, and I was considerably surprised. But I told Exalted Virtue to show her in, and, having straightened my tie, I went to meet her at the door.

Elisalex was wearing an evening coat of black velvet, below which appeared a white satin dress. Her evening shoes were smarter than anything I have ever seen, in that line, in Peking. She declined to take off her cloak, but sat down in an arm-chair, while I gave her a cigarette and lighted the match for her. The flame was reflected in a pair of diamond ear-rings. Elisalex had evidently been dining *en ville*.

She explained the reason of her visit:

'I am going away almost immediately. I came to say good-bye.'

'That is bad news for all of us,' I answered politely. 'And Kuniang will be in despair. Where are you off to?'

'To Harbin, and then perhaps to Russia. But I am not sure.'

'You are going to rule over Kingdom Come?'

Elisalex looked at me in surprise, and then said: 'Ah, of course Kuniang must have told you about it. But do not take it too seriously. There is a Kingdom Come for all of us, if we know how to reach it and how to hold it.'

She spoke lightly, as if the matter was not one that interested her very much. Possibly she would have preferred me not to know anything about it. Then she added:

'I came also because I wanted to speak about Kuniang. She is still nursing that Englishman. Is she not?'

'Yes.'

'What is his name?'

'Dysart. Paul Dysart.'

'Yes. Now I remember. He is having a course of dreams with the Mongol abbot.'

Elisalex seemed very well informed. Kuniang must have told her about Paul. I answered:

'Yes. It is a form of hypnotism that the abbot must have learnt somewhere in the north. The *tung-hudze* are great experts in that sort of thing. The idea was that Paul should find some comfort and forget about his illness. But I understand now, from Kuniang, that he is suffering even in his dreams.'

'When one takes on another personality, it does not follow that it must be a happy one. Does your friend believe in God?'

'I know nothing about his beliefs. Why do you ask?'

'Because, if he does believe, he should have accepted his cross and trusted to the love and pity that will help him bear it. He should not have turned to the East for comfort in his pain. The East is indifferent to pain; it is impassive and aloof. It knows, not love, but only renunciation and withdrawal. Paul Dysart may find that the Christian God is kinder than a Mongol abbot, even than one who some day may become the Living Buddha.'

I stared at Elisalex in surprise, and answered:

'You give too deep a meaning to what the poor boy is doing. He is not trying to escape his fate. But he is young to die, and he seeks an added experience before the end.'

'He may find an added torment. I advise you to bring Kuniang away, as soon as possible.'

'I wish I could. I saw her to-day, and I think she is feeling the strain. But it would be cruel to Paul to take her away. It is towards the end that he will need her most.'

Elisalex seemed to be thinking over what I had said, for she sat there a little while without speaking. Once again, as I watched her, I could not help admiring the grace of her pose and the wonderful elegance of her dress and carriage. I asked myself, not for the first time, what she could be doing in Peking. The explanations I had been given so far did not satisfy me. There must be something still untold.

After a little while she said:

'I do not think you realize how fond I am of Kuniang. I would like to give her all the happiness that I have missed and to spare her all the pain that I have suffered. Yet in this dream, which is about her, there may be even such horrors as I have been through. Do you know anything about the life that the abbot is giving to your friend?'

'Paul told me about his boyhood, and a little of his youth. The abbot must have a vivid imagination to make up all that, even though he is familiar with the places and the people that figure in the dream. But I do not know much about Kuniang's part in it all.'

'Only that she wears the Cross of Alexander?'

'So you know that!'

Elisalex did not answer, and again she sat silent for a little while. I had the impression that there was something she wanted me to understand, but that she found difficult, if not impossible, to tell. At length she asked:

'You write stories, don't you? Eastern stories?'

'Yes. Sometimes.'

'I have heard some Eastern stories since I have been here. And I have noticed that, very often, the story is unfinished. There is a part untold that the reader must guess, if he can. You know part of the story that the abbot is telling Paul in a dream. I wonder if you could guess the rest.'

I shook my head, and answered: 'I doubt it.'

'It all centres round the Cross of Alexander. It might help you, if you knew . . . where that was.'

I looked at her and wondered what she would say next. She did not say anything, but got up from her chair, and stood leaning with one elbow on the mantelpiece. And then, with her left hand, she opened out her velvet coat, showing her slim figure in the white satin. As she did so I was suddenly dazzled by a light that seemed to spring from the front of her dress. It came from a cross of peerless brilliants set on a diamond star.

Again the velvet coat enveloped her, and Elisalex and I gazed into each other's eyes.

'Good night!' she said, and started for the door.

'You cannot go like this!' I exclaimed. 'What does it all mean?'

She stopped and said quietly: 'In the dream Kuniang's taking the part of another woman. I have shown you who that woman was. The rest of the story you must guess, if you can.'

'Well, but . . .'

'And take my advice. Bring Kuniang away before the dream ends. Or stop the dream.'

'But it is not Kuniang herself who is dreaming.'

'Thank God!'

'And in his dream Paul is in Siberia, not in St. Petersburg. All you told me about yourself and Rasputin does not come into it at all.'

'What makes you think that Rasputin was the only lover of a woman such as I? He represents an episode, and he does not come into the life that Paul Dysart is dreaming. That life is more terrible than anything that ever happened to Rasputin. Because I love Kuniang I cannot bear to think of her living through such horrors, even in another person's dream. Should she ever know what Paul has dreamt of her it would haunt her for the rest of her life.'

'To-morrow I will see her. I will do my best to bring her away.'

'I pray you will succeed.'

She held out her hand to me, and this time I did not detain her. I escorted her to the outer door and watched her get into her rickshaw. Even after she had disappeared down the badly lit street, under the Tartar Wall, I stood gazing into the shadows. For a few moments the dusty air of the Chinese hu-tung was fragrant with the scent that she had worn.

III

Kuniang was to have come to me next morning at ten o'clock. But though I waited till lunch-time she never appeared.

At midday Exalted Virtue brought me a telegram

addressed to *Famille de Monsieur Cante de' Tolomei.*
The only person in Peking who could have answered to
such an appellation was Kuniang. But something in the
unusual address made me suspect a tragedy, and I
decided to open the telegram myself.

My fears were confirmed. The local director of the
Kin Han Railway at Kai-feng informed that Signor Cante
had been attacked and wounded by bandits, not far from
the bridge over the Yellow River, while he was proceed-
ing northwards on his work of inspection along the line.
He had died after a few hours. The sad news was
accompanied by the usual expressions of sympathy and
condolence, but it was given without warning. I was
glad that Kuniang had not been there to open the telegram. I might be able to do something to mitigate the
shock. It passed through my mind that her father's death
might justify Kuniang's coming away from the Duke
Lan's palace, as Elisalex had advised.

Poor Signor Cante! He was a modest representative of
that group of *dépaysés* known as Old China Hands.
After a busy and a useful life he had died in harness, in
the way that he himself had predicted: on the banks of
the Yellow River, under a blue autumn sky. Why should
he, a Tuscan, from the hills around Siena, have so lost
his heart to China as to remain on at his post, for his own
pleasure, and at the risk of his life! I wondered, yet I
understood, remembering what he had said to me about
the vast proportions, and the great spaces, which had
become as necessary to him as the air he breathed. He
had loved those mighty waters which came down from
the roof of the world and spread away towards vague,
shimmering horizons. His 'precious bridge', as Kuniang
had once called it, was much more to him than two miles
of iron girders and stone supports above the so-often
flooded plain. It represented his toy and his hobby; its
preservation was his mission in life, and *apologia pro
vita sua.*

When I arrived, at three in the afternoon, at Duke
Lan's palace, Kuniang came out of Paul's room to meet
me. She was looking pale and there were dark shadows
under her eyes. She put her arm in mine and took me into

the garden. It was there that I told her of her father's death, and showed her the telegram. She took it calmly, hardly saying anything at first. Then her eyes grew wet and she repeated once or twice: 'Poor Papa! This is what he always expected.'

After a little while she added: 'He was so pleased when I wrote to him that we were going to get married. I am sure he died the happier for that.'

'One day we will go to Italy and see his old home.'

We talked of him for some little time, and then I remembered to inquire after Paul.

'He is very ill,' she said, 'and the dream is going badly. There is a horror that has to be gone through, at all costs. Even I feel it, when I sit near Paul. I see his face grow all taut, as if he were doing his best not to cry out. Then the abbot will say something in Russian, and Paul will smile, and keep on smiling, but that is worse, for I can see, even though he sleeps, that his smile is a forced one. Quite often Paul will speak. Then I try to make out what is happening from what he says. But I have not succeeded, even though he seems to be talking to himself in English. This morning, when he was awake, I asked him to tell me about it. But he just lay there as if dazed. He hardly seemed to know me. His thoughts are all of the dream Kuniang and not of the real.'

'What sort of things does he say in his sleep?'

'Once he cried out suddenly: "The Cross of Alexander! There is blood upon the diamonds!" And a moment later, almost under his breath, he murmured: "My God, but she is brave!" Another time, he kept muttering: "We have overdone it. Too much success. Now the young Grand Duke wants to be present. He says he will hold the candles." This morning he made quite a long speech, as if he were giving orders, and he repeated it over and over again: "Put soldiers at the door, and at the back of the house. We must not have a riot. Only those may come whom Vassili has chosen. None of the Gospodars, only the moujiks, and let them have vodka. For her, a black dress, very plain and no jewels. For me, my old grey coat and cap. No mask this time. It is the last time. See that the lamps give a strong light." '

Kuniang paused, and I said to her: 'There does not seem to be anything very painful in all this.'

'No. Unless that time when he spoke of blood upon the diamonds. But the pain in his face was dreadful to see. And the abbot's face like a mask. He made me think of a surgeon operating without an anaesthetic.'

'Are you sure that what makes Paul suffer is not the pain of his illness?'

'Quite sure. The waking hours are a relief to him now. Before, it was the contrary. When I left him he was without pain, though he lay on his couch and stared past me, like a wild animal in a cage. The abbot was there, and was just going to make him dream again. I cannot understand the abbot. What is the good of this second life he has given Paul if it is more painful than his own?'

I could give no answer to this question, though the reason why Elisalex had warned me was becoming more clear. There was some horror in Paul's dream-life within the bars of his ivory cage. Kuniang felt it, even though she could not realize all it implied.

Suddenly a cry pierced the stillness. It came from the pavilion where Paul had his couch.

Kuniang started running in the direction whence the sound had come, and I followed her.

Paul's door was open on to the courtyard, and as we drew near another cry rang out, even more terrible than the first.

I entered Paul's room close on Kuniang's heels, but remained near the door. The abbot was there, dressed in the orange and yellow robe of a priest. He was standing a little way from the bed, as if he had stepped back to put a greater distance between himself and Paul. Though the abbot's face was impassive and serene as ever his eyes were on Paul and seemed to hold him captive.

Yet Paul was not lying on his Chinese couch. He was standing with one hand on the wall, to save himself from falling. He wore a black silk dressing-gown over his pyjamas. His face was grey and distorted with pain, or horror, or both. Blood was trickling from his mouth, where he had bitten his lip. His eyes had the unseeing stare of a man in a trance.

Kuniang ran to him and put her arm round his shoulder to support him. As she did so she turned her face towards the abbot. I think she meant to tell him to bring Paul out of his dream. But when she met the abbot's glance her figure stiffened and all expression went out of her face. So, for a moment, we all stood: I at the door, watching; the abbot a little apart, with arms folded under his orange robe, and his glance resting on the other two.

Kuniang had rushed to help Paul, but in doing so had fallen herself under the influence that made him dream. And for a space of time that cannot have been longer than one minute she shared the dream with Paul.

Then the abbot made a pass with his hand, and both Paul and Kuniang became again their normal selves.

But the sequel was yet to come.

Kuniang led Paul back to the bed as if he were a child. And, indeed, there was something in the scene that might have reminded one of a child that has woken up in terror at some nightmare. I could see that Paul's body was all trembling.

'Kuniang,' he gasped. 'My little Kuniang! You are here, here beside me. I am Paul and you are Kuniang, and all the rest is a dream, a hideous dream. But now the end has come and I need dream no more. Thank God! Thank God! Thank God!'

Kuniang helped him to lie down, and placed a cushion under his head. He lay back, smiling at her. 'My little Kuniang,' he said again, but very gently, and then he turned his face sideways on the cushion, and sighed and shut his eyes, like a tired child that is pleased to be in bed.

For a long time he lay still.

The abbot stepped forward and touched Kuniang on the shoulder. She looked up at him, wondering. And he said gravely: 'You must go now. It is all over.'

And he made a sign to me that I should take her away.

20   The Shadow of a Dream

I

Signor Cante's body was brought to Peking and interred in the little cemetery, situated in the south-east corner of the Tartar City, where since the days of the Peking Protocol (1901) Italians, Germans, and Austrians have found a last resting-place, recalling in their common burial-ground the old Triple Alliance.

Paul was buried in the English cemetery outside the Tartar Wall. The necessary formalities were carried through with the help of the Legation. A few days later Kuniang was informed, by the firm of lawyers in Tientsin, that Paul had bequeathed to her the residue of the fortune that Jeremiah Mettray had left to him. Signor Cante also had left his savings to his daughter. Kuniang was now rich and independent. If she married me it would not be out of necessity.

I dislike the idea of marriage in conjunction with a funeral. I feel that it may bring misfortune, as it did to the last of the Tsars. So it was not only out of respect to the dead that I abstained from mentioning marriage to Kuniang in those first days. I might have waited longer if she had taken up again, for a time, the old routine of our life together. But this she was not willing to do. She chafed at all barriers between us, and most of all at the barriers of convention. She hated parting from me at night, and nearly always, when I woke up in the morning, I would find her sitting on the side of my bed. In such a situation it seemed the obvious thing to ask the kind, jovial old friar who acted as chaplain to the Italian Legation, to marry us.

But Kuniang would not hear of it.

It was natural that the double catastrophe, brought home to her suddenly and simultaneously, should have a painful effect on Kuniang's mind. The fact that neither of the two deaths, not even her father's, was entirely unexpected did not diminish the shock, which came at a moment when her nerves had been tried by the eerie and painful experience of Paul's dream. But this sudden and unexpected aversion to marriage was something quite new and, it seemed to me, quite unnatural: almost a case for a Freudian specialist. At first I could not make head or tail of the matter. I asked Kuniang if she did not love me any more.

'Of course I do. But I don't want to marry. I hate the idea of marriage. It is all right for nice, respectable girls, in Europe and America, with reputations to be careful of and families to look after them. But I am outside it all. I have never really belonged to anybody. Only I can give myself away. It has nothing to do with a priest. Please let's do without!'

'But it would be dishonourable of me to take you without marrying. And there would be no end of difficulties. How could we travel together if we were not man and wife? And what about the children, if we had any?'

'We'll think about them when they come. And don't bother about being dishonourable. It is not you who want to do without marriage. It is the other way round.'

'It seems to me that it is always the other way round with you, Kuniang.'

So strange an attitude could not be based on a matter of principle. It was a question of nerves. This being so, I felt it would be impossible to change Kuniang's feelings by any process of reasoning.

There were no psychoanalysts in Peking. I read such books on the subject as I could find. They were all about neurotic symptoms, considered as 'substitutive gratifications of suppressed sexuality', or manifestations of the 'Oedipus complex' (so called because Oedipus murdered his father and married his mother). None of the definitions appeared to cover Kuniang's case. Indeed, the only person, in the Home of the Five

Virtues, to whom my studies on psychoanalysis might have applied was Uncle Podger, who was obviously suffering from a 'superiority complex'.

One evening Kuniang saw me struggling with this highly technical matter. After having read a few lines about the infantile fixations of libido, she asked me what it was all about.

'It is about you,' I said.

'Are you sure? It does not sound like me at all.'

'What I mean is that your mind must have had a wound some time, and I am trying to locate it. But all I can find here is page upon page about repressions of sexuality.'

'I've had plenty of them.'

'You have?'

'Yes.'

'I suppose you would rather not speak about them.'

'I don't mind, if you want to know. It was when Fédor got so difficult to keep in order. I had to repress his sexuality about two or three times a day. He was always trying to . . .'

'It isn't that at all. At least not quite that.'

'What is it then?'

'It is the repression of one's own instincts that leads sometimes to different forms of neurosis. Or else it is the after-effect of some event that is preying upon your mind. This idea of yours, not to be married, even though you love me, is unnatural. It is a typical case of what is called *phobia*. There must be a cause for it, and the reasons you give are not sufficient to explain it. There is some kink in your mind that wants unravelling, and I'm trying to find out what it is.'

Kuniang was silent for a little while, and then she said: 'I think I understand now.'

'And can you help?'

She sighed and said rather wearily: 'Yes, I can help. It is true that I have a painful memory of a marriage.'

'Whose marriage?'

'My own.'

'Good God! Don't tell me you're married already!'

Kuniang laughed. 'How frightened you look! I don't

190

mean that I'm really married. But do you remember Paul's dream, at the very end, when I ran to hold him up?'

'Yes. It seemed to me at the time that you came for a few seconds under the hypnotic influence. It must have been extraordinarily powerful to have caught and held you like that.'

'You say that it lasted only a few seconds. But during those few seconds I was married. Merely to think of it makes me feel quite sick.'

'What was there so dreadful about it?'

'I don't know. That is part of the horror . . . that I don't know.'

'Whom were you going to marry?'

'Kuniang was going to be married, but I was not Kuniang. I suppose that, for one brief moment, I shared Paul's personality. He and I had the same sensations and saw the same things around us, and the same people. I had the sensations of the bridegroom. I was holding Kuniang's hand, and was just going to put on the ring.'

'What a complicated feeling: to be marrying one's self.'

'Yes. I find it difficult to tell about, and to make myself clear. But it all comes to the same thing in one way: that both I, who was the bridegroom, and Kuniang, who was the bride, had the same feelings about it. You see, we were very much in love.'

'That sounds all right.'

'No. It made things worse, a thousand time worse. It was because I loved her that what was coming was so horrible to me, as well as to her!'

'And what was coming?'

'That is just what I do not know!'

Kuniang and I stared at each other in perplexity. We did not seem any nearer unravelling the 'complex' that preyed upon her mind.

'Can you describe the scene to me?' I asked.

'I can describe, but I cannot explain. We were in the open air, in a courtyard, with a house on one side and a wall on the other three. There was a pergola, with a vine

191

on it, or a creeper of some kind. Under the pergola was a long banqueting-table, with people seated at it, all very well dressed and merry; a lot of men in uniform and women in pretty clothes. There were waiters in a gorgeous livery, and other servants in the usual Russian shirt, belted in at the waist, and dark trousers. All this was at some distance from where I stood with Kuniang, near a small movable altar, such as they use for soldiers in camp. There were two girls standing near us. They may have been bridesmaids, though they were not dressed alike. Kuniang was wearing a bridal veil and a wreath of orange-blossoms. She was standing in the sunlight, and the gold of her hair shone through her veil. Does it not seem odd that I should be talking like this about myself?'

'Yes. I don't know how you can keep on saying *Kuniang*, as if it were somebody else.'

'It is because I see the whole picture before my eyes. And she is just opposite me.'

'What I cannot understand is why all this should be dreadful. It was the same with Paul and his dream. He was suffering terribly, but we could not make out why. Can you tell me some more about this vision? Was there any one else in the picture?'

'There were two Russian priests, who were conducting the marriage service. They had tall hats, like chimneys, and long beards. One of them seemed to be half drunk, and the other had an awful, leering face, like a satyr. About ten yards off was a line of soldiers and an officer, standing at attention. They were on the side of the courtyard nearest the house. I think they were a guard of honour.'

'It sounds like an officer's wedding in a country garrison. I cannot imagine why such a scene should inspire horror.'

'The horror was something that had happened before, several times at long intervals, and was going to happen again. During those few seconds I knew all about it. Now, I cannot think what it could be. I forgot to say that there was something very peculiar, and even improper, about the way Kuniang was dressed. Her white satin

192

skirt was very ample and stood out from her hips. There was also some white undergarment that billowed out over the skirt as if it had slipped down from her shoulders. From the top of the skirt upwards, except for the veil, she was naked.'

I gave a low whistle, and remarked dryly:

'You are right in assuming that this must be unusual, even in Siberia. But, still, it is not horrible.'

'For some reason which I could not say the horror is connected in my mind with a great flaming jewel, which was suspended from Kuniang's neck, by a platinum chain. It was a diamond star: probably the Cross of Alexander. It hung between her breasts.'

'Do you think that Kuniang herself felt the coming horror as you did?'

'Yes. Certainly. She kept murmuring: "The last time! You always say it is the last time!" Her face was full of terror. Now the terror is with me. It only leaves me when we are together, you and I. Sometimes I wake up at night and call out to you for help. And you are not there.'

II

Is it the story of Lancelot and Guinevere, or in one of the Nibelungen legends, that the knight lies down with the maiden, a naked sword, *das Schwert*, between them, as a sign that they may not embrace?

That is what I felt like, in those days, with the difference that, except when we separated at bedtime, and retired, each to our respective pavilion, Kuniang so often sought the shelter of my arms. She who had been so independent, so self-reliant, so used to taking everything as it came without complaining, now craved my protection with an almost morbid timidity. I understood that this might be only a passing phase, and that youth would bring its own cure, if Kuniang were well cared for during that difficult time.

Meanwhile I felt all the responsibility for Kuniang's future, and the duty incumbent upon me not to allow her to make mistakes when her nerves were suffering from all she had been through. Yet at times I wondered if my own scruples might not make me unkind. Was it fair to force on her a ceremony of marriage the mere idea of which filled her with a nervous terror? I thought of duty and worldly wisdom and fairness, when all she asked was love. One may do worse things than make mistakes. What matters is to be kind and understanding. Often the things we regret least, when we grow old, are our mistakes.

In the end it was Uncle Podger that decided for me what I should do. Uncle Podger possesses much of the ancient wisdom of the East. If only he did not give himself such airs!

Fédor had come in to see us after dinner, and had spent an hour or so telling us of his future plans.

Fédor had got in touch with some revolutionary leaders in Russia, and was soon to leave for Moscow. He had an invaluable asset, from a revolutionary point of view, in his knowledge of the Chinese language and people. At that time there were not many sinologues in the ranks of the Russian revolutionaries, and Fédor might come in useful on the Russo-Chinese frontier, and elsewhere.

His sympathies were all with the second revolution (which had just overthrown Kerensky), and he posed as one who impersonated the new Russia that had grown out of the old, but his ideas were somewhat vague on the subject of what this new Russia was going to be like. He seemed to think that the most desirable thing for his countrymen would be to cut themselves off from the rest of the world, with its shady financial speculations and its senseless wars, and to live in a cloistered paradise of their own. The only contacts that Russia should maintain, according to Fédor, were with the East.

After he had left us Kuniang had gone to bed. She seemed in better spirits than usual. I remained in my study, reading and writing. When it was about midnight, I got up from my desk and put out the lights, before retiring to my room. It was a dark night, and as I walked down the steps on to the flagged path I almost fell over Uncle Podger. He was sitting there, apparently waiting for me to come out, though Kuniang had taken him to bed with her more than an hour before.

'Podger,' I said, 'come back to your room. What do you mean by leaving your missus in this way?'

Uncle Podger trotted after me, but as we got near to Kuniang's pavilion he ran on in front and disappeared. I followed him and found that the outer door was not quite shut. It was one of those Chinese doors which disprove the French saying: *Il faut qu'une porte soit ouverte ou fermée*. They never seem to be either open or shut. Podger evidently could push his way in and out.

By this time he had disappeared into the darkness of the interior, and I was attempting to close the door after him when I heard a sound that made me stop and listen. The curtain was drawn on the side of Kuniang's bedroom and I could not see in. But I recognized the sound. Kuniang was sobbing.

I walked in and pushed aside the curtain. There was a small reading-lamp lit near the bed. Kuniang looked up at me as I entered. Her eyes were red with weeping. I knelt down and put my arm round her shoulders.

'Darling, what is it?' I asked.

'The dream – Paul's dream. I can't bear to be alone.'

'Always the same scene, in the courtyard?'

'Yes. And sometimes only the cross, the Cross of Alexander. It lies on the ground, in shadow, but it seems to glow like a living thing. And there are red drops on it. I think they must be drops of blood.'

She lay quite still in my arms, and I kissed and soothed her.

'My poor darling,' I said. 'Will you promise not to cry if I go and fetch something? I will be back in a minute.'

'You are sure you are coming back?'

'Quite sure.'

I hurried off to my study and opened the camphor-wood box. From it I took the padded rose-coloured silk in which I had carried Kuniang to her room almost a year ago.

'What are you doing with that thing?' she asked, when she saw me come back.

'It is to wrap you up in,' I answered. And I stood near

195

the bed, holding out the silk, as you would hold out a bath-towel for some one coming out of a bath.

'Where are you going?'

'Only across the courtyards, to my room.'

Her eyes grew round, and the half-moon on her forehead glowed and faded. Then she pushed aside the bedclothes and stood, while I wrapped the silk round her, and lifted her in my arms. She nestled up to me and gave a little sigh of content.

'I always thought it would be much more fun to be a concubine,' said Kuniang.

21   The Untold Story

A marriage abroad is valid, according to the laws in most States, if the forms observed are those of the country where it takes place. It is sufficient to observe the *lex loci*. This legal maxim is, however, subject to notable exceptions.

I asked the British Consul whether a marriage would be considered valid between myself and Kuniang if we observed the Chinese formalities. After he had got over his astonishment at my putting such a question, he answered that he did not think such a marriage could be considered as valid, seeing that we were not debarred, in most provinces in China, from observing the marriage laws of our respective countries. The *lex loci* might be invoked only in cases of necessity. The Italian Consul was also of the same opinion. He said that Kuniang's marriage might be solemnized in a church or in the Consulate. For marriages that did not take place in the Consulate a special register was kept, and the marriage-lines copied out, to be sent later to Italy. These marriage-lines might be of any form, according to the religion of the parties concerned, or the place where the ceremony took place. A marriage in irregular circumstances might be considered valid if nobody contested its validity, so that even a Chinese marriage might be rendered legal by accomplishing the subsequent registration, but any one having interest to contest its validity might do so, and possibly succeed.

My inquiries in this matter were inspired by the desire to go through with some marriage ceremony which would not awaken the horror that was latent in Kuniang's mind. But a symptom of improvement was already manifest in her. She was quite willing to talk the matter over with me and could even laugh at my efforts to legalize our position by a Chinese marriage.

I read out to her the notes on weddings in China which I had collected for my own use in describing ceremonies and customs:

'The bride arrives in a palanquin at the house of the bridegroom, dressed in red and with a special head-dress. On her arrival, crackers are fired off to frighten the evil spirits who may have followed her. The bride must be accompanied by a woman who is the mother of at least one living son. Round her neck she should wear a small looking-glass, in order to prevent any malignant spirit from entering into her body. (The explanation of this is that malignant spirits are so ugly that, if they see their own image in the glass, they are frightened and run away.)

'The bride must cross the threshold with her left foot first and proceed to the family altar, where are the tablets of the ancestors of the bridegroom. Before them she makes the ritual genuflexions, touching the ground nine times with her forehead. The bride and bridegroom drink wine together out of two cups which are loosely tied together with a ribbon of red silk. After which they are considered legally married.'

'I am afraid I have not got any ancestral tablets,' I said, when I had reached this point. 'But I suppose I could have some made, unless old family portraits would do as well.'

'I doubt it,' said Kuniang. 'And I'm sure there is much more to a Chinese wedding than that. I've been to several. They consist in a very long procession through the streets, and then eating for three days. And there have to be all sorts of symbolical presents: a duck, and a carp, and a goose with its head painted red. And all the guests go and tease the bride and make very vulgar jokes about her.'

'Yes, but things are done more in Western fashion

now. The bridegroom wears a dress-suit and a top hat, hired for the occasion. And they have a brass band which plays the Funeral March of Chopin and extracts from the "Merry Widow".'

The ultimate result of such researches and discussions was what I had always hoped it would be. After a few months Kuniang's nerves had quieted down. She expressed her willingness to be married, and not necessarily in the Chinese way. She stipulated only that the ceremony should not be celebrated in Peking, but in Harbin, where the Italian Consul was an old friend of Signor Cante's. She was also pleased at my suggestion that from Harbin we should go to Europe for a year or more, or less, as the fancy took us, before returning to the Home of the Five Virtues, where Uncle Podger and Exalted Virtue might be left in charge.

Railways in China offer a fairly comfortable means of satisfying the *wanderlust*, with the added zest of never knowing whether some marauding war-lord may not stop your train, a hundred miles from anywhere, and take away the engine for his own purposes. But in the spring of 1919 travel was difficult all the world over, save perhaps in America. The Trans-Siberian was practically impassable. One met people who had 'got through', but nobody in his senses would have chosen that route in preference to a journey by sea, even in an overcrowded steamer.

Kuniang and I could hardly have chosen a worse moment for a journey in Europe. Peking and the Treaty Ports of China represented, in those days, a peaceful oasis in the midst of a world which had hardly emerged from the welter of war. We began to realize what we were letting ourselves in for twenty-four hours after we had boarded the Peking-Mukden express in the station outside the Chen Mên. Up to Chanchun (terminus of the South Manchurian Railway) things went pretty smoothly, but after that one entered the region of utter chaos along the eastern borders of Russia.

The trains of the Russian-owned 'Chinese Eastern Railway', which we travelled in after Chanchun, were in a state that made one wonder if the carriages had ever been cleaned since the fall of the Tsarist régime. Most of the windows were broken and the floors were covered, two inches thick, with dust and cigarette ash and odds and ends of rubbish. I even noticed some paper roubles, of no value whatever, lying among the egg-shells and chicken bones and scraps of paper and tea-leaves. There was material there for an interesting archaeological research. But in one way the train service in those days was preferable to that of more prosperous times. The passengers had no fear of being attacked by bandits. No self-respecting bandit would have stopped such a broken-down lot of railway carriages.

All the best part of the rolling-stock was concentrated at Harbin and at Vladivostok, and permanently occupied by a crowd of more or less important people who could not find shelter elsewhere. The goods vans were crammed with refugees; the first- and second-class carriages with officers and officials of half a dozen different nationalities. If what Kuniang wanted was a 'quiet wedding' she could not have found a place where our doings were less likely to attract attention than at Harbin.

II

Not yet having acquired the railway-carriage habit, Kuniang and I made an attempt to find rooms in town. For a long time we were unsuccessful. But in the end we met a Chinese dentist whom I had known in better days and who remembered me. He offered us hospitality of a sort. We passed the night three in a room. Kuniang slept on the sofa, our host on the floor (the sofa was his bed by rights), and I on the dentist's chair.

Getting married was much easier than finding a lodging. Signor Cante's friend, the Italian Consul, who had already accomplished all the preliminary formalities, put the thing through for us in no time. And Kuniang seemed to have forgotten her old *phobia*. The Consul was full of apologies for not offering us a room. But his house was full of officers, who belonged to the Italian contingent of the inter-allied expedition into Siberia. In that contingent had been enrolled many of the *irredenti* whom Kuniang had seen at Shan-hai-kwan.

The Bolshevist régime had not yet extended its sway over Siberia, and all the trains that were eastward bound, as well as all the towns along the line, were full of refugees, flying from terrors that as yet were hardly understood. The line was held by foreign troops: British, French, American, Japanese, Italian. But whose interests they were defending nobody quite knew. The Russians quarrelled among themselves. They were divided into Red, White, and Radishes (red outside and white within). The only thing in which they seemed to agree was to get all they could out of the foreigner.

We were in Harbin for less than a week, but that was long enough for me to appreciate a state of confusion and of misery which has seldom been equalled in our times. Of this situation the Chinese were mildly interested spectators, and they did not fail to draw their own conclusions. Not the least among the causes of the white man's loss of prestige in the Far East was the flight of refugees out of Russia.

One afternoon (it was on the day before our departure for Dairen and Japan) we met Elisalex, coming out of a shop in the Kitaiskaya.

She was looking tired and ill, but her face brightened up when she saw Kuniang. Strange to say, she asked no questions as to why we were in Harbin or where we were going. Possibly she knew all about us already.

'I thought you were in Kingdom Come,' said Kuniang.

'I am going there to-morrow, or, at least, to-morrow is the day I start. I do not know if I will ever reach it.'

'But does it really exist?'

'I will let you know when I get there.'

'And where are you living now?'

'In a railway carriage, like everybody else. Don't tell me that you have found a lodging in town!'

I described my nights in the dentist's chair, and she laughed.

'You are luckier than most,' she said. 'It is a pity that I am leaving to-morrow morning early or I might have offered you a compartment in my railway carriage. You are welcome to it for one night, if you do not mind being turned out on to the platform at six to-morrow morning.'

'But that would be splendid,' exclaimed Kuniang. 'We are leaving ourselves for Dairen to-morrow. Our train starts at seven.'

In a few minutes the requisite arrangements were made. The dentist's laboratory which formed our habitation (and where patients were received during the day) was close by. It did not take long to pack our scanty luggage, which consisted of three suit-cases. These were piled into a very dilapidated equipage, drawn by a woolly Mongolian pony. We perched ourselves as best we could on the narrow seats and proceeded jerkily to the station.

When we got there we called somebody to carry the suit-cases, and followed Elisalex through the station buildings, which, as usual, were crowded to suffocation with people who had the indescribably miserable look of refugees. On the platform we passed close to a pretty girl, talking to two American soldiers in uniform. She was speaking English with a slight foreign accent. I said something to Kuniang about wondering who she could be, and Elisalex, who was walking on ahead, overheard my remark. Without turning round she said casually:

'She is probably a daughter of the Tsar. I am told that the place is full of them.'

'A daughter of the Tsar! What do you mean?'

Elisalex was wending her way between the railway lines. In order to hear her explanation I had to hurry after her, tripping over the rails and the wooden sleepers.

'There are no end of destitute girls,' she said, 'who have reached Manchuria somehow. They have lost their parents, their homes, everything. They always make straight for the foreign officers, and often begin by saying that they are daughters of the Tsar. Even if the officer does not believe, he may be good for a meal and a bed.'

The next moment Elisalex stopped before a railway carriage and started to mount the steps, which were high up off the ground. An official in uniform, who appeared to be on guard, saluted her as she passed him. Kuniang and I climbed up in our turn. The carriage was an ordinary first-class sleeper of the Chinese Eastern, and Elisalex occupied two compartments. She cleared out one of these, with our help, taking away some boxes and bundles of papers. Then she told us to make ourselves at home. There were some officials in the other compartments. But we saw nothing of them except the smoke of their cigarettes, which filled the corridor. The whole carriage reeked of stale tobacco. But it was fairly clean. I was glad not to have to pass another night in the dentist's chair.

Elisalex did not seem to be able to take her eyes off Kuniang. She looked at her with all the pride of an old nurse meeting a young charge of other days who was grown up.

There was an attendant in the carriage, a *provodnik*, who made himself useful in various ways. But Elisalex insisted on making tea for us herself, fetching the hot water from a lighted samovar which stood at the end of the corridor. Instead of cups, we used big glass tumblers in metal holders.

'Lemon or milk,' she said, 'have I none. But there is some sugar in this box.' She took down a biscuit-tin from the rack, and handed it to me. It was half full of lump sugar and biscuits, all mixed up together.

'They were better teas you gave us,' she added, 'in your house in Peking.' And it seemed to me that in her voice there was a touch of regret, as for pleasant days that would never come again.

III

Even though there were no sheets on the bed, but only blankets, I was far more comfortable in the sleeping-carriage than I had been on the previous nights in the dentist's chair. Nevertheless, I could not get to sleep, though Kuniang slumbered peacefully on the berth below. Every now and then I looked down at her. In the faint light that came from the open window I could just see the shape of her head and arm.

It was strangely silent in spite of the fact that all around us, in the railway carriages, were many hundred people, possibly over a thousand, who had made a home for themselves on the sidings of that big shunting-yard. Once, in a carriage farther down the line, I heard a man's voice singing, and other voices joined in and dropped out again. It was a melancholy song, evidently Russian, and soon it died down. For an hour or more I heard the gentle hiss and throb of an engine under steam, and then it moved away.

I kept thinking about Elisalex. She had said nothing more about Kingdom Come, and I knew no more about her than I did on that night in Peking when she came to see me, and drew aside her cloak to show the Cross of Alexander.

An hour after midnight I heard some one moving about in the corridor. I felt restless, so I got up, and slipping on a coat went out, closing the door gently behind me. I found Elisalex putting some papers in order by the light of a candle (the car being isolated there was no electric light). She was fully dressed and seemed to have no intention of going to bed.

'I will get all the sleep I want to-morrow,' she said, 'on the way to Manchuli.'

I went into her compartment, and for a while we talked, and she smoked cigarettes, one after the other.

'So Paul Dysart is dead,' said Elisalex. 'I understand that in the end the dream killed him. I am not surprised.'

'Yes, and it hurt Kuniang. Your warning came just too late, even supposing that I could have done something. But, tell me: how is it that you never gave that warning to Kuniang herself when she told you about Paul's dream?'

'Kuniang never spoke to me about Paul's dream, and I did not want to tell her what I told you. The less we say to Kuniang on that subject the better.'

'I do not understand. How could you have known all you did if you had not talked it over with Kuniang? She was the only person, except Paul himself, who could have told you what the dream was about.'

Elisalex did not answer, but looked at me rather strangely. Then she stretched out her hand to a small suit-case that lay on the floor beside her, and lifted it up on to the seat between us. She opened it and began searching among the contents, which, as far as I could see, consisted entirely of papers. From these she took a large envelope, apparently full of photographs, and, having selected one, she handed it to me to look at.

'Does that explain anything to you?' she asked.

The photograph was that of a group, and as soon as my eye fell on it I recognized the strange scene that Kuniang had described to me: the scene in which she herself had figured as the bride in a marriage ceremony with Paul. There, in the background, was the long banqueting-table, with people seated at it (they were all a little out of focus). There were the soldiers, lined up as if to form a guard of honour. There were the two priests, with long beards and tall black hats (they were not an attractive pair). There were the two girls, who may have been bridesmaids. One of them was very pretty. And there, in a bridal veil and billowing skirt, was, not Kuniang, but Elisalex. The veil fell from her head in two straight lines. It hid her shoulders, but left her torso bare, with the diamond star shining between her breasts.

I had never expected to see a photograph of the scene which had left such a painful impression on Kuniang's mind. But so far the details were those which she had described. It was the figure of the bridegroom that brought home to me, in a sudden blinding revelation, a fact which I had never guessed, never even dimly suspected. There could be no mistaking the tall, fine figure in the skirted Cossack coat, belted round a slim waist; the impassive face, with the slanting Mongol eyes; the beautiful hands, of which one held up the hand of the bride. Paul, of course, it could not be. But how was it that I had never understood, never imagined, that in his dream Paul had lived the life of the abbot?

The truth is that I had never believed in the reality behind Paul's dream. Yet Elisalex herself had told me that she was the woman whose part Kuniang had taken. I had seen the wonderful cross of brilliants, set on a diamond star: the same that had appeared and reappeared throughout the dream. Elisalex had given me an added proof when she warned me of the danger that Kuniang ought not to be exposed to, lest the horror of it should haunt her for the rest of her days. The warning had not been an idle one. Yet it had all seemed too fanciful, too unreal. Such things could only be 'shadow-pictures': dreams that passed through the gates of ivory, and never came true.

There was one thing – one little thing – that ought to have helped me to guess the truth. It was the scent that Elisalex wore: the scent that had lingered in the street, under the Tartar Wall, that night when I had watched her, in her rickshaw, disappear among the shadows. How was it that I had not recognized that scent, though I had noticed it and wondered how it could be so familiar: the scent on the note-paper, when I had picked up the two walnuts and the letter that lay under the lilac bushes in the little courtyard of the Lama Temple? That same scent was around me again, as I sat beside Elisalex in the railway compartment, in the shunting-yard at Harbin. I realized now that it should have formed a connecting link between Elisalex and the abbot, 'the Prince Dorbon Oirad', to whom her letter had been addressed. It should have told me the reason for her coming to Peking: to be near him.

I had been blind and stupid. But I had one excuse: my faculties were dulled, because my thoughts were elsewhere. I had thought always and only of Kuniang. Shall a man solve riddles whose mind is steeped in love?

Now I gazed at Elisalex in petrified astonishment, feeling stunned as if by an explosion. It was only after several minutes that I began to gather my scattered wits, and even then I could only ask stupidly:

'Was it he that made Paul dream?'

'Yes. Of our life together.'

Their life together! I saw it now. For in my hand was the photograph of the man whose life Paul had followed almost day by day. And sitting beside me in the railway compartment was the real woman whose part Kuniang had taken in a dream: the girl who had fallen under the influence of Rasputin; who had loved a Mongol prince and joined him in his far-flung Eastern province. That woman's story and the dream were one, and both were true. And Elisalex sat there and watched me, smiling, through the smoke of her cigarettes.

IV

I handed the photograph back to Elisalex, and with my finger I indicated the abbot, where he stood beside the bride.

'Can you tell me more about him?' I asked.

'I could tell you lots more about him. But I do not know that you would understand him any better than you do now. I know something of his ambitions, a little of his philosophy, much of the man that underlies them both. And yet in many ways he remains a mystery even to me.'

'Has he really carved out a kingdom for himself, like Semenoff and the others?'

'It is already there. As I told Kuniang to-day, Kingdom Come has always existed. It is the only unspoiled part of the world: the grass-lands bordering the desert, the tundra, and the steppes. Semenoff and Koltchak and this Baron Ungarn, whom they are beginning to talk about, are only rulers of an hour. The Mongol princes were there before Gengiz Khan, their songs go back to the days of Ogotai and Tamerlane. They have no fixed abode, but the highlands of Asia belong to them, even though the standards of Russia or of China may fly over their possessions.'

'But when we saw this prince of yours in Peking,' I objected, 'we were told of monasteries that had been pillaged and burnt down. He was seeking funds to rebuild them. Was that not true?'

'True enough, I dare say. And money is always useful. But that is not the point. Marauding tribes from the north have always given trouble, and to them are now added disbanded soldiers out of China. The real danger is very different. What matters the looting of a few monasteries to a people whose ancestors have sacked the cities of two continents? My prince, as you call him, is struggling to preserve the true independence of his country. But the enemy is not represented by the *tung hudze*, or by the Chinese, or the Russians, or even by the Japanese, who are pushing westward through Manchuria. The enemy is civilization. It threatens to destroy the old aloofness, the old detachment. I do not think that any one who has not lived on the roof of the world can understand the horror that is represented by the encroachments of modern conditions in a country which has always been isolated and unsullied by the march of so-called progress.'

'It is an idea,' I said, 'that could only be understood by those who love Nature, even where she is repellent, and who love solitude.'

'To many people I have no doubt that it appears merely silly. I once found it expressed in a rather amusing way in a Russian book called *Dal Zoviet*, which means the lure of far horizons. The author is Galinischef Kutuzoff, and he tells of a man in Northern Mongolia who goes out of his yurt every morning to breathe the free air of the steppes and enjoy the immensity and the solitude. But one day he feels an unaccountable sense of oppression, almost as if he could not breathe. He looks about to find the reason. And there, across the undulating grasslands, is a line of telegraph poles. After that the place is never the same to him again.'

'And does the abbot feel that way about it?'

'I think so. He has seen something of the world. He knows the old civilization of China and the new civilization of Russia. Of the two, he prefers the old. But he wishes to keep them both out of Mongolia. To see his country civilized would give him a sense as of Paradise lost.'

For a few moments I thought over what Elisalex had told me. It was a strange ideal that she had described, and possibly a hopeless one. Yet I could sympathize with the abbot. What I could not understand was what part she had in the struggle. How could she be an ally of such a man? Would she not appear to him rather as an enemy within the camp? Was that perhaps her tragedy? She who was beautiful and desired of men to be put aside for an ideal in which love could have no part? In that strange mind which was the abbot's, she might even give the impression of the telegraph poles in Kutuzoff's book! I have noticed that most dramas, in Russia, as in China, end in an anticlimax.

I asked her: 'What are you to the Prince Dorbon Oirad?'

'I was married to him once. But I doubt if the marriage was legal. I can only think of him as my lover.'

'Has he been kind to you?'

'I cannot say that he has.' Elisalex smiled somewhat bitterly. 'No one can be more gentle, and the wild animals come to him, as they did to St. Francis. Yet he can watch those he loves under torture, and remain serene and impassive.'

'You loved him. Do you love him still?'

'I am beginning to feel towards him what your friend Paul Dysart might have felt if he had lived out his dream to the end. Though I am only twenty-five, I am exhausted. I have been through too much. I am tired of emotion. It is as if I had lived, not one life, but many. And one of these lives was only a dream with a rude awakening. Yet the drama was so intense that I feel as if I had outlived all my years of passion. Now I would like to lie awake and rest.'

We were both silent for a little while, and then I said:

'I am trying to imagine the abbot as a lover. He is a fine figure of a man, and that magnetic charm of his must add to his attractions.'

'When he first came to St. Petersburg all the women lost their heads about him. I was proud that he should have chosen me. But when he left for his eastern post he would not take me. *He* never lost his head. His passions never rose above the level of his eyes. His brain remained cool and untroubled. He is very much like a god in some ways. It is safer to have a more human lover.'

'Such as Rasputin.'

Elisalex laughed. 'You must think that I have a strange

209

taste in – what is the expression? – boy friends!'

'You attract men with exceptionally magnetic person-alities. You have one yourself.'

'Have I? After Dorbon left me I met Grishka. I was not feeling very magnetic at the time, but lost and lonely. There was a political background to that love-affair, as you know. When the crash came I fled to my former lover, in his fortress, and begged for protection. He gave it willingly. But after I had been with him a month he received some orders concerning me, or he said he did. He was to suppress me and to make sure that I was never heard of again. I have often wondered who those orders could have been from: the Empress, or Grishka, or the *Okhrana*? Sometimes I ask myself if they were not an invention of Dorbon himelf to get rid of me.'

'But what did he do?'

'Exactly the opposite to what he had been ordered. He did not suppress me, and he made my name a byword all over Russia. And that is what Paul Dysart dreamt of.'

'It must have been a terrible business, judging by the effects on Paul.'

'It was. And to this day I do not really know if Dorbon wished to save my life by a ruse or merely to satisfy some latent cruelty in his own character, some strange lusts of his own.'

'Do you mean that it was all what the Chinese call *look see*?'

'Yes. We staged a series of events, much as Hamlet staged a play in Elsinore, or Scheherazade told tales to save herself from death. The idea was so subtle that it could only have been born in the East. For me the hor-ror lay in the fact that, once we had begun, we could not stop. As Dorbon said: "He who rides the tiger cannot dismount".'

I started, and Elisalex asked me: 'Do you know that saying?'

'Yes. It is an Eastern proverb. And what happened then?'

'The plan succeeded beyond all expectations, and the story of what we had done swept over the crumbling Empire, from Archangel to Odessa and from Warsaw to

Vladivostok. The soldiers told it round their camp-fires. The Buriats made a song of it. At Peking, the Cossacks of the Legation Guard used to wait about to see me pass. And your servants wrote anonymous letters about me.'

'Will you not tell me the story? You see, I never heard it!'

'You had other things to think about. You and Kuniang were living in an older, sweeter story of your own.'

'Does she not know it either?'

'No. And I will tell it to you only on condition that you never tell it to her.'

'I promise that.'

'But you are an author. You will write it, and she will know.'

'I promise that I will not write it.'

And then she told me.

I am sorry that I gave that promise. For now my life and Kuniang's, and this book, seem to circle round a story that I may not tell. It is made up of the immortal elements: love and courage and suffering and shame. The abbot told it in a dream. I doubt if I could do it justice. But I would like to try.

Now I must be content with humbler subjects: with quiet courtyards and a sheltered garden; with myself and Kuniang and Little Lu; with Uncle Podger and the Russian family down the street.

Like Ah-ting-fu, I call myself a Maker of Heavenly Trousers, but my wares are celestial only in name. Paul Dysart might dream of a life that was too terrible to live out to the end. Kuniang may still feel the horror of the marriage ceremony with Paul. Such fierce drama is not for me. All I can attain is a certain quiet philosophy, while I cherish a happiness, multiplied by two, like the character Fu, in my crystal seal.

Yet at times, while I write of these things at my desk, I seem to see the abbot and Elisalex looking down at me. The abbot wears the black skirted coat of a Cossack. From the waist upwards Elisalex is naked, under a bridal veil. And the Cross of Alexander sparkles between her breasts.

211

As in Pirandello's *Sei Personaggi in cerca d'autore*, they must search for another author who will give them life. I may not tell their story.

Carducci says that what was a note of the eternal poem, while it hovered unexpressed in his brain, became only one small verse when he wrote it down.

. . . Fu una nota del poema eterno
Quel ch'io sentiva e picciol verso or è.

For me, the untold story is a note of the eternal poem. And such it must remain.

V

When I left Elisalex and went back to my own compartment I found Kuniang in trouble with the bedclothes, which kept slipping down on to the floor, as they so often do in sleeping-carriages. The first glimmer of dawn was showing through the window.

'I dreamt I was back in Peking,' said Kuniang, 'with Natasha in the schoolroom. We had got into awful trouble with Matushka. I woke up just in time!'

At half-past five I told the *provodnik* to call me a porter (or a refugee) from the station, and to have our luggage taken on to the platform, while our train was being made up. Meanwhile Kuniang and I watched Elisalex's carriage being coupled on to the train which was bound for Manchuli.

We did not talk much. It had begun to rain, and a little northern station, in the early morning, is not conducive to conversation. We were very sleepy. Elisalex smiled at us from the window, and just as her train was about to move off she handed Kuniang a tiny parcel wrapped in an old piece of newspaper.

'It is a wedding present,' she said. 'Do not open it now. Wait till you are alone.'

Kuniang thanked her and waved her hand as the train moved out towards the west.

Our compartment in the Dairen train was crowded to

212

suffocation with Russians, whose half-tanned boots smelt to heaven. A few minutes before our departure a nasty little accident happened. A small boy of about five years old, for whom there was no seat, was climbing about on the knees of his parents and other passengers when he slipped and fell heavily on to a basket that lay on the floor. The basket was tied round with a dirty piece of cloth, and the jagged edge of a badly opened tin stuck out at the top. The child fell on this and cut his wrist. And then pandemonium broke loose! The child yelled. His mother yelled. His father snatched him up and shouted. Everybody offered advice in different languages. Meanwhile the child was bleeding over everything and everybody.

At last the parents got out with the child, to seek medical aid, and, for reaons that I could not fathom, a fussy and short-tempered railway official promptly turned out all the other occupants of the carriage, except Kuniang and myself. So we started with the compartment to ourselves.

Kuniang had been a little upset by the scene with the wounded child, whose wrist had bled over her skirt and over the little paper parcel that Elisalex had given her. She asked me to get her suit-case down from the rack. While I did so she opened the parcel:

'I hope there is nothing inside to spoil,' she said.

The next moment I heard something drop and then a piercing scream. I turned quickly to see what was wrong.

Kuniang was leaning with her back against the door of the carriage. She was deadly pale and appeared to be shrinking in horror from what lay at her feet.

I looked down.

In the dust and dirt of the carriage floor something shone and sparkled like a living flame. It was a diamond star, and on the diamonds there were drops of blood.

22 Golden Slippers

I

We never went to Europe. The diamond star, blood-stained at her feet, brought back to Kuniang all the horror of Paul's dream, with much the same consequences as before. I thought, at first, that a change of scene and the bustle of travel might be good for her. So, after a week at Star Beach (on the coast between Dalny and Port Arthur), I took her to Japan, where we stayed for a time on the island of Miyajima, on the Inland Sea. It is a pretty place, with a strange local tradition. No one may be born there, and no one may die. Women who are expecting a baby are requested to leave the island in good time. People who fall ill are hustled into a boat and taken to the mainland till they get better.

Kuniang seemed quiet and contented. We sailed up and down the coast and took walks, and she fed the tame deer in the temple grounds. But, as after Paul's death, she would not let me out of her sight. I suggested reserving a cabin on a C.P.R. steamer for Vancouver, but she appeared reluctant to start. She said she was homesick for Peking. Could we not go to Europe some other time?

So we embarked on a little steamer, the *Ajiwa Maru*, for Tang-ku, and returned to the Home of the Five Virtues a little more than a month after we had left it.

The servants and Uncle Podger appeared pleased to see us. They do not get much 'squeeze', or tit-bits, when we are away. But, even apart from such considerations, I do not doubt that their friendly welcome was sincere.

The first thing I tried to do, after I arrived home, was

to get in touch with Elisalex, in order to return to her the Cross of Alexander. Kuniang and I could well appreciate the generosity of that wonderful gift. But the associations were too painful, and the jewel itself was too valuable for us to accept it. Yet, how could we get it back to its rightful owner? It seemed impossible for any communication of ours to reach a person, without any permanent address, who was living with a nomad tribe, somewhere on the north-eastern Asiatic plateau.

I asked my friends the priests in the Lama Temple to help me, and gave them a letter for the abbot, enclosing one to Elisalex. But the months passed and I got no answer. As a matter of fact I hardly expected to.

And then one day, at the beginning of summer, the post brought me a bulky grey envelope, with a French stamp. It contained a letter from Donald Parramoor, half a page of a musical score, and a tiny pair of baby's shoes in knitted wool and silk, with a gold thread running through the wool.

The letter ran as follows:

'DEAR MAKER OF HEAVENLY TROUSERS,

'I once promised I would send Miss Kuniang a pair of golden slippers, if our revue turned out a success.

'It has. It ran for three months in Paris and five in London. The costumes were just too cunning! Your Uncle Donald surpassed himself, and the girls were not unshapely.

'So here are the slippers. You may say that they are too small. But I don't know what size Miss Kuniang takes in shoes. Besides, I hear you have married her. Bully for you! So I have had the shoes made for the Baby, when it comes. Mammà can sing it the old coon-song, when she rocks the cradle. I enclose the score.

'I have been hearing about you from a Russian lady, who says she saw quite a lot of you in Peking, and met you afterwards in Harbin, where you were busy getting married (why Harbin, of all places?). She calls herself Princess Dorbon Oirad, and is a peach. I can't quite make out who Dorbon Oirad is. He seems to be running for the post of Living Buddha, somewhere east of Suez. And the lady is getting a divorce. Meanwhile she is living in Paris, and has the most stunning clothes. I designed a frock for her myself: white lace, with bunches of grapes in black velvet.

'Like a good many other refugees, the Princess D.B. has opened a shop in Paris. Hers is not a shop, really; it is a Russian cabaret and a Chinese restaurant, all in one. The restaurant is on the ground floor, and the cabaret is in the basement. It is quite close to the Luxembourg. The place is called *Crodiachaja sobaka*. I believe there is a place of that name in Moscow. It means *The Stray Dog*. Any stray dog may loaf in, and they most of them do, after the performance is over at the Odéon. I guess Elisalex (did I say her name was Elisalex?) is making a good thing out of it, for last month she went for ten days to the Riviera.

'Elsie has married her French officer and they have a baby. It is she who got me the golden slippers here enclosed.

'I have taken a flat in the Avenue Junot, and Norah keeps house for me.

'Have you bought any more silks recently?

'Has the Old Lady retired into her coffin yet?

'Love to you all

'Ever yours

'DONALD PARRAMOOR.'

I handed the letter and the enclosure to Kuniang. She picked up the little shoes with an exclamation of delight.

'How clever of Donald! How could he know?'

Then she took the score of the coon-song and hurried off to the Russian family; she would ask Matushka to play it on the piano, and teach her the tune.

I remained in my study with Donald's letter and the little woollen shoes lying on my desk. Like other writers, I see the world as a book of short stories. The golden slippers represented the end of one and the beginning of another.

But what about Elisalex?

For her also had come the end of story. The abbot was in Mongolia and she in Paris, the Mecca of so many aristocratic Russian refugees.

Rasputin and the abbot, her 'boy friends', as she had once called them, were not men who could bring happiness into any woman's life. Though possibly, after such lovers, any other would seem very dull indeed!

I smiled as I told myself that Elisalex had better marry Donald Parramoor and enter into a paradise of clothes. We would send her back the Cross of Alexander to remind her of old times.

And the abbot: what was his destiny?

During our generation perhaps he might still keep the highlands of Asia uncontaminated by Western civilization: one last stronghold of the old world of thought in a new world of action. But in the end the uplands would be submerged by the encroaching tide. Even now motorcars traverse the desert and aeroplanes sweep the sky. Doubtless the time must come, in the world's evolution, when a man seeking solitude will find it only within himself:

'Noise is not in the market-place, nor quiet in the hills . . . but in the ever-changing hearts of men.'

Late that afternoon Kuniang and I were together in the garden. Uncle Podger was snuffing round, as usual, in the bushes, and Exalted Virtue was clearing away the tea-things. Kuniang sat on a deck-chair and hummed the tune she had just learnt:

Golden slippers on a golden stair,
    Golden slippers on my tirèd feet.
Golden slippers that we all must wear,
    Because dey am so sweet!

Then she stopped and spoke to Exalted Virtue:
'*To-tai.*'
'Yes, Missy.'
'When I was a *hsiao kuniang*, quite small, I had Little Lu to play with.'
'Yes, Missy. You play-play allo time.'
'But Little Lu is quite a big Lu now.'
'Yes, Missy. Velly big.'
'I was thinking that, when my baby is born, in the autumn, there ought to be also a Chinese baby about the

217

place for company. Could not the Family of the Five Virtues produce one from somewhere?'

Exalted Virtue thought the matter over as he collected the cups and saucers on a tray. The ghost of a smile passed over his impassive face. But he answered gravely:

'Yes, Missy. Can do!'

THE END

Queen Lucia
E.F. Benson

'We will pay anything for Lucia books'
NOEL COWARD: GERTRUDE LAWRENCE: NANCY MITFORD:
W.H. AUDEN

Queen Lucia is set in the middle-class, garden-party world
of the 1920's, a society dominated utterly and ruthlessly by
the greatest arch-snob who has ever existed. Lucia and her
cohorts – Georgie with his dyed hair, embroidery, and
piano duets, Daisy Quantock with her passion for the new
and exotic – capture the mood and flavour of a whole
period, and the nuances and rivalries of English life are
described engrossingly and with a rapier wit.

If the pens of Evelyn Waugh and Jane Austen had mated,
Lucia would have been the offspring.

'At long last, here she is again, the splendid creature, the
great, the wonderful Lucia'
NANCY MITFORD

'To describe her as a snob would be to describe Leonardo
as a talented man'
MICHAEL MACLIAMMOR

0 552 99075 2

BLACK SWAN

Lucia in London
E.F. Benson

Lucia, Queen of provincial society, now launches herself onto the London scene. The *crème de la crème* of social climbers, Lucia never falters as she dons her real (seed) pearls and prepares to attack the beau monde, wheedling her way into parties where she has not been invited and coaxing the rich and titled to come to tea.

Lucia in London is the second of the famous Lucia books by E.F. Benson. Comic masterpieces, these novels of manners are brought to life by sharp, satirical social observations and are as deliciously funny today as they were when first published in the 1920's.

'He was a master of a certain kind of light fiction, and he can delight even though one knows that his satire is ultimately friendly . . . He is clever and funny, but he writes for his victims'
THE SPECTATOR

'The flow of his comic inspiration never dwindles'
ELIZABETH HARVEY

'Here she is again, the splendid creature, the great, the wonderful Lucia . . . I must say I reopened these magic books after some thirty years with misgivings: I feared that they would have worn badly and seem dated. Not at all; they are as fresh as paint. The characters are real and therefore timeless'
NANCY MITFORD

0 552 99076 0

BLACK SWAN

Miss Mapp
E.F. Benson

'The flow of his comic inspiration never dwindles'
ELIZABETH HARVEY

Here is the redoubtable 'triumphantly arch of all arch
villainesses', Miss Elizabeth Mapp of Tilling – a schemer, a
woman of fine habits and low cunning who spends her days in
the delightful bow window of her delightful period house, light
opera glasses in hand, noting and annotating the business of
her neighbours. Not a thing escapes her gimlet eyes, from the
purchase of a basket of over-ripe red-currants, to the
unfortunate drinking habits of Captain Puffin.

Miss Mapp is the third in the sequence of the famous Lucia
novels. Deliciously funny, outrageously U, quintessentially
English, Benson's comic characters have come alive again for
another generation.

'He was a master of a certain kind of light fiction, and he can
delight even though one knows that his satire is ultimately
friendly . . . He is clever and funny, but he writes for his
victims'
THE SPECTATOR

'My greatest reading pleasure in 1967 was the discovery of E.F.
Benson's 'Lucia' novels . . . I enjoyed them so much that I
borrowed (and was tempted to steal) two more of the series. I
confess myself a Lucia addict'
TERENCE DE VERE WHITE

0 552 99083 3

BLACK SWAN

Mapp and Lucia
E. F. Benson

'I have not laughed so much at any novel as *Mapp and Lucia* since I read the early Waughs'
TERENCE DE VERE WHITE

At last they meet — the two most formidable ladies in English literature collide in genteel and deadly enmity. Lucia, now widowed, shakes the dust of Riseholme from her elegant feet and, with Georgie Pillson as devoted courtier, prepares to conquer the high society of Tilling. She brings her musical evenings, her Italian, her poetry, and her ambitious snobbery. And Miss Mapp, her features corrugated by chronic rage and curiosity, can only prepare to defend her position as doyenne of Tilling. The town is split in an exciting and scintillating war of garden parties, bridge evenings, and staggeringly simple little dinners.

Mapp and Lucia is the fourth of the Lucia novels, a chronicle of life in two English country towns described with malicious delicacy and wit.

'I might have gone to my grave without ever knowing about Lucia or Miss Mapp. It is not a risk anyone should take lightly'
AUBERON WAUGH

0 552 99084 1

BLACK SWAN

Lucia's Progress

E. F. Benson

"I might have gone to my grave without ever knowing about Lucia or Miss Mapp. It is not a risk anyone should take lightly"
AUBERON WAUGH

Once more the society of Tilling is locked in exquisite trepidation as Lucia and Miss Mapp — now Mrs Benjamin Mapp-Flint launch themselves into a fresh foray of deadly civilities. For Mrs Benjamin Mapp-Flint, triumphant from her honeymoon in Monte Carlo, is *too* triumphant, and Lucia has delicate designs of Borgian dimensions to reduce Tilling's new bride to her rightful place.

Lucia's Progress is the fifth in E. F. Benson's delicious, satirical, sparkling and malicious Lucia series.

"I reopened these magic books after some thirty years with misgivings; I feared that they would have worn badly and seem dated. Not at all; they are as fresh as paint. The characters are real and therefore timeless"
NANCY MITFORD

0 552 99087 6

BLACK SWAN

Trouble for Lucia
E. F. Benson

'Whenever I stopped reading to laugh aloud, I measured
the pages still unread, not to see how much more I had to
accomplish, but from a simple fear that my pleasure was
drawing to an end . . . A Cranford of 1930'
TERENCE DE VERE WHITE

Lucia's lofty ambitions are at last to be fulfilled.
For as Mayor-Elect of Tilling it seems she has come to her
highest calling. The tearooms of Tilling quiver with delicious
gossip as she reigns from Mallards — formerly the home of
Mrs Benjamin Mapp-Flint — with dear Georgie Pillson as
her consort.

But Lucia's position as the town's *premiere* socialite is in
danger. For, concerned with her civic dignities, 'Dear
Worship' is inclined to forget the subtle nuances and quaint
customs of Tilling society.

Trouble for Lucia is the last of E. F. Benson's Lucia novels,
a delicious study of outrageous snobbery, essentially English
and consistently entertaining.

'The art of these books lies in their simplicity. The jokes
seem quite obvious and are often repeated; we can never
have enough of them'
NANCY MITFORD

0 552 99088 4

BLACK SWAN